Priests Without People

Priests Without People

a novel

Nicholas P. Cafardi

The Ross House Press

The Ross House Press
389 Lincoln Ave
Woodstock, Il 60098

Edited and designed by Phil Rice

www.RossHousePress.com

ISBN: 978-0-9971695-8-4

The chapters of this novel are set in the fictitious Dioceses of Rocksburg, USA and Rome, Italy. Except for the final chapter, they take place in 1968-1970, reflecting the turmoil in the Church in those years just after the Second Vatican Council. All the characters and places, even those that appear under historical name, and all of the events in this novel are creations of the author's imagination, and no resemblance to any person, living or dead, or to actual places or events is intended and should not be inferred.

For the Rev. Louis F. Vallone

Friend, Teacher and Priest
who is never without his people

Contents

Principal Characters
In the Order of Their Appearance

John Rooney, Bishop of Rocksburg, later Cardinal Prefect of the Congregation for Clergy at the Vatican in Rome

Terrence "Sparky" Larkin, pastor of St. Teresa Parish in Rocksburg

Marty Phelan, auxiliary bishop, then diocesan bishop of the Diocese of Rocksburg

Tony Capresi, assistant pastor of St. Teresa Parish in Rocksburg

Connie Amoroso, parishioner at St. Teresa Parish in Rocksburg

Joe Amoroso, parishioner at St. Teresa Parish in Rocksburg

Henry Da Silva, chancellor, then auxiliary bishop of the Diocese of Rocksburg

Bill Tuigg, priest of the Diocese of Rocksburg, secretary to John Cardinal Rooney

Cornelius "Corny" Sheehan, priest of the Diocese of Rocksburg, Professor at St. Gregory's Seminary in Rocksburg

Arthur Darner, student in Theology at St. Gregory's Seminary in Rocksburg

Fred Gacious, student in Theology at St. Gregory's Seminary in Rocksburg

Barney Ramage, student in Theology at St. Gregory's Seminary in Rocksburg

Mike Krebs, priest of the Diocese of Rocksburg, sometime Professor at St. Gregory's Seminary

Thomas "Cal" Kennelly, monsignor, priest of the Diocese of Cape Forneau, pastor in residence at the North American College in Rome

Jake Whelan, priest of the Diocese of Rockville Center, instructor in Moral Theology at the North American College in Rome

Andy Guelph, Bishop and Rector of the North American College in Rome

Richard Giordano, second year student from the Diocese of Brooklyn at the North American College in Rome

Sal Caputo, deacon, fourth year student from the Diocese of Brooklyn at the North American College in Rome

Joe Denzer, deacon, fourth year student from the Diocese of Rocksburg at the North American College in Rome, then priest at St. Teresa Parish in Rocksburg

Don Himmelreich, Rector of St. Gregory's Seminary in Rocksburg

Archbishop Luigi LaMonde, Apostolic Delegate to the United States

Francis X. Tooley, wealthy parishioner at St. Teresa Parish in Rocksburg

Jerry Donnelly, pastor in the Diocese of Rocksburg

Carl Kalina, pastor in the Diocese of Rocksburg

Peter Brennan, deacon, fourth year student from the Diocese of Sheboygan at the North American College in Rome

Mark Merolac, deacon, fourth year student from the Diocese of Santa Anna at the North American College in Rome

Tom Bumbaucher, first year student from the Diocese of Rocksburg at the North American College in Rome

Monsignor Phil Rogers, priest of the Diocese of Syracuse, Vice-Rector of the North American College in Rome

Sister DeeDee Moriarty, SVD, religious sister studying for her M.S.W. at Rocksburg University

Augustus Diamond, priest of the Diocese of Nogaces

Jim O'Hara, retired, parishioner at St. Teresa Parish in Rocksburg

Ernie Daniels, sixth grade student at St. Teresa grade school in Rocksburg, grandson of Jim O'Hara

Ben, a patient at the Veteran's Hospital in Rocksburg

Priests Without People

I

Appointment in Rome

John Rooney was being kept waiting. It was an odd experience for the Bishop of Rocksburg. People did not often keep him waiting. Usually, it was the other way around.

He was almost always late for meetings and appointments. Not out of a lack of concern, or even disorganization. He was a highly organized person, and he often said that the secret to success in life was to develop a daily schedule as a young man and stick to it thereafter.

The reason was people. Wherever he went, when he was recognized, his disarming affability seemed to invite people to approach him and burden him with the secrets of their lives. This happened to him in hallways, on street corners, in airports.

But making time for these encounters meant that he would inevitably be late for wherever he was going.

At least, he thought, this is a sumptuous place to count the minutes. He looked at the walls, covered in a plaited beige fabric, stretching from the green marble baseboard to the coffered ceiling. The modern wall covering had been installed by the current pontiff, replacing the faded red brocade that had hung there for nearly a century. John Rooney wondered if the pope knew how much it resembled the brown grocery paper that his fictional predecessor, Hadrian the Seventh, had pasted on the walls of the Vatican apartments. Somewhere in the afterlife, he thought, Baron Corvo, the louche Scottish author who had created Hadrian, was chuckling.

But then, how dotty am I going, he wondered, comparing that imaginary rascal Hadrian VII to the very real Paul VI. That's what comes from having such a case of the nerves. Why in the world does he want to see me?

He got up from his chair and paced the anteroom. At the window, he pulled back the sheer curtains and looked down on the San Damaso courtyard. The sluggish fountain shot a few languid trickles into the air. Four flights up, in the Apostolic Palace, the splash of the water in the fountain's basin could barely be heard, but the effect was a pleasant one.

How often, back in Rocksburg, had he daydreamed about the fountains of Rome? Tucked away in courtyards and small, angular piazzas, they were meant to surprise the eye as a person came through an archway or around a corner. The unexpected, seemingly unorganized beauty of the city was one of the joys of Rome that he remembered from his student days.

He wished that the apostolic delegate had been more expansive when he had called. Archbishop LaMonde had simply said that the Holy Father wanted to see him in Rome on a certain date. No why or wherefore, just a simple, "Won't you please arrange your schedule to be there?"

Suddenly the door to the papal library sprung open. Out shuffled an old Italian cardinal. John Rooney recognized him, Ettore Fischetti, the Cardinal Prefect of the Sacred Congregation for Clergy.

The man was almost blind. He was being led at the elbow by a very solicitous younger priest. John Rooney went to greet them as they passed, but the younger priest steered his cardinal-ward past the American bishop as if he did not exist.

Puzzled, John Rooney heard the papal chamberlain say that His Holiness would see him now.

John Rooney admired Paul VI. During the recent Vatican Council, he had come to know him almost as well as anyone knew the reserved and reticent pontiff.

In his pre-seminary days, John Rooney had been a cub reporter and this accident of his background won him the assignment of running the makeshift news conferences at the Council. They were lively affairs, and John Rooney's quick wit was more than a match for most reporters. The pope prized this bishop who could handle the difficult media, especially the insistent American press.

When he entered the papal library, Paul VI came forward to meet him. John Rooney bent over to kiss the Fisherman's ring, as the pope looked down with an embarrassed expression.

"*Eccelenza,*" Paul greeted him.

"*Santità,*" John Rooney responded, saying "Holiness" in the impeccable Italian he had learned over thirty years before as a seminary student in Rome.

The pope motioned him to a chair. Their conversation continued in Italian. Paul VI for all his erudition had never mastered English.

"Thank you for attending us, dear friend," Paul said. "We are sorry you were kept waiting. The last audience was a difficult one."

"Cardinal Fischetti?" John Rooney said. "I saw him leave. He and his companion seemed upset. They ignored me entirely. I can't imagine why."

"Oh, that is easy," the pope smiled. "They are displeased with you."

"Me? Why?"

"You will have his job."

"I do not understand, Holiness."

"We have it in mind to appoint you Prefect for Clergy. Will you accept?"

John Rooney was flabbergasted. Of all the reasons that he could guess for being summoned to Rome, that would have been the last.

The pope saw the confusion on his face and hurried on. "We said it frequently during the Council. There are too many persons of one nationality in the Curia. They have operated the Church for so long that they permit no other point of view. The only way to change that, dear friend, is to change them. There are no Americans at the head of any Congregation. It would please us to appoint you."

"But, Holiness, there are many others more qualified."

"Qualified? How? We have seen your work. We know how much you love this city and its bishop who sits in Peter's chair."

John Rooney knew that the pope had read him well. As with the poet Browning, it was equally true of him, "Open my heart and you will see carved inside of it, 'Italy.'"

"But, Holiness, I am only the bishop of a small city in America."

"We will be announcing a consistory next month. Although it is under pontifical secret until the official announcement, for your country, we have it in mind to give the red hat to Chicago, St. Louis and yourself. You will be a cardinal."

"Holiness, I am overwhelmed."

"You will accept?"

"As I said, I am overwhelmed, stunned. What you propose is a great honor."

"Then you accept?"

"Holiness, I am taken by surprise. Is it possible that I may have some time to think about this?"

"You are thinking about your diocese, this small city in America?"

Again, the pope had read him well. He was

thinking about Rocksburg where he had been
bishop for ten years. The priests, at first, had not
warmed to him, "a wise man from the East," im-
ported from Boston to be their bishop. They would
have preferred one of their own after the rigid
Clevelander who had led the diocese for years. But
the people of Rocksburg had received him with
generous hearts and he had reciprocated, going
everywhere and doing anything he was asked.
Eventually the priests came around as well, won
over by his natural charm. He had many friends
in Rocksburg now, priests and people. It would be
hard to leave.

"Yes, your Holiness. I am."

"If what we propose is such a 'great honor,'
what is there to consider?" the pope asked. "No,
Giovanni, you are too diplomatic. You know it is
not so much *'un onore'* we are proposing as it is a
Calvary, *'un Calvario'.*"

Paul picked up a pile of red-ribboned dossiers
stacked on the corner of the huge library table
that he used for a desk, and he let them fall with
a heavy thump. "Do you know what these are,
Eccelenza?"

John Rooney shook his head.

The pope continued. "These are the files of
priests asking to be relieved of their priesthood.
After the Council, there are many. Every week the
Holy Office sends us dozens. Many of them—most
of them—are Americans."

"I am aware, your Holiness. Even in my own
diocese …"

"These men who would leave the ministry of
Christ are our own personal cross, Giovanni. We
need help to bear it. We cannot do it alone."

John Rooney looked up at the man. He thought
that he saw tears welling in the large round eyes
perched above the pontiff's little bird's nose.

Funny, he thought to himself, if you asked
anyone where the power was in this world of ours

today, surely this room in the Apostolic Palace would show up on the list, along with that mansion on Pennsylvania Avenue and the yellow stuccoed office building inside the Kremlin's walls. Yet, here is the incumbent feeling and acting very powerless.

"But Holiness, dismissal from priesthood is not in the competency of the Congregation for Clergy. That is the Holy Office. How could I help you as Prefect for Clergy?"

"Yes, the Holy Office does them, but their approach is always to punish, to punish." The pope slashed the air with his right hand as he said this.

"These priests who ask us to be relieved of the burdens of their priesthood need help, Giovanni, not punishment. Your Congregation, that of Clergy, must assist them with counsel, with guidance, with the support of the universal church, and perhaps their hearts will be changed. We have not done enough for them in the past, these troubled men," Paul said as he ruffled the edges of the dossiers on his desk. "Will you help us to do it?"

"I need some time, Holiness. What you propose is an awesome task. It will change my life drastically. I need to pray and think."

"We know that we are asking much of you, but we have already told his Eminence Fischetti that he must resign and that you are the probable successor. The walls have ears, *caro amico*. It will not be long before everyone is whispering."

"I shall not take long, Holiness. A day, no more."

"A day we can give, dear friend. Go and pray hard."

On the way down the winding travertine stairs that led from the papal apartments to the Bronze Door and out to St. Peter's Square, John Rooney felt a bit of vertigo and grabbed onto the marble railing several times to steady himself. When he was outside in the Square, the bright sun of the late Roman spring almost blinded him. He felt light-headed and disoriented.

Slowly he made his way up the long, shallow stairs to the basilica. The shade inside refreshed him as he walked its length, past the seated statue of St. Peter, and down the stairs to the tombs of the popes.

John XXIII, who had died five years ago, was buried there as was Pius XII, who had made John Rooney a bishop. Pius's tomb was bare and John's was covered with flowers.

Across from Pius's resting place, there were some prie-dieux drawn up in front of the tomb of Peter, the first pope. John Rooney knelt there in prayer.

As he did so often in his conversations with the Lord, he found himself laughing. The world will think this is a great honor, Lord, being made a cardinal and called to Rome, he prayed. But You know and I know it would be easier for me to stay in Rocksburg. I am sixty-four years old. If I am fortunate, I have a dozen or so good years left. I really do not want to spend them fighting bureaucratic battles at the papal court. Yet, it is not what I want, but what You want. Help me, Lord, to see and do Your will.

Hoisting himself from the prie-dieu, he slowly ambled toward the front of the basilica and the ground floor exit, past the remains of the old Constantinian wall that formed the foundation of the renaissance church above. He was back in the bright, sunlit Square again, surrounded by the forest of Bernini's columns, reaching out like two arms to embrace the world.

He walked through the massive colonnade and into the gray Piazza del Sant'Uffizio, the headquarters of the Holy Office, the Vatican department that handled discipline in the Church, including the resignation of priests. What had the pope said? Their approach was always to punish. If I take this job, he wondered, how many fights will I have with these folks?

Why, why should I want to give up my own

diocese and come here, his mind questioned. The hardest part would be leaving his people. He loved to be with them, to preach to them in his cathedral, to talk with them in meetings and social gatherings. If he came to Rome, he would be bishop of no one, a priest without people, and the thought alarmed him. Was it worth giving that up to be a courtier at the papal throne?

No, he was not being fair to his Holiness. The job that he was being offered was more than that.

The crisis in the priesthood was real. He knew it from his own experience in Rocksburg. Priests were just men, earthen vessels asked to convey a supernatural treasure. But that weighty cargo did not come without its pressures and sometimes the human clay cracked.

It was not just the weak, not just those who lost their sense of the holy, who left. Sometimes it was the best—the most devoted and devout, deprived of intimacy for too long or suffocated by a soul-crushing nearness to the Eternal—who sought a different life.

What, he contemplated, could he do from Rome to change this? He had not been very successful in Rocksburg with changing the minds of his own priests who had decided to leave. He had met with them, cajoled them, prayed with them, offered them special assignments, and all to no avail. To his great sorrow, they had left anyway.

His life in Rome would not be easy. The city had changed greatly from his student days. It was much more disorganized and unlivable now. Suddenly he caught himself laughing again. Of course Rome was more organized when he was a student here in the 30s, he thought. Fascism will do that. No, he would prefer modern Italian disorganization over the orderliness of a dictatorship anytime.

But where would he live? Most of the cardinals resident in Rome lived in cramped apartments in the Mussolini built structures that surrounded the Vatican. Some senior prelates had nicer places in the older palazzos, but even those apartments lacked modern plumbing and ventilated bathrooms. It would be a far cry from the pleasant suburban house that Rocksburg had for its bishop.

The dampness in Rome, the rainy winters, the way the thick brick and plaster walls held their moisture—that would not be good for his arthritis. Already he felt his hips stiffening in their joints, and he had barely been here for two days.

He was overweight, which also was not good for his hips, and lately he had been having trouble with his digestion. Some form of nervous colitis, his doctor said. Where in this land of spiced sauces and rich wines would he find the bland food that his aging body demanded? And he loved Italian food so much.

What if he were to get sick here? Time moved fast as a weaver's shuttle. In a twinkling he would be old. Illness would not be unexpected. In Rocksburg he had his doctors, a private suite in the Divine Word Hospital, and the special treatment afforded an ailing diocesan bishop.

Rome had none of these. Italian doctors, he knew, were long on theory and short on clinical experience. The hospitals were not antiseptic and the nurses were undertrained. Sick prelates staffing the Church's headquarters were supernumerary. If he ever became ill, he would have to pray that his body gave him enough warning to get on the first plane for America.

He re-examined his thoughts and realized the temptations that self-preoccupation brought. All of his concerns were for himself, and not for the Church that he had promised to serve so many years ago.

He was a priest of Christ and Christ's vicar had called him, yet he was vacillating. How much different was he than the priests who left, thinking only what he must do to save himself?

He remembered what looked like tears in the pope's eyes and he knew it was that memory, more than anything, that would make him say yes. What a sentimental sap I have become, he thought. All of my New England flint has turned to Italian cheese. Ah well. It was obedience that made me a priest and it will be obedience that makes me a cardinal.

And with his mind all but made up, he began singing, softly to himself, "*Ridi Pagliaccio, sul tuo amore infranto*–Laugh, Clown, for your breaking heart ..." as he walked slowly down the streets of the city where, he knew now, one day, his earthly life would end.

II

One Time King

"It's a mistake, I'm telling you, Marty. This is an Irish parish," Sparky Larkin, pastor of St. Teresa's Parish, barked into the telephone at Martin Phelan, auxiliary bishop and vicar general of the Diocese of Rocksburg.

Sitting in the diocesan chancery, five miles away in downtown Rocksburg, Martin Phelan shook his head. Sparky Larkin had always been an excitable sort.

Many people thought that his temperament was the source of his nickname, but Martin Phelan and Sparky Larkin went back a long way, to St. Gregory's Seminary in the 1930s, and Marty Phelan well remembered the day Sparky Larkin got his nickname.

It was visitors' Sunday at St. Gregory's, the one day in the month when the seminarians' parents, spiffed up in their Sunday best, were permitted by diocesan ordinance to drive out to the countryside, to the remote location of St. Gregory's Seminary, and salute their offspring.

On such a Sunday, a group of parents was sitting on the park benches, in the shade of the huge sycamores that lined the walk to the chapel building, visiting with their sons, when Terrence Larkin, still vested in his altar boy's red cassock and white surplice, sprung down the chapel steps and away to the dormitory building on what appeared to be an urgent errand.

Someone's mother, her identity long since forgotten, had remarked at the sight of the running seminarian in his red and white altar boy's regalia, "Why he looks just like a sparkplug."

And she was right. In his short, stocky form, with his red bottom and white top, Terrence Larkin did look just like a Champion brand sparkplug.

Word of this utterance immediately spread and within the day everyone on the seminary campus was calling him "Sparkplug Larkin." In time, the name was shortened to "Sparky," and so it had remained these last three decades. Now a senior pastor, in his late fifties, at one of the largest parishes in Rocksburg, Father Terrence Larkin was "Sparky" to one and all.

"Sparky," Bishop Phelan shouted back into the telephone, "this is 1968. When was the last time you looked at the stats on St. Teresa's? When was the last time you even did a parish census?"

That was a trick question. Both men knew that diocesan statutes required a parish census every three years and both men knew that Sparky had not had the energy to do a census since he had become pastor of St. Teresa's over a dozen years ago.

"I don't need a census to know my parish, Marty. And you ought to know better, too. You were born and raised right down the street in Soho."

"That's why I know it's not an Irish parish anymore, Sparky. Hasn't been for donkeys' days. If you'd been paying attention, you'd've seen that most of the people moving into St. Teresa's are the coloreds in the projects on the Hill. All the Irish are gone away to Brookline."

"So that's why the diocese is sending me this dago, to take care of the coloreds? That's just what

I would expect from John Rooney. Too bad we couldn't have one of our own a bishop here."

"This isn't Bishop Rooney's appointment, Sparky. He's in Rome with the Holy Father."

"I shoulda guessed that," Sparky Larkin said. "A fine bishop who's never in his own diocese. So are you the one sending me this spaghetti bender, Marty?"

"Sparky, you know as well as I do. Appointments come from the personnel board. You've got a choice. It's Father Anthony Capresi or it's nobody. Which is it to be?"

"He'll be a sad replacement for Jack Donahue," Sparky lamented in reference to his most recent curate, who had been named pastor of a small rural parish in the May changes that were sending the newly ordained Tony Capresi to St. Teresa's as assistant pastor.

"Which is it to be, Sparky?"

"I can't believe that you are doing this to me."

"Sparky, there are pastors in this diocese who would give their Christmas collection for a live, healthy assistant. Now do you want the man or not?"

"I guess I'll give him a try. You've really left me no choice."

It did not help things when Father Capresi arrived at St. Teresa's the following week driving a bright red 1968 Chevrolet Impala.

Just what you'd expect from a dago, Sparky Larkin thought. Showy.

"Priests usually drive black cars, Father," Sparky Larkin had said when he greeted his new assistant at the front door of the rectory. "Black or dark blue."

"It was a gift from my parents, Father Larkin. For my ordination. They picked the color. It's my mother's favorite."

"This is a working class, Irish parish, Father.

Displays of wealth, especially by the clergy, are not welcomed by the parishioners."

"Gee, Father, I never thought ..."

"Well, you'll have to be thinking about those things, about how things will look in the people's eyes."

"Sorry. It was a gift. Is the color that important?"

"Red is flashy, Father, and around here appearances count. Take my word for it. Appearances count. Now that you're a priest, you'll be living your life in a fish bowl."

"I didn't mean to criticize, Father," the young man said, angling his suitcases past the older priest. "Is my room upstairs? Where shall I put my stuff?"

"Upstairs and second door to the right," Sparky Larkin said.

On his way up the stairs, Tony Capresi sensed a frightening stench. He wasn't sure if it was coming from upstairs or if it permeated the whole house. Whatever the smell was, and wherever it was coming from, it was foul. It smelled like hell had opened up its jaws and belched. The young priest was hacking and sneezing before he got to the top of the stairs. Oh great, he thought, I'm allergic to my first parish.

He pushed the door to the second room on the right open with one of his suitcases. The room wasn't very big, and was furnished with a bed, a bookcase, a lamp, and a reading chair. Tony Capresi opened an inside door, expecting it to be an attached bathroom, but it was only a clothes' closet. He put his suitcases down and quickly opened the only window in the room, which was over the front porch of the rectory, in order to air the place out.

Then he went exploring. The door across from his had a wooden plaque on it, with the figure of a golfer, and beside it, engraved in a cursive scroll, Sparky Larkin's name. Just past Tony Capresi's room was a large room that looked like a library, although there didn't seem to be many books in it.

Across from that was another bedroom. Tony peeked in. It was bigger than his room, and it seemed to be unoccupied, although there were a few books and odd clothes about. When he pushed open an inside door in the room, he saw that it had its own bathroom. That was curious.

He went downstairs. Sparky Larkin was out in the driveway, kicking the tires on his assistant's new Impala.

"Father, did you say the second door to the right or to the left?" Tony Capresi asked.

"To the right, I said. It's that room there." Sparky Larkin pointed to the window over the front porch.

"I was just wondering. Who gets the second room on the left, the one with the bath?"

"It's being saved for visiting priests, and besides, I told Father Donahue he could leave a few things in it for the time being. I hope you didn't disturb any of his belongings."

"Jack Donahue, your former assistant, the man I'm replacing?"

"Yes."

"That was his room?"

"It was, but now that he's moved out, I thought I'd make the change. Nothing to do with you, Father. It was just a convenient time."

"And my bathroom, where is that?"

"You passed it. It's that door at the top of the stairs, just before your own door."

"So I'll be going out in the hallway to get my shower and all?"

"You did that in the seminary, didn't you, Father? Unless they remodeled St. Gregory's since my day."

"What if somebody sees me?"

"On your way to the shower?"

"Yes."

"No one except priests is allowed up there.

That's one of the rules you'll have to be learning about St. Teresa's. No one except me and you and our fellow priests is allowed on the second floor. Too much trouble is caused in rectories by having people in the priests' quarters. It's a good rule. Jack Donahue didn't have any trouble with it."

"Who cleans up? Doesn't the cleaning woman ever go up there?" As soon as he asked the question, Tony Capresi had his doubts. He recalled the fetid smell on the stairs and shuddered. Maybe the cleaning woman never does go up there. Maybe there is no cleaning woman.

"She does, on my day off, which is Wednesdays, by the way. You'll have to pick another day — Saturdays and Sundays excluded of course."

"So what if she's in the hall on Wednesdays?"

"Look, Father, Jack Donahue never had that problem."

"Father, Jack Donahue had a room with a bath in it."

"Don't get excited, Father. I think I see the problem. Just arrange your schedule around hers or something on those days."

Tony Capresi opened the back door of his car and removed the clothes hanging there. Perspiring in the heat, he made several trips back and forth between his room and the car. Every time that he came back, Sparky Larkin was examining another part of his car. When he returned to get the last item, his stereo turntable that had been perched precariously on the back seat, Sparky Larkin had the hood open and was examining the motor.

Tony Capresi took the turntable carefully from the back seat and began to carry it toward the rectory. He smelled the dog before he saw it. The stink made him wince and, in an instant, the dog was upon him, a huge German shepherd that had a worse scent than anything he had ever smelled before. He quickly recognized it as the odor that pervaded the rectory. He immediately started sneezing in spasms.

The dog was prancing all around him, jumping up and trying to lick his face.

"Father, could you get the dog?" he said. Sparky Larkin did not hear him, his head buried under the Impala's hood.

The dog must have sensed his fear, and it became more aggressive, barking loudly and snapping at his legs.

"Father," he said, his shaking hands holding tightly onto his turntable, "could you get the dog, please?"

There was still no answer. The man must be deaf, he thought. If I run the dog will know I'm afraid and that will be worse. I'll just walk calmly but quickly. "Nice doggie … nice doggie," he said as he tried to take a step and sneezed again.

The dog kept circling around him, barking and barking, and would not let him move.

"Father Larkin," he yelled. "Could you come and get the dog, please?"

He heard the hood slam and Sparky Larkin's voice call, "Rex!"

The dog went to his master. This is my chance, Tony Capresi thought, as he started to run for the rectory door.

It was a mistake. At the sight of the running man, Rex did a u-turn and went after his terrified quarry.

The dog was on him in a leap, knocking him down from behind. The turntable went flying into the air and landed in smithereens on the concrete driveway. Among the shards of plastic, wire, and metal, Tony Capresi lay face down with Rex barking over him, a paw planted firmly on his back.

"Rex, Rex," Sparky Larkin said, as he grabbed the dog's collar and pulled him away. "Look what you've done. Bad boy, bad boy," he remonstrated as he led the dog, whining, off behind the rectory.

Tony Capresi was picking up the pieces of his turntable when Sparky Larkin returned.

"I've got him chained up in the backyard. I guess it's broke, huh?"

"I don't think I can play any records on it," Tony Capresi said.

"You shouldn't a run. It's the running that sets him off. He's a good dog, mostly. He keeps the coloreds away from this place. St. Teresa's has never been broken into."

"Father, I just got this thing. Now it's ruined."

"It was an accident. You shouldn't a run. It won't be that way when he gets to know you."

"And what am I supposed to do about this in the meantime?" he questioned, holding up the twisted record plate from his turntable.

"Look, go to the Diocesan Purchasing Commission. Get a new one. Tell them to put it on the parish account."

"Thanks."

"That's okay. You can pay the parish back from your first monthly check, and the next time you're with the dog, be friendly. The dog's a good judge of character. If he doesn't like you, there must be a reason. He never had a problem with Jack Donahue."

Dinner that night, and every night at St. Teresa's, was a hot dish brought in by one of the ladies of the parish. Seated at the dining room table, Tony heard loud slurping sounds coming from the kitchen.

"What's that?" he asked.

"Rex is eating out there, so's he won't bother you," Sparky Larkin said.

"He's in the house a lot, is he?"

"Evenings mostly. He usually has dinner with me, and then we watch TV together in the den. I like to keep him inside nights, for burglars, you know."

"Father, I'm not so sure that's a good idea. Dogs and I don't get along. I was never allowed to have one as a kid and I'm kind of afraid of them."

"You should never show a dog you're afraid of it. Worst thing you can do."

"I'll try to remember that. But what are we going to do about things in the meantime?"

"You'll get used to him."

"I don't know if I can."

"Well, he was here first."

"Father, I'm the assistant pastor in this parish. What are you saying?"

"I'm saying, Rex serves a purpose. He serves a purpose. And if there's any getting used to around here, it's *you* should be getting used to *him*."

They spent the rest of the meal in silence. Tony Capresi wanted to watch television that night, but when he got to the den, Rex was firmly ensconced besides Sparky's La-Z-Boy and Tony was afraid to enter the room.

He stuck his head in to see what show was on. Sparky Larkin was pouring some of his beer into Rex's dish and feeding him some potato chips from the big bag on his lap. Sparky did not notice the door opening, but Rex did. He looked up and growled. Tony Capresi sneezed before he could close the door. He decided to go upstairs and read himself to sleep.

He woke in the middle of a nightmare. Wherever he went in his dream, even when he was on the altar to say mass, Rex was there, growling and snapping at him. He was in a cold sweat, and he had to go to the bathroom. He got out of bed and opened his bedroom door. There across the hall was Rex, sleeping outside Sparky Larkin's door. Maybe he won't hear me, Tony Capresi thought, as he took three steps toward the bathroom door, but then he sneezed. The noise awoke the dog, and, as soon as he saw Tony, he began snarling. Tony quickly hopped inside the bathroom and closed the door.

He prayed that by the time he was done the dog would be back asleep. After he flushed the toilet, he slowly opened the bathroom door. In a flash, Rex was there growling. Tony Capresi closed the door.

For the next half-hour, Tony Capresi kept peeping out of the bathroom door, in the hope that Rex would fall asleep and that he could safely go back to his bedroom, but that did not happen. Every crack of the door caught the dog's ear and brought him standing to attention outside.

Almost unconscious from his lack of sleep, Father Tony Capresi finally gave in and, on his first night in St. Teresa's rectory, he went to sleep in the bathtub, with a rolled up towel for a pillow.

He was stiff when he woke up the next morning. He stretched and slowly opened the bathroom door. Down the hall, the door to Sparky Larkin's room was still closed, but there was no sign of Rex. Thank God, Tony thought. I can at least get my shaving kit and shower.

Downstairs, at breakfast, he peered cautiously around every corner for the dog. Although his stench was everywhere, the animal was gone. I guess it'll just be the nights, the young priest thought. That won't be so bad, if the dog's not around most of the day. Maybe I can get used to it.

He was walking over to the church for his early morning mass, staring up at the tall brick towers of the structure, lost in a world of contemplation, when he heard the skitter of unclipped toenails scurrying on the concrete. It was Rex, barking his head off, chasing after a chipmunk.

Thank God for another victim, Tony Capresi thought. But when Rex saw a far bigger prize than the one he was after, he left his small quarry and headed for the priest. Tony Capresi knew not to run, so he just kept walking slowly, not looking at Rex.

Then he remembered a trick, one he had used as a little boy to keep strange dogs at bay. He bent over, pretending to pick up a stone, and curved his arm in a throwing motion, as if he were going to whale a good-sized rock at the dog.

Miraculously, it worked. Rex, confused that his playmate might want to hurt him, backed off several yards. It was all that Tony needed to make it to the church door.

After mass and some brief chats with the few parishioners who could attend a weekday liturgy, Tony Capresi peered out the church door for any sign of Rex. Nothing.

He was halfway to the rectory before the dog saw him and came running. Tony stooped again, pretending he was picking up a rock, and again the dog backed off.

But Rex was patrolling the rectory and every attempt that Tony Capresi made to approach the building, the dog headed him off. Stupid dog, he thought, he doesn't remember that I live here. This is nonsense. I can't spend the next five years of my life afraid of going to the bathroom or of walking from the church to the rectory, he thought, as he stubbornly headed for the rectory door.

Rex was quickly at his heels. Despite his fear, Tony Capresi lunged out, trying to kick the animal with his right foot. The dog was too fast for him. He dodged the priest's shoe and came back at him from the other side, grabbing hold of his left ankle. In terror, Tony Capresi realized that the sensation he felt was the dog's teeth against his skin. He could feel the pressure and it hurt. He panicked.

With a quick push from his right foot, he freed himself and started to run. But Rex, the guard dog, was between him and the rectory. There was no place to go but the street.

Tony Capresi darted between two parked cars and into traffic. A large van nearly clipped the priest, and the driver leaned on his horn in anger and fright that he had almost run someone over.

But the van blocked Rex for a while and Tony made it to the other side of the street well in advance of the dog. He looked for a place of refuge. The side of the street across from the rectory was lined with small brick houses, all with wooden front porches, all identically-shaped to their neighbors, but separated from each other by their driveways. Where could he run for help? Not a person was in sight.

Then he saw her, in her driveway, wearing shorts and a halter top, washing her car. It was a beautiful bright red Corvette convertible. It looked like a '57. Gosh, it was in great shape, Tony Capresi thought.

By then the dog was across the street, barking loudly and looking for the priest.

Tony Capresi shouted, "Help me," as he ran down the woman's driveway.

The woman saw the man, dressed in clerical clothes, being pursued by the huge dog. She acted instinctively, pushing the man inside her car and turning the hose, nozzle on full pressure, at the dog.

It caught Rex square in the face and knocked him back a yard. Again, Rex advanced toward his quarry sitting in the car, but again the woman let him have it with the hose full in the face.

"Rex," she shouted, "go, get the hell out of here."

The dog stopped in his tracks. "Rex, go," she said and pointed authoritatively back to the rectory. The dog looked at her and the man in the car sorrowfully. Nobody wanted to play. He went home.

The woman opened the door to her Corvette and said, "It's safe to come out. He's gone."

"Thanks," the priest said as he emerged from the car. "You saved my life."

"I'm not sure about that," the young woman said.

He lifted up his pants leg. There were red scratch marks all around his ankle and some of them were bleeding.

"Stupid dog," she said. "That looks nasty.

Come in the house and let me take care of it."

"Thanks," Tony said. "By the way, I'm Tony Capresi, the new priest at St. Teresa's."

"Yeah, I figured. Connie Amoroso, pleased to meet you." She stuck out her hand and they shook. "Come on in."

She made him sit on the couch in the front room while she went to her medicine cabinet. She came back with two brown bottles, some cotton swabs, and bandages.

"Just relax now," she said as she rolled the priest's pant leg up and his sock down. "This might sting a little. It's peroxide, but it'll take care of whatever gunk that dog had on his teeth."

Tony looked down at her as she swabbed his scratches, put some mercurochrome on them, and bandaged them. She was very attractive. Pale blue eyes, square shouldered, and about five foot six or seven, he guessed. Her strawberry blonde hair was pinned back on either side of her head with red plastic barrettes. Her body looked strong and he could not help but notice, as she bent over his ankle, that, inside her halter top, she was very well proportioned.

The feeling of her fingers on his bare leg made him feel giddy and languorous.

"Amoroso," he said, "that's Italian, isn't it?"

"Yeah, it is, but I'm not. That's Joe's name. My husband. I'm a polack, Connie Kowalski, originally."

"Do you guys belong to St. Teresa's?"

"That's a long story."

"Oh?"

"I'll tell you sometime."

"What's wrong with now?"

"In case you didn't notice, I was doing something when you ran down my driveway. I'd like to get back to washing my car when I'm done playing Florence Nightingale here."

"That's a great car. A '57 Corvette, right? Where'd you find it?"

"Joe bought it from one of the kids at the

university. We've been restoring it for almost two years now. We really enjoy it."

"Is that where he works, your husband, at the university?"

"Yeah."

"What's he teach?"

"No, he's in counseling and advisement."

"Sounds interesting. And you?"

"I work here. I'm a 'homemaker,' as they say."

"Any kids?"

"No."

"Oh."

"Don't 'oh' me, Father. I meant none yet."

"Tony. You can call me Tony."

"Sure. Tony. Fine. It's a sensitive subject."

"Is that your problem with the Church—the pill?"

"Hell no, that's not it. I was married before."

"Oh."

"You know, you sure have a way of putting a lot of disapproval into a simple 'oh.' They teach you that in the seminary?"

"No. I mean, I'm not disapproving. Whatever your situation is, I'm sure there are reasons."

"Yeah, there are reasons. Look. You're all done, good as new. Time for us both to go back to work."

She stood from her crouching position and helped the priest up from the couch.

He trod gingerly on his ankle.

"I think you fixed it. Thanks a lot."

"You're welcome."

"Are you going to wax the car when you're done?"

"No. I just wash. Joe waxes."

"That's a nice division of labor. Maybe I could bring my Impala over sometime."

"Your Impala? I saw it yesterday. That's a pretty nice car."

Tony Capresi turned a bright red. "Did you see the whole thing yesterday?"

"Half the street saw yesterday. With the heat, there were a lot of people sitting on their porches when you drove up."

"God, how embarrassing."

"Yeah. Larkin can be a real fool, can't he?"

"I don't know. I just met the man. Why don't you tell me more about him?"

"Say, you really don't want to go back across the street, do you?"

"No, I don't. I'm scared to death of that dog."

"Hell, that dog's a coward. He's the joke of the parish. Last fall, I saw Rex tree a squirrel in front of the rectory. Only the poor squirrel got so confused at Rex's barking, he came running back down the tree. When Rex saw the squirrel change directions, he took off like a shot. You haven't seen anything as funny as that huge dog running away from a tiny little squirrel. That dog's the original all bark and no bite."

"You couldn't prove it by me," Tony said as he lifted his left foot slightly.

"It really looks worse than it is. I'm sure he was just playing with you."

"I can't take that kind of playing. This is only my second day here and already I'm a nervous case. I hardly slept at all last night and now I can't get into the rectory."

Connie Amoroso started laughing. Tony Capresi looked at her in disbelief.

"This isn't funny. I'm afraid to go back to the rectory and I have to live there the next five years of my life."

Looking at him and giggling, she said, "But are you a man or are you a squirrel?" She was bending over with laughter now.

"I don't know why you think this is so hilarious."

"You are a man. Rex is a dog. A very dumb, fat, stinky, cowardly dog. You should be able to outsmart him. Look, the thing with a dog is, you have to show who's in charge."

"How do I do that?"

"Did you ever have a dog?"

"No, never. We weren't allowed. That's why I'm so afraid of him."

"People who train dogs have little tricks. Like whenever we got a new dog at my house, when I was small, my dad would keep a newspaper rolled up, and every time the dog did something he shouldn't, my dad rapped him on the nose with the paper. Pretty soon, all my dad had to do was wave the rolled up paper at the dog, and the dog knew to stop doing whatever ..."

"Yes?" the priest said, wondering why she had stopped.

"Oh, nothing. I just realized that my dad did the same thing with us kids. Anyhow it worked."

"So what are you telling me, carry a rolled up newspaper all the time?"

"A newspaper or something. Look. I think I have an idea. Give me a second." She left him in the front room and ran up the stairs. She was back in a few minutes, beaming from ear to ear, carrying a cane.

"Joe used this last year when he sprained his ankle," she said. "Why don't you borrow it?"

"I don't get it. What will this do?"

"Pretend it's your newspaper, dummy. Every time Rex gets too close, rap him in the shins or the nose with the cane. In a day or two, he'll get the message and stay away."

"You think it'll work?"

"What have you got to lose?"

"Only my ankles. Thanks. I really appreciate this," he said, taking the cane and practicing walking around the room with it. "I hope I can return the favor someday."

"I'll call you the next time my car needs washed."

"I meant maybe I could help you regularize your marriage."

"Get going," she said. "My marriage is fine."

She gave him a confident pat on the back as she pushed him out the door. Her touch on his shoulder made him feel a bit light-headed.

He stopped at the top of the porch stairs and turned around. "Thanks again," he said as he waved the cane in a circle beside his head.

Connie Amoroso stood there watching his progress. Why, she wondered, do I feel like a mother who has just seen her only child off for his first day of school?

As soon as Tony Capresi had crossed the street, Rex came barking and running up to the priest. The cane flashed and Rex went scrambling away. Tony Capresi made it safely to the rectory's front porch, turned and saw Connie watching him.

"It worked," he shouted and waved the cane again.

Stupid priest, she thought, and went back to washing her car.

"What's wrong with your leg, Father?" Sparky Larkin asked at dinner that night when he saw the cane.

"Your dog bit me on the ankle. It's very tender and I need the extra support."

"Did you see a doctor?"

"No, a woman across the street bandaged me and lent me the cane."

"Who would that be?"

"Connie Amoroso. Do you know her?"

Sparky Larkin regurgitated a small piece of dried out pork chop onto his plate. "You stay away from her. That woman is trouble."

"Why is that, Father?"

"Number one, she's divorced and remarried outside the Church, which means she's living in adultery. Number two, she's forever challenging and making a mockery of the teachings of the Church."

"Which teachings, Father?"

"All of them."

"Really?"

"All of the important ones."

"You mean like the Incarnation and the Resurrection?"

"No, I mean like sex and marriage. That hussy tries to sneak to Communion every so often. But I'm ready for her. I'll keep refusing her until she gets her excommunicate soul back in line with the Church."

"You mean, she comes to mass?"

"Yes, she comes to mass. She even takes envelopes. And she flaunts it. Sits in the front pew. Not only on Sundays, but sometimes during the week. Last year, she got herself nominated to parish council, but I struck her name from the ballot."

"That sounds pretty devout to me. Have you tried talking to her?"

"Devout? It's all a show, a lousy dago show. And she doesn't want to talk. All that woman wants to do is argue."

"I don't think she's Italian, Father. Amoroso's her husband's name. She told me she was Polish."

"I know that. Isn't she my parishioner? What I meant was, it's all the same."

"Being Polish is the same as being Italian?"

"That's not what I said. What I said was the polacks like to put on a good show, just like the dagos."

"Oh."

"Any way, you stay away from her. That woman is trouble."

The cane was a miracle rod. Not for Tony Capresi's ankle, which really did not need the extra support, but for his safety. Rex was terrified of the thing. He never went near Tony when he carried it and so Tony took to carrying it all the time.

Some parishioners asked why he always walked with a cane. In response, he mumbled something about a congenital defect and hung his head, giving the impression that it was not something he felt comfortable talking about.

Tony Capresi's life at St. Teresa's soon became very much of a ritual. He had the early mass every day because, as Sparky Larkin explained, pastors had earned the right to sleep in. He took care of the school and all the youth activities because, as Sparky Larkin explained, those things needed a younger man. He handled the drop-in business and phone calls at the parish because, as Sparky Larkin explained, pastors shouldn't be answering doorbells and telephone calls.

Once, when he asked Sparky Larkin just what his duties as an assistant pastor were, Sparky told him, "That's easy. You do everything that I don't want to do." That appeared to be a pretty accurate description. About the only thing they did do together was to hear confessions at the same time, every Saturday afternoon, at three o'clock in the parish church.

It was only gradual at first, but after Tony Capresi had been in the parish for just over a month, the trend was undeniable. The line for his confessional was always much longer than Sparky's.

At first, Sparky Larkin had tried to joke about it. "What are you doing in there, Father," he had said, "giving out lollipops?"

But then it became a matter of ego, and it started to grate on Sparky Larkin's nerves. Jack Donahue's line had never been longer than his. He's doing something in there, Sparky thought. What could it be?

He found out one day in August, the weekend before the feast of the Assumption. Like all the Saturdays before a feast day, the lines for confession were a bit longer than usual.

A woman knelt down with a hurried thump in Sparky Larkin's box. "Forgive me, Father, for I have sinned. It's been one month since my last confession," she began. "Since then, I was unjustifiably angry with my children at least twenty times, Father, but there are five of them and that's easy to do. I have used bad words, but not the Lord's name, a dozen times. I got extra change at the Food Lion once, and I did not tell the cashier. It was only fifteen cents, Father, and I figure they've probably overcharged me at least that much in the past. And I am on the pill. I know you said last time I didn't have to confess that if I didn't think it was wrong, and I don't, I truly don't. I would die if I had another kid, but I feel better mentioning it. I am sorry for these …"

She did not get a chance to finish. Sparky Larkin roared like a wounded lion. "What do you mean I said not to confess birth control? It's the greatest of sins."

"Oh dear," the woman said. "I got in the wrong line. Sorry, Father."

Sparky Larkin heard the door to his confessional open and shut. The woman was gone. He was stupefied. How dare she leave in the middle of a sacrament, he thought.

The person on the other side of his confessional had started his confession. Sparky turned to him and said, "Be quiet. I'll be back," and he sprang from his confessional and strode across the church to the line at Father Capresi's.

"Who just left my confessional?" he shouted. "Whoever it was, you just get right back there. This is the Catholic Church. You can't pick and choose your priests. Whoever it was, you get right back there and finish that confession."

No one moved, but all of the people in line looked terrified.

"All right, you won't admit it. Fine, fine," he ranted as he stomped back to his own confessional.

That night, at dinner, before they divided up the veal cutlets and mashed potatoes that had been left to dry out for them on the rectory stove, he started. "What have you been telling them in the box about birth control, Father?"

"Excuse me?" Tony Capresi said.

"What is it? Don't you understand a simple question?"

"Not that one. What are you talking about?"

"In the confessional. What are you telling people about birth control?"

"Father, I tell them what they need to know to form their consciences and make a good confession."

"You do? Then why are people telling me that you're saying it's not a sin."

"Father, I don't judge what's a sin or not in the confessional. Only the penitent can do that."

Sparky Larkin was stymied. He did not have direct proof, and in the absence of an admission of guilt, there was little he could do.

"Well, don't let me be hearing that you're doing otherwise. The Church teaches one thing about birth control and one thing only. It's a serious sin. You've been spending too much time with those heretics across the street. I warned you about them."

"Father, Connie and I wash our cars together. And sometimes Joe and I watch the baseball games on TV. Besides, they're parishioners here. Instead of trying to make them feel unwelcome, you should get to know them better."

"And you should get to know better what the Church teaches."

"Have you read *Humanae Vitae*, Father?" Tony asked about Pope Paul VI's new encyclical letter on artificial contraception.

"I've read the highlights, Father. Not the whole thing," Sparky Larkin blustered.

"Maybe you should read the whole thing. You might discover that it's based on a highly cultural interpretation of natural law that a lot of theologians say is mistaken."

Sparky Larkin was perplexed. "Sweet Jesus," he

finally said. "You'd at least expect the dagos to stick with the pope. Wait till they hear that one downtown."

"What do you mean, 'downtown'"?

"At the chancery. They suspended all those priests down in Washington, D.C. who wouldn't go along with the pope on birth control. Maybe Marty Phelan will do the same for you."

"Father, this was just rectory talk."

"Now, you say. No, it's too late. I'll be calling the chancery tomorrow when they open."

"Father, don't do that."

"It's too late now. The die are cast."

Tony Capresi spent a sleepless night. He tried to tell himself that the chancery would not get upset about what he had said. Maybe just a warning and that would be all. Or maybe they would suspend him. No, they wouldn't. His thoughts went back and forth as he tossed and turned, pursuing a reluctant drowsiness.

Early the next morning, Sparky Larkin was on the phone to Marty Phelan, who had just been appointed apostolic administrator of the diocese while they waited for the Vatican to pick a new bishop. The previous bishop, John Rooney, had been made a cardinal and summoned to Rome by Pope Paul VI to head up the Vatican department on priests.

"Marty, I want you to suspend my assistant, that Tony fellow," Sparky Larkin began.

"His name is Capresi, Sparky."

"I know that."

"Is there any specific reason that you want me to do this, Sparky, or is it just because his last name is too hard for you to pronounce?"

"Marty, the man's a heretic, just like all those priests down there in Washington, D.C."

"How is he a heretic, Sparky?"

"He's questioned papal infallibility. He's been saying that that new thing on birth control from the pope is wrong, that somehow it's based on bad theology."

"Have you read *Humanae Vitae*, Sparky?"

"The highlights, Marty. I just read the highlights. Running a parish is a full time job. I don't have a lot of time for fancy reading like you chancery folks."

"If you had read it, Sparky, you would know that, nowhere in the document, does the pope claim it's an infallible teaching."

"Oh."

"So if Father Capresi questions it, he's not saying that the pope is not infallible."

"He's not?"

"No. So he's not a heretic."

"All the same, Marty, we can't have these young priests going around saying things against the Holy Father."

"Who's he been saying these thing to, Sparky? Has he criticized the Holy Father from the pulpit?"

"No, not exactly."

"Where then? Did he tell it to the Christian Mothers? The Knights of Columbus? The kids in school?"

"No, not exactly."

"Sparky, I'm tired playing '20 Questions.' Where, when, and to whom did Father Capresi say something against the pope?"

"Last night, he said it to me at dinner."

"What?" Bishop Phelan shouted so loudly at the other end of the line that the receiver vibrated in Sparky's hand. "Do you mean to tell me that you called to report a private conversation in the rectory between two priests of this diocese? What do you think this is, Russia? My God, if two priests can't talk to each other, who can they talk to? I won't have you reporting such nonsense."

There was silence at Sparky Larkin's end.

"Did you hear me, Sparky?"

"Yes, Marty. I heard you. I think you're wrong on this one, but I heard you."

"Good, Sparky. I'm going to do you a favor and forget that you ever made this call."

Sparky Larkin put the receiver down, fuming.

Damn that Tony whatever his name was. He had
got him into trouble again. If the chancery wouldn't
help him, there had to be something he could do
himself. He went into the den to reflect. He did his
best thinking there, in front of the television.

Rex was in the room, eating the remains of a
pepperoni pizza that they had shared as an after
dinner snack the night before. Sparky eased himself into his recliner and patted Rex on his head.
The poor thing had been a bit skittish lately, ever
since that Tony fellow had moved in with his cane.
As Sparky massaged between the dog's ears, he
mewed gently and rubbed his head against his
master's leg.

"Rex, ole pal, we got a problem here," Sparky
Larkin said to the dog. "That fellow's not fit to be
a priest, and we're the only ones who can do anything about it. Thing is, what can we do?"

He put his La-Z-Boy all the way back to do
some deep thinking, and, as he slid into his mid-
morning nap, he felt the wisp of an idea overtaking
him.

Tony Capresi spent that day going about his
usual routine, waiting in terror for a call from the
chancery, but no call ever came.

That night at dinner, Sparky Larkin was overly
polite. One of the parish ladies had made spaghetti
and meatballs for them, and they were very good.
Tony waited for Sparky to bring up their conversation of last night, but he never did.

Tony was surprised when Sparky invited him
into the den after the meal. "Rex will be outside
tonight, Father. Maybe it's not so good for him
to be inside all the time, what with you and your
allergies and all."

Tony could not believe the man's kindness.
Maybe that's what comes of standing up to him, he
thought. He joined him in the den that had obviously been sprayed, heavily, with some kind of
disinfectant, and he was even more surprised when

Sparky Larkin offered him a beer. They had never had a drink together before. They watched television and after an hour or so, and a few more beers, a tipsy Tony Capresi made his way to his bedroom.

He dreamed that he saw a bright light in the middle of the night. It almost brought him to consciousness, but not quite.

He woke next morning and started for the bathroom. As soon as he opened the door, he saw Rex outside in the hallway. The animal advanced, growling. The priest began to sneeze as he quickly closed the door.

That's odd, he thought. Didn't Sparky say that he would be keeping Rex outside? Probably he just forgot. We both had a little bit too much to drink last night. No matter. I'll just get my cane.

He turned to the corner, beside the bookcase, where he always kept his cane. It was gone. He was in a panic. I know it was there, he thought. I put it there last night. Suddenly it dawned on him. Sparky Larkin's unanticipated kindness, the beers, and the bright light in the middle of the night. He had been set up.

The dog was still snarling in the hallway. Tony Capresi felt his bladder about to burst.

He quickly piled his clothes into his two suitcases, lowered them from the window and let them drop to the ground below. Then he climbed out of the window, onto the roof of the porch, and did a hanging jump down to the ground. He carried his suitcases across the street to Connie and Joe Amoroso's house and rang the doorbell.

"I've run away from home, and I have to use the bathroom," he said when Connie answered the door. She looked at his quickly packed suitcases, odd items of clothing sticking out, and, laughing uncontrollably, she motioned him inside.

Tony Capresi continued to function as the assistant pastor of St. Teresa parish, he just did not live in the rectory. He lived across the street.

Joe and Connie bought him a shiny new metal cane to replace the one Sparky Larkin stole, and he had no trouble from Rex whenever he crossed parish territory on his way to the church or school, as long as he carried the cane.

He hardly ever saw Sparky Larkin. Even on Saturdays, the pastor somehow found a way to get to his confessional after Tony and leave before him.

Connie Amoroso was an excellent cook, and Tony Capresi especially enjoyed their meals together and the chance to sit and talk with Connie and Joe afterwards. He felt a bit awkward at first, but they did everything they could to make him feel at home.

At the end of August, when Connie and Joe were about to set off for their vacation on the Jersey shore, they invited him along. He hesitated, but then gave in when they accepted his offer to drive them in his Impala. Three people could never have fit in their Corvette anyway.

Finally, during the vacation, Tony did get them around to talking about their marriage. They were walking on the beach, in their swimsuits, the three of them, Joe and Tony, with Connie in the middle.

"I really married Tommy to get out of the house," Connie Amoroso said. "I was only eighteen. He was just the first guy to happen along. My folks were so happy to see me go, they gave us a nice church wedding at St. Teresa's. Well, as nice as it could be. Sparky Larkin made a big deal about Tommy not being a Catholic. But the trouble started right away. Tommy drank, and he fooled around. The last straw was when this woman starts calling up, asking for back child support. Turns out he was married before and had a kid with her."

"That first wife," Tony Capresi said, "do you know what she was? Catholic, Protestant?"

"She was Methodist, like him, I'm pretty sure."

"Were they married in their church?"

"Yeah. After I threw Tommy out, I found some pictures of their church wedding he kept in the back of a drawer."

"Listen, did Sparky Larkin know about this guy's first marriage when he married you?"

"How could he? I didn't even know about it."

"He never asked if Tommy was married before?"

"The subject never came up."

"Gee, Connie. That's a prior bond. 'Ligamen' they called it in the seminary. If Sparky had done his homework, he couldn't have married you because of Tommy's first marriage, at least not until Tommy got a Catholic annulment. All we have to do now, when we get home, is fill out some papers, run them through the chancery and you and Joe can get married in the Church."

"You mean everything is okay because Sparky Larkin shouldn't have married me and Tommy in the first place?"

"He had no business marrying you because Tommy had a prior marriage that was not dissolved by the Catholic Church."

"But it was dissolved. He had to be divorced to marry me."

"Doesn't matter, Connie. Our Church doesn't recognize civil divorce."

"I can't wait to see the look on Sparky Larkin's face," Connie said as she threw one arm around Joe and the other around Tony. "I love you two guys, you know that? And Tony, when we get back, and you take care of these forms, Joe and I want you to marry us, right, Joe?"

"Right. Definitely right," Joe answered.

When they returned from Cape May, Tony kept living with Connie and Joe Amoroso. The arrangement was the talk of the parish. Before long, the news reached the diocesan chancery.

It was a happy time in the building because it had just been announced by the Vatican that the auxiliary bishop of Rocksburg, and a native son, Martin Phelan, would be the new bishop of the diocese. After two foreigners, one from Cleveland and one from Boston, the Rocksburg chancery was proud to have one of its own in charge again.

Bishop Phelan began his job mid-stride. The truth was that he had been running the diocese for years. John Rooney, the previous bishop, had been rather peripatetic, spending a good deal of his time away from the diocese. Part of that was understandable, since three years had been taken up by the Second Vatican Council in Rome, and then there were the national bishops' meetings, the talks and conferences for which he was in high demand.

Bishop Phelan made the telephone call himself. "Father Larkin," he said, "I want you and Father Capresi in my office tomorrow at ten."

"What about, Marty?"

"You know what about, Sparky."

"Well, I'll come, but I don't know if what's his name will be there."

"See that he is."

"Marty, I don't even see the fellow anymore. How will I tell him? He doesn't live here."

"How you tell him is your problem, Father. Tomorrow at ten. The two of you. In my office."

Sparky swallowed hard as he hung up the telephone. Marty didn't sound happy. Well, he hadn't done anything wrong. That damn fellow had a nerve, sneaking out of the rectory and moving in with parishioners. This was all that Capry fellow's fault, and he would make Marty Phelan see it that way tomorrow.

Meantime, how was he going to tell him about the meeting? I guess I could just walk across the street, he considered. Nights, what's his name was usually out on the porch with Connie and Joe, talking with the neighbors.

No, I'd rather die, he thought. All those people sitting on their front porches would see me. It'd be a sign of weakness. Let me see. They should be in the book. He dialed the number.

By the third ring, he decided to fake it. Joe answered the telephone.

"This is the Rocksburg chancery calling," Sparky Larkin said in a high and squeaky voice that he thought sounded feminine. "Please tell Father, uh, Carpy that he has an appointment with Bishop Phelan here at ten a.m. tomorrow morning. Good-bye," and he hung up.

Joe walked back outside where Connie and Tony were sitting on the porch swing. "That was the strangest call," he said.

"Who was it?" Connie asked.

"It was Sparky Larkin, but he was talking like he had a hernia or something."

"What'd he want?" Tony Capresi asked.

"He says the bishop wants to see you at the chancery tomorrow at ten."

"Did he say why?"

"No, he just said the time and place and hung up."

"Do you think you're in trouble, Tony?" Connie Amoroso asked.

"I don't know. I guess I'll see tomorrow."

Tony Capresi got to the chancery a few minutes early. Sparky Larkin was already sitting there in the waiting area.

"I didn't know you would be here, Father," Tony Capresi said.

"Look, you got a lot of explaining to do, fellow," Sparky Larkin said. "The bishop's gonna wanna know why you're not living in the rectory."

"*You* know ..." Tony started to say, but he was interrupted by the bishop's secretary, beckoning both of them into the bishop's office.

The bishop was not alone. Monsignor Henry DaSilva, the new chancellor and vicar general of the diocese, was there with him.

"Sit down, Fathers." Bishop Phelan said. "I've

asked Monsignor DaSilva to join us, since he will
be handling personnel matters."

"It's good to see you, Marty," Sparky Larkin
said. "I can't tell you how happy I was when you
were named bishop. One of our own. The Vatican
got John Rooney out of here just in time. After ten
years, he was learning enough of the ropes to be
dangerous. You know what I mean?" Sparky asked,
laughing.

"Why don't we get started?" Martin Phelan
asked. "Father Larkin, do you want to tell me why
your assistant pastor is not living in the parish
rectory?"

"Ask him," Sparky Larkin sputtered. "He's
here. Ask him. I don't know what possessed the
man."

"Do you want to tell us, Father Capresi?" the
bishop asked.

"I can't live there. The place stinks to high
heaven. It needs to be fumigated. The dog, his dog,
has the run of the place, and the dog hates me. He
already bit me once."

"And that's why you won't live in the rectory?"
the bishop asked.

"No, that's not all. He stole my cane."

"What?"

"I used to have a cane to keep the dog away,
but he snuck into my room one night while I was
sleeping and he stole my cane."

"Is that true, Father Larkin?" the bishop asked.

"Marty, I never did ..."

Bishop Phelan put his hand up. "I know we've
known each other for quite a while, Father, but for
purposes of keeping this meeting as business like
as possible, why don't we use our titles?"

Sparky Larkin looked puzzled for a moment.
"Oh, sure," he finally said. "It's like I was saying,
uh, Bishop, I never did such a thing and he has no
proof."

"Who else could it have been?" Tony Capresi

asked. "There's only the two of us in the rectory. When I went to sleep, the cane was in my room. When I woke up, it was gone. And it couldn't've been burglars because his mutt is a watch dog."

"Rex is not a mutt. He's a pedigreed German shepherd. I have papers."

"Excuse me, Father Larkin," Monsignor DaSilva interjected. "What did you say the dog's name was?"

"It's Rex," Sparky Larkin snorted.

"I thought I heard somewhere that his name was Christus Rex. That would be blasphemous, of course, naming a dog after Christ the King," Monsignor DaSilva said.

"I never did such a thing. A few years ago, some twit at my forty hours says I treated the dog like he was Jesus. Said his name shoulda been Christus Rex, just cause I let him eat in the same room with the clergy that day. That's how rumors get started in this diocese. But it's not true."

"I'm glad to hear that explanation, Father," Monsignor DaSilva said.

Sparky Larkin was beginning to wonder who was on trial here. He thought he should get things back on track,

"Mart ... uh, *Bishop*," he said, "this young man has some very unorthodox theological views. It's been very painful watching him lead my parishioners astray."

"We've been over that before, Father, and unless you have some proof of Father Capresi's unorthodoxy, I don't want to hear it."

Tony Capresi reacted at the exchange. So Sparky *had* called to report him.

"The proof is that every blessed Saturday his confessional line is ten times longer than mine," Sparky Larkin said. "Now he must be doing something wrong for all those people to be coming to him."

Monsignor DaSilva looked up from a book that

he was poring through. "Sounds like maybe he's doing something right," he said.

Sparky scowled at him. He hadn't been happy when he walked into the meeting and saw DaSilva there. He had never been fond of DaSilva, whom he thought John Rooney had brought into the chancery to laugh at his intellectual Boston jokes. He was surprised to see Marty Phelan working with him. What did they see in this slimy little dago, he wondered, and what had happened to the days when all the Irish stood together?

DaSilva did not flinch at the scowl. He just stared placidly back at Sparky and then returned to his book.

"Tell them, tell them both, what you're saying about birth control in the box," Sparky insisted.

"In the box?" Tony Capresi asked.

"You know what I mean," Sparky said. "In the confessional."

Bishop Phelan intervened. "Father Larkin, what happens in Father Capresi's confessional is between him, the penitent and almighty God."

"I don't want to be knowing the sins," Sparky Larkin said. "I want to know what he's saying."

"Bishop, all I do is try to help people. I'm very faithful to what the Church teaches. Maybe the reason more people come to me is that I don't yell at them in confession," Tony Capresi said.

"I don't do that," Sparky Larkin shouted. "I very seldom yell in the box. And when I do, it's well deserved, I can tell you."

"We are not here to discuss your divergent styles in the confessional," Bishop Phelan said. "We are here to find out why a priest of this diocese is not living in a rectory, with his pastor, and why the pastor has allowed that situation to go on."

"It's the dog and the smell, Bishop" Tony Capresi said. "I'd be happy to move back if they were gone."

"What do you say to that, Father?" Bishop Phelan turned to Sparky Larkin.

"I love Rex, Marty, uh, Bishop, I mean. He's like

family to me. I don't think Father, uh, Capry, uh, gave him much of a chance."

"Bishop," Tony Capresi said, "I can't help the way I was raised. My mother thought that animals were dirty, that houses with animals were dirty. I was never around animals, and I can't get used to them. I feel very uneasy around dogs, large dogs especially. Then there are my allergies."

"Why should he have his way?" Sparky Larkin asked. "I'm the pastor. I should have the last say."

"It's not a matter of who gets their say, Father," Bishop Phelan answered. "We have a scandalous situation on our hands, a priest living with parishioners because he's uncomfortable in the parish rectory. It can't go on. What do you think, Monsignor DaSilva?"

DaSilva was still paging through the same old book he had been perusing for the last part of the conversation. "I think we have an answer, Bishop. It looks like the diocesan synod in 1948 covered this matter. We have a diocesan statute on rectories, Statute 112 of 1948. It says that, as to rectories, only priests assigned to the parish shall have regular residence there. It says very clearly that a priest's family or pets cannot live in the rectory."

Bishop Phelan looked at Sparky Larkin, whose shoulders had just slumped. "It looks like the dog goes, Father."

Damn those canon lawyers, Sparky thought of DaSilva. Wouldn't you know he'd find a loophole to help his *paisan*? "Marty, uh, Bishop," he said, "it's not right. The dog was there when he got there."

"There's no such thing as squatter's rights in the synodal laws," Monsignor DaSilva said.

"I'm sorry, Father, but the dog has to go," Bishop Phelan said to Sparky. Then turning to Tony Capresi, Bishop Phelan said, "Father, I take it that you will return to the rectory, with the dog gone?"

"As soon as it's gone and the rectory is fumigated,

Bishop. I'm allergic to the animal's hair or something, and it's all over the place."

"Well, if the dog can't stay, neither can its smell. You'll take care of that, Father Larkin?"

Sparky could only nod affirmatively. It was a complete loss for the home team.

Then Bishop Phelan stood up and the meeting was over. They all shook hands, like gentlemen, but Sparky could see DaSilva and what's his name smiling at each other. Well, at least those two dagos stick together, he thought.

It took Sparky Larkin a week to find a place for Rex. Bringing him to the Animal Rescue was out of the question. Sparky knew that they only kept animals a few weeks or so, and if no one adopted them, they put them to sleep. He could not let that happen to Rex.

Instead, he put an ad in the Sunday parish bulletin. "Loving dog, housebroken, good guard dog, needs a loving home. Contact Father Larkin." But everybody in the parish knew that the dog was Rex and there were no takers.

It finally came to a kennel. He had no other choice. Sparky Larkin inspected a few before he found one that would be right for Rex. He wanted to make sure it was clean, with room to run around, that the food was good, and that the kennel was conscientious enough to separate the male dogs from the female dogs.

He chose one in Glenfield, right off the highway. It was fifty dollars a month and Sparky Larkin shuddered as he forked over the first month's rent and the last month's as a security deposit.

He hugged Rex as he left him with the attendant. The dog started to whine as Sparky walked away, but Sparky was too choked up to turn around. Instead, he just hurried to his car, cursing what's his name, the bishop and Monsignor DaSilva. "Don't worry, Rex," he said out loud. "We'll get even, pal. We'll get even."

Tony Capresi did not move back to the rectory right away. He stopped in after he saw that Rex was gone and sniffed around. At the first whiff, he bent over in a spasm of sneezes. He could feel an allergy headache coming on. Before he left, he taped a note to the refrigerator, where he knew Sparky Larkin would see it. "I'll move back once you get the place cleaned and fumigated."

The note bothered Sparky. But he knew that Capry fellow had him over a barrel. He could still hear Marty Phelan saying, "If the dog has to go, so does his smell."

Let them laugh. Let them laugh now. He and Rex would have their day.

It cost over two hundred dollars to have the cleaning company come, but at least the parish paid for that. The hardest part was watching what's-his-name move back to the rectory with his two friends, Connie and Joe Amoroso, helping him.

Sparky Larkin nearly had a conniption when he saw the couple heading towards the rectory, helping his assistant carry his belongings.

"Father," he had called Tony Capresi into the kitchen, "what are those two excommunicates doing here in my rectory?"

"They're helping me move back, and besides they're not excommunicates. The marriage you performed, when Connie married her first husband, wasn't valid. There was an impediment—a prior bond. You forgot to ask if her first husband was married before. As soon as I get the okay from the chancery, I'll be celebrating their marriage for them."

"So you'll be making a fool of me downtown again, telling them I performed an invalid marriage?"

"Father, I don't want to make a fool of you. I just want to help these people get right with the Church."

"I have a good record downtown. I don't want any blots on it."

"Father, I'm not trying to blot your record."

"And where is this marriage to take place?"

"Here at St. Teresa's. They're parishioners."

"These people, are they going upstairs now?"

"I need help with my things, Father, and my room is on the second floor."

"Listen, mister, you know very well that I have a rule about that."

"Father, this is my house, too, and I have a right to feel comfortable here, like Bishop Phelan said. And by the way, I'll be moving into 'Jack Donahue's room.' You can give my old room to that visitor if he ever shows up."

Sparky Larkin never got headaches, but that day he had a headache. He took two aspirins and lay down in his room while he waited for the abomination to be over.

There has to be a way, Rex, he kept repeating to himself. There has to be a way.

The Amoroso wedding was a grand affair. Joe's Italian family was very large, and Connie's Polish family was even bigger. The reception was in the parish hall and it could barely hold the crowd. The cookie table was over-laden with Polish nut-horns and Italian pizzelle.

Sparky Larkin arranged to spend the whole day away at a bowling tournament. He could not have stomached the event.

Tony Capresi said the wedding mass and gave a moving homily on the perseverance of love, using Connie and Joe as examples. At the reception, he gave the invocation.

He was standing with the crowd when the dancing started, and after the bridal party dance, he found himself swept onto the floor to dance with the bride.

He was a clumsy dancer without much experience, but Connie led him. Her long gossamer veil enveloped his shoulders as they swirled around the floor, and the citrus and floral scent of her perfume was overpowering. He felt a little woozy and almost lost his balance as the dance ended and they let go of each other.

The next morning in the rectory, as Tony was pouring himself a bowl of cereal, Sparky Larkin, who had not been to the event, knew all about it.

"So you're a dancer now, is it? That's a bad example, Father, a bad example for the people of this parish."

"What? To see that their priests are normal?"

"It's another man's wife, Father. It's bad enough she has the eyes for you without giving emphasis to the fact."

"Eyes for me? What are you talking about?"

"Surely you've noticed? I saw it the day she helped you move back in here. Every step you took, she was watching you. That big lummox of a husband may be too stupid to see it, but I saw it, and other people of the parish saw it last night too. You be careful of yourself, Father. That woman has set her cap for you."

Tony Capresi was thunderstruck. How could something like that be true? It couldn't be true. Besides, Connie was married, very married now that he had validated her vows to Joe in the Church.

Sparky Larkin watched the expressions change on his assistant's face as Tony pondered the thoughts that Sparky had just given birth to. He saw his confusion and chuckled, "There's no doubting it, Father. That woman is desirous of you."

The thought that a woman as wonderful as Connie could have any feeling for him made Tony feel giddy. All the week she was gone on her honeymoon, he found visions of her intruding into his thoughts.

Once she and Joe were back, he was a frequent visitor to their house. He found himself watching her at odd moments to see if she was watching him, like Sparky Larkin said. Sometimes she would catch him at it and just smile.

One night, a month after the wedding, Sparky

Larkin made it a point to be out in the front yard of the rectory when Joe was walking by on his way home from the university. The priest motioned him over, and began talking in a whisper, his arm over Joe's shoulder.

"Joe, my boy, now that you're truly married, in the Church, I want to help you. I think there's something going on between Father, uh, you know, the assistant, and your wife."

"Is this some kind of joke?" Joe said, pulling away.

"I wish it were, son. I wish it were. I've only lately taken to noticing that days, when you're at work, he seems to be spending a lot of time at your house. I can only tell you, look to your affairs, my boy, look to your marriage. I think that Father, uh, you know, has the hots for your wife."

Joe shook his head as he walked across the street. Larkin's bonkers, he thought. Connie and Tony? But then he remembered all those times he had caught them smiling at each other, and he wondered, what were they smiling about?

Joe lived with his worries for a few days before he decided that he had to talk to Connie about it. It was one night after Tony had been over for dinner, while they were cleaning dishes.

"Tony's a great guy, isn't he?" Joe started.

"Sure," Connie said.

"You know, we really see a lot of him," Joe continued

"Why not? He's probably our best friend," Connie said.

"Does he ever, you know, stop over when I'm not here?"

"Sure."

Joe looked at her apprehensively. "He does?"

"Joe, he lives across the street, for goodness sake. He comes over, we have coffee. We wash our cars together, you know that.

"What do you talk about?"

"Joe, what is on your mind?"

"I don't know, Con. This is embarrassing, but shoot, it's been bothering me and I have to ask. That crazy fool Larkin stopped me on the way home from work the other day and told me that Tony had the hots for you and was spending afternoons with you."

"He what? I'll kill him. I'll kill the old bastard."

"I take it that's a denial."

"You bet your ass it's a denial. Joe, how could you ever...I mean, look at him," she said pointing to the place at their empty kitchen table where Tony habitually sat. "He looks like a little kid. His clothes are all a size too big, and he needs mothered. I mean, he acts so lost sometimes."

"So what do you talk about?"

"Oh, Joe, things, life. Did you know he was only fourteen when he entered the seminary? He never was on a date, in his whole life. He knows nothing about women."

"He told you that?"

"Sure, why not?"

"I don't know. It seems kind of personal, Con. You sure he's not coming onto you?"

"Joe, don't you think I would know that, if he was?"

"Cause some women would find that attractive, a guy who wants to be mothered."

"When I become a mother, Joe, it will be with the kid you and I have together."

"That's my girl," Joe said as he grabbed Connie and held her tight to him.

She looked up at him and laughed. "Did Larkin really say Tony has the hots for me?"

"His exact words."

"The old fool doesn't know what the hots means."

The rectory bell rang and rang before Sparky Larkin went to answer the door. Joe Amoroso practically knocked him down as he pushed past him into the rectory.

"Is he here?" he yelled.

"Is who here?" Sparky Larkin said.

"You know who I mean. Tony. Is Tony here?"

"Joe, calm down. You look mad enough to kill."

"If I get my hands on that son of a bitch, I will kill him. Is he here?"

"Joe, you can't just come barging in here. Anyhow I don't think Father uh Capry is here right now. If he was, he would've answered the door. That's his job."

"Are you sure?" Joe said as he ran up the stairs to the second floor.

Sparky Larkin followed him up. "Hold on right there, Joe. No one except priests is allowed up there. Those are private quarters."

Joe was already halfway down the corridor to Tony's room. The door was open and he went in, Sparky Larkin trailing behind.

"Joe, I know you're upset. I don't know why you're upset, but I can see it. These are private quarters, though, and you have to leave."

Joe ignored the priest as he threw open closets and pulled out dresser drawers. They were all empty.

"He's gone," he said, "he's gone," and he sat down on the bed, his shoulders hunched up, and he started to cry.

"Now what are you blubbering for?" Sparky Larkin said. "A big man like you?"

"It's the same at my house. All her drawers, all her closets, empty."

"Joe, you're not making any sense."

"You warned me. You warned me and I didn't believe you."

"Joe, what the devil are you talking about?"

"Isn't it obvious? They're gone. The both of them, Tony and Connie. They've run off together."

"No, it can't be," Sparky Larkin smiled. "Father

uh Carpy and your wife? No, it just can't be."

Sparky Larkin waited a week to be sure, but Joe Amoroso had been right. His assistant had disappeared and so had Connie Amoroso. He called the kennel and told them to get Rex ready, that he would be there for him in an hour.

It was a joyous reunion. Rex leaped and jumped all over his owner as Sparky Larkin led him away from the kennel. The priest nuzzled the dog and gave him some big spearmint gum drops from the bag he kept in his car.

"We're back in the saddle again, Rex," the priest sang, as he let the dog into the front seat of his dark blue 1968 Lincoln Continental. "Back in the saddle again."

III

On Ovid's Feast

Marco Gualtieri was holding a cigarette and watching the cars whirr past on the nearby autostrada.
He drew the last smoke from the Marlboro into his
lungs and exhaled it slowly through his nostrils.
His Vatican job allowed him to buy such luxuries
without Italian custom duties or taxes.

The chauffeur was awaiting his charges. The
thin young priest was pacing near the limousine.
The old priest was still inside the gas station, in the
servizio. There was time for another cigarette.

Finally, he heard the young priest call, "*Marco,
siamo pronti*," saying that they were ready. Marco
flicked his half-done cigarette onto the asphalt, ground
it under his shoe, and returned to the Mercedes.

The old priest, wrapped in a heavy black wool-
en cape against the wind that whistled down the
Apennines, had just emerged from the men's room.
The chauffeur started the diesel engine chugging
quietly as the old man entered the car door that his
secretary held open.

Once he heard the doors close, Marco checked
the rear view mirror, then roared into the autostrada
traffic.

"I wish he would learn to drive more slowly,

Bill, or I may never live to reach my dotage," the old priest said.

The young priest motioned down with his hand so that Marco could see him in the rear view mirror through the glass partition that separated the chauffeur from his passengers.

Che peccato, what a shame, Marco thought, not to take full advantage of a machine like this. *Questi americani*, these Americans, they don't know what an automobile is for.

"Are you feeling any better, your Eminence?"

"Immensely so, Bill, but I need to practice more self-control with the twin temptations of Italian food and Italian wine. Either that, or get a new digestive apparatus."

They were returning—cardinal, priest-secretary, and chauffeur—from a diocesan *festa* in Sulmona in the Abruzzo region of central Italy. John Cardinal Rooney, the Prefect of the Vatican's Congregation for Clergy, was a sought after speaker at these country affairs. His flawless but heavily-accented Italian flattered the natives, who were always surprised that a foreigner, especially someone as important as *Su' Eminenza*, could speak their language so well.

On the way to Sulmona that morning, the cardinal had asked his secretary whose feast they were going to celebrate that day. In an unusual lapse of memory, the young priest could not recall the saint's name, but then, it had been a bad morning.

His failure of memory did not stop Bill Tuigg's inventiveness, though, and in response to the cardinal's question, he said they were going to celebrate Ovid's feast.

"Ovid?" the cardinal asked. "When was he canonized?"

"I'm not sure. He was born in Sulmona, you know."

"Yes, I know my Ovid, Bill," the cardinal said. "One of the benefits of a classical education. *Sulmo mihi patria est.* Sulmona is my homeland. Do you remember the rest?"

"Very rich in icy streams—*gelidis uberrimus undis,*" Bill Tuigg replied.

"Fine. Now tell me why you think that the author of antiquity's most salacious guide to carnal love merits Catholic sainthood?"

It was the sort of classical banter that both men enjoyed, and when they were done, the cardinal never remembered that his first question had gone unanswered.

Six husky men had carried the heavy statue of the saint, who turned out to be St. Pamphilus, patron saint of Sulmona, dressed in his holiday silks, through the Piazza Garibaldi, under the medieval aqueduct, and down the street to the cathedral.

There was the obligatory, but uncontrolled liturgy, presided over by a scatter-brained Italian monsignor, who gave all of his instructions in Latin and who insisted on pulling the cardinal around the altar by his vestments.

Afterwards, outdoors in the aqueduct-bound piazza, there was the huge *festa* meal. Buoyed by the applause that his remarks received, the cardinal had over-indulged. The last gas station had been their second stop, and Rome was still far.

But, since the cardinal insisted that he was feeling better, the young priest settled into their routine for the end of a busy day on the road. He turned on the lights that lay just below the level of the front seats, and he lifted his briefcase onto his knees. From within, he retrieved a pile of correspondence and handed the cardinal a letter from the packet.

Somehow, earlier that day, the secretary had found time to open the cardinal's mail and choose what the prelate would want to see. From his seminary days, Bill Tuigg was accustomed to finding a twenty-fifth and twenty-sixth hour in the day, that were his alone, to get such extra work done.

Thwap. The sound of a hard-hit rubber ball burst into his memory. He was back at St. Gregory's, his college seminary, playing hand ball with his best friend and classmate, Tony Capresi.

"Whose point was that?" he asked.

"Mine," Tony had replied. "And that's game."

Tony bent to pick up the ball and started to leave the court.

"Where are you going?" Bill Tuigg asked.

"We have Corny Sheehan's church history exam tomorrow," Tony answered. "Some of us have to study. I know you've probably reviewed every-thing three times already, but ..."

"What do these people want, Bill?" the cardinal was asking, putting the rather lengthy Italian letter down without finishing it.

"They'd like a bishop."

"Why are they writing to me?"

"They've already written to the Congregation for Bishops, but since the diocesan administrator is not a bishop, just a senior monsignor from the diocesan curia, Bishops told them to write to you at Clergy."

"Pass the Roman ball. It will take us a while to learn how to play that game, Bill. How long have they been without a bishop?"

"Almost two years."

"Why?"

"From what I could tell in the file, Bishops is planning on merging this diocese with another. It's just too small, only about eight thousand faithful."

"So, instead of saying that, the Congregation for Bishops says they should write to us. I will never understand why these fellows delay making decisions that they know are inevitable. Who is the administrator?"

"Monsignor Ottavio Occhiomorto. He's become a hermit in the chancery. The last time he went to a parish, someone tried to stab him. I guess they think he's part of the plot to deprive them of a bishop."

"Let's write to the poor fellow, Bill. Tell Monsignor Occhiomorto to come see me, if he can get to Rome safely. Maybe I can buck him up. Meanwhile, draft an answer to these vigilantes. Tell them Bishops is considering merging their diocese, and that's the reason for the delay. A little sunshine won't hurt the situation."

"These people won't like that, your Eminence. At the end of the letter they remind you that their diocese was founded by St. Paul himself, and that this is the first time in two thousand years they haven't had a bishop."

"St. Paul? When was he in Campo Marino?"

"It seems he stopped there on his way from Pozzuoli to Rome."

"For a fellow under arrest and in chains, he was pretty busy on his way to Rome. It's a good thing for the Church that he didn't land further south."

Smiling, the young priest passed a second letter to the cardinal. "This is one you'll appreciate, your Eminence. Monsignor Himmelreich at St. Gregory's Seminary is still using the old diocesan stationary with your coat of arms on it."

"Don Himmelreich is one of the most miserly priests I know, Bill," the cardinal said, "which is why I appointed him rector of that hard-to-heat Gothic horror that Rocksburg calls a seminary. And do you know, he's the first man who was ever able to pay the oil bills."

The old man glanced quickly over the brief typewritten paragraphs. "So the group from St. Gregory's will be back in Rome for the Christmas archeological tour."

"Yes, your Eminence. This is their fifth year, but the first since you've been here."

"Did you ever make that trip, Bill?"

"No, your Eminence. I was already a student

in Rome when St. Gregory's started them."

"The letters are in the boxes," he could remember one of his classmates shouting down the hall at the college dorm of St. Gregory's that day in late May of 1964. Seminarians rushed from their rooms to the mail center. In their mailboxes were the official letters from the Rocksburg director of vocations, telling them where they would be going to study theology for the next four years before their priestly ordinations.

"What's yours say?" Bill Tuigg asked Tony Capresi

"Four more years at St. Gregory's. That's not so bad. You?"

"They're sending me away," Bill Tuigg said.

"Throwing you out? I always said you were too smart for them."

"Not that, you idiot. They're sending me to Rome, the North American."

"Don't you think so, Bill?" the cardinal's question ended his secretary's reverie.

"What, your Eminence?"

"That this notice of the St. Gregory's arrival date is an angle for an invitation?" the old man repeated, wondering why his secretary was so unusually distracted.

"I'd say so."

"Check my calendar for the last week of December and schedule a mass and meal with them. It will be good to see some faces from home."

"Yes, your Eminence," the young priest replied as he exchanged letters with the cardinal, scribbling 'mass and meal' on the back of the St. Gregory's letter before handing the old man a letter from Mexico.

The cardinal was only half way into the letter when he broke off. "This is serious," he said.

"Yes, your Eminence."

"If what these people say is true, even with my imperfect Spanish, this priest is a monster. How can the local bishop have allowed this sexual abuse to go on?"

"By all accounts the priest involved is a very effective fund-raiser, and this religious order that he has started has numerous vocations."

"None of that cancels the harm here. Draft a letter from me to the bishop. Tell him he must suspend this priest and start a canonical investigation immediately, and send me a copy of the findings."

"Yes, your Eminence," Bill Tuigg said as he made notes on the back of the letter the cardinal had just returned to him.

"Are there any others?" the old priest asked and nodded in answer to his own question at the last letter over which his secretary was nervously drumming the fingers of his left hand. The young priest looked down at the scribbled sheets, trying to wish them away.

"Bill?" the cardinal asked again, and his secretary slowly passed him the hand-written letter.

The frown on the cardinal's face knit tighter as he read. He dropped his head onto his chest. The extra folds of his chin lined his face on his cape. Sclerotically, he reached out to the glass divider and knocked, motioning the chauffeur off at the approaching gas station.

Marco was enjoying another cigarette while the secretary paced near the *servizio*, trying not to be impatient with the old man's weakness.

The chauffeur had finished one cigarette and was on to another when the *servizio* door opened and the cardinal came out. They quickly rejoined the traffic on the autostrada, rushing on again in the darkness.

"Did you know this man, Bill?" the cardinal asked, waving the last letter.

"We were in the college seminary together for four years, at St. Gregory's."

"It's true that I ordained him, then?" the cardinal asked, rubbing his palms together fretfully.

"Yes, your Eminence. He was ordained for Rocksburg last year."

"Bill, you are familiar with the ordination procedures I followed in Rocksburg. How can this man write that he was under duress at the ordination ceremony?" The cardinal turned to face his secretary, as if by facing him he could convince him. "I required every man I ever ordained in Rocksburg to ask for orders months in advance of the day, in his own hand. I even had them all psychologically tested. I think I was one of the few bishops in the country who did that."

"Yes, your Eminence."

"Did you know his family situation?"

"I visited a few times."

"Did you ever see any of this 'subtle family pressure' that he mentions?"

The young priest recalled the free Sunday afternoons spent at Tony Capresi's home because his own parents' house was too far from St. Gregory's. He remembered the huge Italian meals, Tony's hovering parents, his teasing younger sister.

"I'd say there were the normal expectations that a Catholic family has when one of its sons decides to become a priest," he began to answer, then quickly added, "but they could have been inordinate. They could have been. Maybe they were."

"I thought as much. Do you know what this letter says to me, Bill? That for the first time, in his twenty-six years of life, this fellow has noticed a woman. Now what did he think they were before he was ordained?"

"She's attractive, isn't she?" Tony Capresi asked. He and Bill Tuigg were sitting in his dad's powder blue 1959 Chevrolet Biscayne at the Park and Eat on South Park Boulevard in Rocksburg. The car hop, in her crisp white blouse and crimson slacks, had just attached a tray with their order to the driver's door and was walking away. Tony passed a milkshake and a hamburger to Bill.

They had not seen each other in two years. Bill was back in Rocksburg for the summer, for the first time after he had been sent to Rome for theological studies. Tony had spent those years at Rocksburg's diocesan seminary, St. Gregory's. The two best friends had written frequently at first, but then time and the press of events near at hand had cut the pace.

"I guess."

"You weren't even looking."

"I haven't had a real hamburger in two years."

"I wish I had gone to a regular high school, like you."

"Why?"

"You know, dating, proms, some kind of social life."

"You didn't miss much."

"I'm thinking about taking a leave from St. Greg's. You know, getting a job, trying life out."

"Tony, if that's what you think you should do, then you should do it."

"But it would kill my folks, if I left the seminary. It'd break their hearts."

"I don't know, your Eminence," the secretary brought himself back to the present, answering the cardinal's question that did not require an answer.

How *do* these things happen? Why hadn't Tony written to him before? Surely the idea of leaving the priesthood did not just now occur to him. It was the sort of thing someone like Tony would mull over for months before deciding.

Tony's letter to the cardinal that he had read and re-read that morning and had rehearsed in his mind the rest of the day, was not much help. Leave it to Tony, at such an important time, to lapse into triteness. The priesthood was "limiting my ability to love," he wrote. What on earth did that mean?

He wished that he could have talked to him.

This letter was so unexpected; Tony's final salute to the Church before he left. *Fugituri te salutamus,* he might have punned at a happier moment. "We who are about to bug out, salute you." But what was behind it? He wished he knew. Maybe then he could have helped.

"I take my priesthood very seriously," the old priest said, imprinting his right thumb deeply into the cleft of his folded left hand. "And although there is no strict theology to it, I hold myself personally accountable for those men whom I have ordained, because it was my act, my judgment that admitted them to Christ's priesthood." He sighed. "Bill, I feel responsible for this man's sorry state of mind."

"Your Eminence ..." he began. If only he had the courage to add: This man was my best friend, and whatever official language on whatever official form it will take to suspend his allegiance and end his divided mind's agony, we must send him.

"The stewardship is mine, Bill, and I will be judged on my exercise of it." The cardinal handed the letter back to his secretary. "In his confusion, this fellow has written to the wrong Congregation. We don't do laicizations. That's Doctrine of the Faith. Write this man that I have referred his petition to the proper Congregation."

The secretary reluctantly accepted the letter from the cardinal's hand, praying that the old priest would say something more. In that moment, the young priest's thoughts faltered, and he sensed a strange loss of equilibrium, as if suddenly transported to a place of great height with no support. In a lapse of infinite seconds, he felt that he was falling and he arched his body instinctively to protect himself. "Is that all, your Eminence?" he finally asked when he regained the earth.

"No, Bill. You can take the letter to the Congregation yourself tomorrow. Tell them it's important to me and ask them to hurry it along."

"Thank you, your Eminence."

"Thank me?" the old priest queried, eyebrows circumflected. "This man is more than just a former classmate, isn't he, Bill?"

"We were very close friends, once."

"There is no thanks due me. I take my priesthood seriously, and someone who no longer wants it, is likely to misuse it. I would prefer to avoid that."

Unnoticed, Marco had taken the Mercedes up to one hundred and forty kilometers. They tore past the Tivoli exit and were soon on the Via Tiburtina. As they encountered Rome's congestion, the chauffeur decreased his speed, for he knew that the cardinal did not appreciate the time-honored Italian custom of dodging traffic with his limousine.

Meekly, they followed the flow of traffic alongside the train station and around the Naiad Fountain in Piazza della Repubblica. Down the neonized Via Nazionale they traveled, through the Venezia and onto Corso Vittorio Emanuele. After they crossed the Tiber and were onto the broad lantern-lit expanse of the Via della Conciliazione, the cardinal turned to the young priest.

"Have him drop me at the apartment first, Bill. You can go on to the garage with him and bring back the liturgical gear."

"Do you feel all right, your Eminence?"

"I'll feel better when I'm home."

The old priest was safely inside the *palazzo* door before the Mercedes pulled away from the curb. The garage was not far and the young priest was soon unloading the case with the cardinal's red cassock, miter and collapsible crozier from the trunk.

"*C'e qualcos' altra da fare, don Guglielmo?*" Marco inquired, asking the priest if there was anything else to do.

"No, Marco. I can handle this myself," the priest answered in Italian. "Thank you."

"*Prego.*" The chauffeur said he was welcome,

snapping the garage door closed.

"*Ci vediamo domani.*" The young priest said he would see Marco tomorrow, as, bobbing his head in parting, he headed back to the cardinal's apartment with the liturgical accessories.

"*Buona notte*" Marco said and, lighting a cigarette, he set off towards the Trionfale and his own apartment where, he knew, his wife and children would be waiting.

IV

New Year's Eve 1970, Roma

The students from St. Gregory's Seminary in Rocksburg had been in Rome since December twelfth.
Christmas was already a confused memory of midnight Mass at St. Mary Major and the pope the next
day in St. Peter's Square and the skirl of shepherds'
pipes at the Spanish Steps. Today was New Year's
Eve, and another holiday to celebrate away from
home.

Their trip was winding down. Only a week
remained of their inter-semester study trip to Rome
before their return to St. Gregory's and the start of
the second semester.

That morning, their subject had been the Roman ruins beneath the church of St. Clement's,
beyond the Colosseum. Down the sacristy steps
they had trekked behind Father Cornelius Sheehan,
Professor of Latin and Ancient History at St. Gregory's, to view the remains of the fourth century
basilica of St. Clement that underlay the twelfth
century church above.

Deep underground, Father Sheehan pointed
out the frescoes on the fourth century basilica's

walls. One image, he said, could be the earliest
representation of the Assumption of the Blessed
Virgin Mary into heaven, thus disproving the
Protestant criticism that the doctrine, announced
by Pius XII in 1950, did not come from the ancient
church. Another fresco, Father Sheehan said, had
the earliest recorded use of an Italian swear word,
but he didn't translate the swear word for the
seminarians.

In the back corner, past the altar where St.
Methodius, Apostle to the Slavs, was buried, he led
them to a pair of metal steps. "Boys," his stentorian
voice dropped to a stage whisper, "I have a surprise for you. Follow me down these stairs."

On the steps, they heard the rush of water, as if
they were descending into the deluge.

"That," Father Sheehan half-turned to shout
back, "is the running water of a Roman aqueduct.
Amazing, isn't it,that it is still functioning after
two thousand years?" he chuckled as he continued
down the steps.

At the foot of the stairs, Father Sheehan went
on. "Going down those steps, we have just tra-
versed three centuries. We have left the fourth
century church above us, and we are now in first
century Rome, just outside an apartment building
that had a pagan temple on its first floor. Boys, look
in there," he said, pointing to a door-sized iron
grate, "and you will see the remains of a first century temple to the pagan god Mithras."

As the seminarians crowded by the door to see,
Father Sheehan continued. "As you know from
class, during the early growth of Christianity, in the
first centuries after Christ, the major religion of the
Roman world was no longer the province of Jupiter
and Juno, Mars, Venus, Apollo and the other Olym-
pian gods.

"No, by that time, their worship had fallen from
vogue. It had become too abstract and passionless.
More emotional, more human, and hence more

popular mystery cults from the eastern part of the empire had replaced them.

"Chief among these mystery religions was the cult of Mithras. Mithras was the son of the god, Ahura Mazda, from Persia. Mithras was considered the mediator between God and man, and, just as the Christ of St. John's Gospel, he was also considered the principle of light.

"His followers celebrated his birthday at the winter solstice, or roughly December twenty-fifth," he paused, smiling at the surprise on his students' faces.

"The Mithraic religion was hierarchic, with a chief pontiff and orders of celibates serving the god. Daily sacrifice would be offered at this altar you see in front of you, and during the sacrifice, those present would share a ceremonial meal of bread and wine.

"Now, boys, the similarities of this particular mystery religion to Christianity are fairly obvious, and as I see it, we could evince two explanations.

"The first is that the Mithrains knowingly borrowed Christian beliefs and ritual. This, however, is not very likely, since from all historical data, it is rather evident that Mithraism predates Christianity by a few centuries.

"The second, more likely, explanation is that the Mithrains were a part of God's eternal plan to prepare the hearts and minds of men for the similar practices of the true faith of His Son, our Lord and Savior, Jesus Christ. And now, boys, follow me for something even more exciting."

He led them around a corner and through an opening cut into a wall of chunky brown stones. The way was well-lit, and except for the dampness, they could have been above ground. They were gathered in a small, low ceilinged brick room when Father Sheehan resumed his commentary.

"Boys, we have just crossed an alleyway from the apartment house, where the Mithraeum was, to a first century Roman home. This house is the reason that the fourth century church was built on this site, because you are standing in the ruins of the home of St. Clement himself. You know, from our history classes, that all of the churches in the first century were in people's homes.

"From the Roman canon in the Mass, remember that, in the line of early popes mentioned there, 'Linus, Cletus, Clement,' Clement is the third successor of St. Peter, and so the fourth pope. It was Clement's house, where we are now, that Peter and Paul would have visited when they were in Rome. Think of it, boys," his voice trembled, "the princes of the apostles were in this very room where you are standing now."

And some of his audience did think of it, and for them, the herring-boned orange floor tiles and the dank brown walls seemed more awesome, now that history had given them meaning. But others of Father Sheehan's students were tired, tired of his history with homilies at every site, and tired of being called "boys."

They were all in their second or third year of post-university training for the priesthood, and except for the fact that they had to take the old priest's test for credit when they got back to St. Gregory's, they would have tuned him out days ago.

The tour assistant, Father Mike Krebs, sometime professor at St. Gregory's, shared this view. That afternoon, he met three of the Rocksburg seminarians, Arthur Darner, Fred Gacious and Barney Ramage, for drinks at an outdoor cafe in the Piazza Navona for a sympathy session. The large oval piazza, with the breathtaking Fountain of the Four Rivers in the middle, and two minor fountains, one at each far end, was lined with carnival booths for the annual Christmas fair. The booths were a strange assortment of stands selling nativity figures for Christmas mangers, candy, toys, and games of chance, including a couple of target shoots. The incongruence of target shooting booths alongside figurines of the Baby Jesus, Mary and Joseph was evidently lost on the Roman crowds.

With their glasses of vino spumante in front of them at a cafe near the Fountain of the Four Rivers, Barney Ramage asked Father Mike Krebs, "Hey Mike, did you believe that stuff about Mithras, today?" Father Krebs had encouraged them to use his first name, and unless Corny Sheehan was around, he did not wear his Roman collar.

"What's to believe? It's history, Barney," Mike Krebs answered.

"We borrow a ton of things from the cult of Mithras, and that was part of God's eternal plan?" Barney Ramage said. "Sounds made up to me. They were the competition and we stole their stuff, plain as pie."

"I am sure some anti-Christian historians would say something along those lines," Father Mike Krebs replied.

"Hey, Mike," Arthur Darner said, "I don't think Barney's an anti-Christian. Are you, Barney?"

"Yeah, that's why I spent six years in the seminary so far. I'm infiltrating for the pagans."

"Y'know," Fred Gacious said, "my guidebook says that story about St. Clement's house is really a legend. They think those rooms are just part of some old Roman warehouse."

"I don't think I would put that answer down on Corny Sheehan's test, if I were you, Fred," Father Mike Krebs advised. "Not if you want ole Sheehan to pass you."

Their glasses were empty now and Mike Krebs suggested another round.

"Nah," Barney Ramage said. "I want to go try one of those shooting galleries. You guys want to come?" Barney's family, from the farm country south of Rocksburg, were all hunters and he had been raised with a rifle in his hands.

Father Mike Krebs said, "You fellows go. I'll be happy here with another cigarette and some more vino spumante."

"How can you smoke those things? They stink," Barney Ramage said as Mike Krebs was shaking another cigarette out of his pack of M.S. brand Italian cigarettes.

"They don't have Winstons in this crazy country," Mike Krebs said. "Besides, these are cheap."

The three seminarians, Barney Ramage, Arthur Darner and Fred Gacious, circled the piazza until they settled on a booth run by a kind-looking Italian grandmother type. The air-powered rifles spewed out little pellets, ten at a pull, almost like buck shot, and the targets were small metal bulls-eyes on a moving belt that fell over when they were hit.

The big sign over the targets said, "100 Lire *La Pallina*," which they thought was a very good deal, 100 lire, or about 15 cents a shot. After shooting ten rounds or so, they had learned the rhythm of it, and a crowd of curious Italian youngsters had gathered to watch the sharp-shooting Americans. "Cowboys, *Americani*," they heard someone in the crowd say. Soon, Barney, Arthur and Fred each had a big, floppy stuffed animal in front of them on the counter.

The trouble started when they tried to pay up and leave with their prizes. The grandmotherly owner of the game, a short stocky woman wearing a leather apron full of coins, told them they owed her not three thousand lira each, but thirty thousand each.

"That's almost fifty dollars," Fred Gacious said.

They tried to tell her that she was mistaken, that they had shot thirty rounds each, not three hundred, but she kept wagging her finger in front of them, saying "terty t'ousan." It seemed to be the only English that she knew.

"How could it be ten times as much?" Arthur Darner asked.

"Here," Barney Ramage said to her, shoving his

stuffed giraffe at her, "take back the prizes. We don't want them. They're not worth fifty dollars each."

But the grandmother would have none of it. "Terty t'ousan, ev'ry one," she kept repeating.

"Look," Barney Ramage said to his friends, "Let's just get out of here. She's trying to cheat us."

The three of them started sidling away from the shooting booth, but in a sprint the woman was out from behind the counter holding onto Fred Gacious's left ear lobe.

"Yowh," he screamed.

"Hey," Barney Ramage said to her. "Leave him alone."

But all the woman replied was, "Terty t'ousan, ev'ry one," still holding onto Fred Gacious's ear.

A carabiniere, on the look-out for pick-pockets at the crowded fair, walked over to the fracas from across the piazza.

He spoke with the woman in Italian. She immediately let go of Fred's ear. The three seminarians from Rocksburg looked on in complete incomprehension as the two Italians conversed. Then the carabiniere turned to them. Very tall, in his black uniform, with thick red stripes down the sides of his pants and a holstered revolver on his hip, he was an intimidating figure.

He spoke in English, "You owe this woman money. You must pay."

"Thank God," Barney Ramage said, "One of them speaks English. Look," he said to the carabiniere, "we owe her three thousand lire each, and she says she wants thirty. These crummy animals aren't worth fifty dollars each."

Again the carabiniere turned to the woman and exchanged a word with her. He nodded his head as if he understood, then he turned back to the seminarians.

"How many times are you shot the rifles?" he asked them.

"I don't know, but not more than thirty shots

each. Thirty shots times 100 lire is three thousand lire. That's all we owe her," Barney Ramage said.

The carabiniere smiled. "You are mistaken. The sign say 100 lire the pellet—*la pallina*. Each shot are ten *palline*, each pull, each shot make one thousand lire."

"Oh my God," Arthur Darner said. "He's right. We've been had."

"Here," Barney Ramage began handing the prizes to the carabiniere. "We don't want these. She can keep her cheap prizes."

But the carabiniere backed away. He would not take the stuffed animals. "I am sorry," he said, "but the sign is the truth."

"What are we going to do?" Arthur Darner said. I don't have a hundred and fifty dollars on me. Do you guys?" He turned to Barney Ramage and Fred Gacious.

"I have it back at the hotel," Fred Gacious said. "Maybe they'll let me go back and get it while you guys wait here."

"Sure, Fred," Barney Ramage answered. "Let us stay hostages while you get lost on your way back to the hotel."

"Look," Arthur Darner said, pointing across the piazza, "there's Mike Krebs." He started shouting and waving both arms, "Mike, hey, Mike"

But he did not seem to hear them. Finally, Fred Gacious thought to shout, "Father Michael Krebs! Father Krebs!"

The priest, who had been staring at the giant fountain of the Four Rivers in the middle of the piazza, finally heard his name being called. When he saw Arthur Darner, Fred Gacious, and Barney Ramage in the custody of an Italian carabiniere, he hurried over.

"Mike, are we glad to see you," Arthur Darner said. "These people are trying to cheat us. In a jumble, the three seminarians told the priest their story.

The priest turned to the carabiniere. "They did

not understand the sign. Surely, we can arrange something. I understand that the Italians are a generous people."

"Terty t'ousan, ev'ry one," the old woman shouted in the priest's face.

The carabiniere motioned her aside. Father Mike Krebs reached into his wallet and took out five twenty dollar bills. The old woman snatched the money out of his hand.

"That is all you deserve," Father Mike Krebs said to her, then turning to the carabiniere, "Do you agree?"

The carabiniere nodded his head. The old woman began to say something but the officer unleashed a stream of vehement Italian at her and she got very quiet.

The seminarians and the priest started to leave when Father Mike Krebs remembered the stuffed animals. He took them from the counter and gave one to each of the seminarians as he marched them off. "Here," he said. "The spoils of war. It would be a shame to leave them behind."

The three young men looked out of place carrying the large stuffed animals through the piazza. An Italian family, a man pushing a baby in a stroller, and his wife holding the hands of two toddlers, was circling the booths and stopped at one selling Christmas toys. The young children were looking wide-eyed at the display. The man looked to the woman who shook her head, no.

Barney Ramage saw them and said, "Hey, let's give these things away," and through a combination of sign language and smiles, offered the stuffed animals to the family. The toddlers were delighted at their gifts and the father could not stop saying "*Grazie*" to the Americans.

"That ended happily," Father Mike Krebs said as they walked away. "That was very generous of you fellows."

"No, Mike," Barney Ramage said. "It was

generous of you. You paid for it."

"We're glad you saw us there, Mike. Otherwise, we'd probably be in some Italian jail right now," Arthur Darner said.

"We'll pay you back, Mike, as soon as we get back to the hotel," Fred Gacious said.

"And, Mike, there's no need to mention this ..." Barney Ramage started to say.

"To Corny Sheehan?" Father Mike Krebs asked. "No problem there. He would probably tell me I was responsible. If you haven't been noticing, he treats me like one of 'the boys' too. No offense, Art, but he's making me, his fellow priest, share a room with you because it was too much money otherwise. But he has a private room because he's 'too old to share.' I don't know, maybe when you're past seventy everyone under forty looks like a boy."

"No offense taken, Mike," Arthur Darner said.

"I'm heading back to the hotel to rest up for tonight," Father Mike Krebs said. "I want to be ready for John Rooney's party." He was referring to John Cardinal Rooney, former bishop of Rocksburg, now a cardinal living in Rome. He had invited the group from the seminary in his former diocese to celebrate mass and have a meal with him that evening.

"It will be good to see him again," Arthur Darner said, as they all headed back. "I kind of miss the old guy."

Mass was at six that night at the American church of Santa Susanna, in anticipation of the feast the next day, January 1st, the Solemnity of Mary. The cardinal was the main celebrant, but he asked Corny Sheehan and Mike Krebs to concelebrate with him. The cardinal's secretary, Bill Tuigg, was the master of ceremonies.

After Mass, the group of them walked down the Via Barberini, past all the brightly lit airline offices, the cardinal with them. He had asked his chauffeur to follow them to the restaurant with the car, just

in case his ailing hips would not let him finish the
journey on foot.

The night breeze was slightly chilled, that last
night of 1969, but the *tramontana*, the harsh north-
erly wind from over the Alps, had not yet reached
Rome with its full force, bringing the bitter winter weather with it. The cardinal chatted with his
visitors as they strolled, although Corny Sheehan
seemed determined to monopolize the cardinal's
attention.

Father Bill Tuigg walked behind with Father
Mike Krebs. "I hear that you are at St. Teresa's
now," Bill Tuigg said.

"Yeah, I got sent there in an emergency when
Tony Capresi took off. You two were classmates,
weren't you?"

"Good friends," Father Bill Tuigg said. "Is it
true that he ran off with a parishioner?"

"That's only part of the story, Bill. I think
Sparky Larkin drove him crazy first. I know he's
trying to drive me nuts."

"A hard case to live with, huh?"

"Very hard. The sooner I get out of there, the
better off I'll be. That's why I'm along on this trip.
I've been teaching some courses at St. Greg's, and I
might be going there as vice-rector. This is sort of a
trial run."

"Why do they let guys like Sparky Larkin get
away with the things they do?" Bill Tuigg said.

"Hey, Bill, your man there," he pointed at
Cardinal Rooney, walking ahead with some of the
seminarians, "was bishop of Rocksburg for ten
years. Why didn't he do something? He knew how
crazy Larkin is. Everybody does."

Father Bill Tuigg shrugged his shoulders. There
was no answer.

The group walked past Triton, blowing his horn
in the spray of the fountain in the Piazza Barberini, up the Via Quattro Fontane and down the Via
Rasella, to Gino's Restaurant where Father Bill

Tuigg had made reservations for the group.

The restaurant was ready for them and had set up a long table down one side of their main dining room. The cardinal sat at the middle of the table, and asked Father Bill Tuigg to make sure that the chauffeur got something from the kitchen.

The cardinal was in an ebullient mood. He spoke in his elegant Italian to all the waiters, who made quite a fuss over the prelate. The site of faces from home seemed to raise his spirits and he regaled the group with his favorite Rocksburg stories, mostly about Monsignor Don Himmelreich, the rector of St. Gregory's Seminary.

"You see, lads, Don Himmelreich is one of the brightest priests I ever met in Rocksburg," the cardinal said. "Also one of the cheapest. And it was for both of those reasons that I appointed him rector of St. Gregory's.

"One day, he asked for an appointment to see me. He was very excited. For years, the seminarians had been complaining about the antique showers and other bathroom facilities. He had this plan to remodel all of the jakes at St. Gregory's and to do it at no cost to the diocese.

"You see, lads," the cardinal continued, "it had occurred to Monsignor Himmelreich that all the marble wainscoting and the marble stall and shower dividers in the nineteenth century bathrooms at St. Gregory's were a hidden treasure. His plan was to replace the marble with Masonite and sell it for enough profit to do the remodeling.

"Of course, I gave my permission, and, you know, lads, he was right. He sold the marble to some company in Rocksburg that remade them into coffee tables, mantles and fireplaces, and all that money went to buy new showers and so on for the seminarians at St. Gregory's. Somewhere in Rocksburg tonight, some very wealthy people will be putting their New Year's cocktails down and lighting their holiday fires on old urinal separators from

St. Gregory's Seminary," the cardinal laughed.

Story followed story, and one of the seminarians in the group said, "Hey, Fred, why don't you tell the cardinal about the old lady who almost tore your ear off today?"

Arthur Darner and Barney Ramage glared at Fred Gacious. He had blabbed. But it was too late. Corny Sheehan's ears perked up, and he said, "Yes, Frederick, I would like to hear that story."

Soon the details were out in a raucous retelling of the sharpshooting incident and how Father Mike Krebs had ridden to the rescue. They were all laughing, even Corny Sheehan, but the cardinal was not.

"I don't like to hear stories like that," the cardinal said. "It makes the people of this city look bad, and they are not that way. Most are industrious, hard-working folks. How much did you pay, Father Krebs?"

Reluctantly, but unable to ignore the cardinal, Mike Krebs said, "A hundred dollars, your Eminence."

Cardinal Rooney took out his wallet and passed some large Italian lira notes down the long table to where Father Krebs was sitting.

"Here, Father, you take these. Let me make up for your poor impression of this marvelous city."

"Your Eminence, it's really not ..." Mike Krebs began to say,

"Nonsense," the cardinal said in a tone that allowed no alternative. Father Mike Krebs took the money and put it in his pocket.

It was just after ten o'clock when the meal ended, and the restaurant needed the tables for the midnight revelers to come. Cardinal Rooney thanked his fellow Rocksburgers for their company and wished them a Happy New Year. He said that he was sorry to leave them before midnight, but he had a busy schedule on the feast day tomorrow.

"Be careful as you walk the streets tonight,

lads," the cardinal warned. "The Italians have a quaint habit of saluting the New Year by ridding themselves of the old, often by throwing things out their windows at midnight."

"What kinds of things?" someone asked.

"Oh, ashtrays, cigarette packs, pots and pans, records, broken furniture, pictures of old lovers, anything with bad memories of the year gone by. You may even hear some gunshots, since firing a gun at the moon is an acceptable alternative to heaving the family sofa onto the street from your third floor window," the cardinal laughed.

The group from St. Gregory's said good-bye to Cardinal Rooney and Father Tuigg on the street outside the restaurant, where the cardinal's limousine was waiting.

Corny Sheehan waved goodbye and turned to the group. "I think that the old man is losing it, boys," he said, ignoring the fact that he was the cardinal's elder by a decade. "He's confusing Rome with Naples. The Romans are too sophisticated to jettison their belongings for sentiment's sake. The emotional Neapolitans might do that, but not the Romans."

The group broke up, with most of the seminarians and Father Sheehan returning to their hotel where they had a few bottles of bubbly wine on ice standing by to celebrate the New Year.

Father Mike Krebs collared his roommate, Arthur Darner, and said, "It's kind of early to be heading back, Art, don't you think? Let's stop for a drink somewhere."

"Gee, Mike, after all the wine we just had at dinner ..."

Barney Ramage saw Father Mike Krebs and Arthur Darner standing together on the sidewalk and he came over to them. Fred Gacious joined them.

"Geez, did you hear that about the gunshots?" Fred asked.

"What are you worried about, blabbermouth?

If I were you I'd be more worried some little old lady was going to pull my ear off," Barney Ramage said.

"Leave him alone, Barney. Even Corny Sheehan laughed at the story," Arthur Darner said.

"Besides, why are the best sharpshooters in Rome worried about a few gunshots?" Mike Krebs laughed.

"Okay, Mike. At least you got your money back," Barney Ramage said.

"And I am dying to spend it," Father Mike Krebs said. "Look, you guys interested in a drink? There's no way I want to face Corny Sheehan over a glass of spumante back at the hotel. He will have this endlessly boring story about how St. Peter stomped the grapes or something, and I couldn't face that, not on New Year's Eve."

"We're with you, Mike," Barney Ramage said, his face flushed.

That decided it, and soon the four of them were headed back to the Piazza Barberini where the Via Veneto began. They strolled slowly beneath the bright lights of the Veneto to regain their breath after their prodigious repast and too much Frascati wine. In a darker spot, where the Veneto curves, near the Polish Airlines office, beneath the huge sycamore trees, they encountered a cluster of heavily scented women standing there, their legs apart, their long winter coats open.

"Hey, look guys, a bunch of hookers," Barney Ramage said, a little too loudly. "Let's see how much they cost."

"Barney, get serious," Arthur Darner said.

"Barney, stop it. I have my Roman collar on," Mike Krebs said.

"S'okay, s'okay," Barney Ramage said. "Just let me ask one, for curiosity." He turned to the closest girl and said, "*Cuanto cuesta, senorita?*"

Father Mike Krebs grabbed Barney and pulled him away. "That wasn't even Italian, you idiot drunk."

Barney mumbled, "Spanish, almost the same."

The girl approached them. She saw Father Mike Krebs's Roman collar and said, in heavily accented English, "A special price for you, Father."

The offer was so direct and so guileless that the three seminarians broke into hiccupping laughter. Mike Krebs, pushing and pulling, hauled them away from the women, herding them up the Veneto.

"That wasn't funny, Barney," Mike Krebs said. "You need to settle down. C'mon guys, somebody from Rocksburg told me there's a bar at the end of this street that makes a decent Manhattan. Let's have that nightcap."

He herded them to the top of the Veneto, and at the end, near the Porta Pinciana, he led them into Harry's Bar.

It was a clean, well-heated place and starting to become crowded, and they did not feel comfortable until they removed their topcoats.

The maitre'd sat them towards the back, near where the dining section began. They settled into the low-lying leather chairs and ordered a round. Through the sheer-curtained windows, between the high wooden paneling, amid the haze of the smoke-filled bar, they could see the bright Veneto traffic.

They were surrounded by the height of Roman fashion. Women in highly-patterned midi-skirts or very short hot pants were talking to men in dark suits with trim waists and broad shoulders. The priest and the seminarians from Rocksburg felt a bit out of place. When he thought that he saw some people staring, Father Mike Krebs quickly removed his Roman collar.

"Wow, would you look at that one?" Barney Ramage said, tossing his head towards a tall, beautiful, long-haired brunette, in a short skirt and diaphanous blouse, standing at the bar. She was surrounded by Italian men, cigarettes and drinks in hand, laughing, joking, vying for her attention.

He had spoken more loudly than he had intended, and the other three broke into a lurching laughter. Some people nearby turned to look, but in the crowded room, above a jabber of upper-class Italian, not many people noticed, although the growing red on Barney's cheeks made him feel as if everyone in the room was staring at him.

Round followed round, and soon the lights in the bar were blinking. It was midnight. On the sound system, a solo saxophone was playing "Auld Lang Syne."

The couples in the bar leaned into each other, linked by a promise of intimacy to follow, as they kissed. The priest and the three seminarians looked at each other.

Lifting his glass, Father Mike Krebs said, "Well, gentlemen, shall we share the click of peace?" And they touched their glasses round.

"Happy New Year," Fred Gacious said.

"To us," Barney Ramage added.

"Those like us, damn few and they're all dead," Arthur Darner added, downing his glass just after the others.

After they lingered for a while, Mike Krebs looked at his watch and said, "We should be going, guys, before Corny Sheehan thinks we've all been corrupted by the Roman night."

They had their wallets out to pay the bill, but Mike Krebs tossed a pile of Italian lire on the plate. "The cardinal's money," he said.

Out in the chill evening air, they hurried down the Veneto to hunt a cab to take them back to the hotel. It was a quiet ride. No one felt like talking.

When they got back, they found the rest of their group huddled about Corny Sheehan, who was sitting in a big lobby chair, with a towel wrapped around his head. There was some blood dripping down his left ear.

Father Mike Krebs asked what happened.

One of the seminarians said, "He was saying that Cardinal Rooney's story, about how the Romans celebrate New Year's Eve, was for the birds. That nothing much happened in Rome at midnight. We were outside in the street here," he jerked his head towards the hotel door, "in front of the hotel, and he got wacked by a picture some bozo tossed out their window. Here it is," the seminarian said, handing Mike Krebs a twisted silver picture frame, its glass broken, with the photo of a bride and groom inside, in tatters.

V

The Wings of Morning

Brightly the sun flashed on the wings of the DC-8.
The light awoke the short, nearly bald man in seat
10-A, and he leaned forward to look through the
porthole. Beneath him, the Atlantic shimmered in
the dawn. How clean and pure the water looked.

He mumbled a morning offering when he realized that he was awake. Then he reached under the
seat, into his carry-on, for his breviary. He flipped
the red-edged pages to the prayers for the day and
he began to read the words of Psalm 139, "If I fly on
the wings of morning, to the uttermost ends of the
sea …" That's appropriate he thought, a fugitive,
just like me.

A stewardess interrupted him with breakfast,
and, soon after the red seat belt sign blinked on,
a voice advised the travelers that they were thirty
minutes from Rome's Leonardo Da Vinci airport,
and would they please fasten their seat belts.

The plane came quickly to the earth. It taxied
about the tarmac and then parked, without reason,
away from the terminal.

Somehow it seemed normal, now that the plane
was in Italy, to slow down the pace of things. After
a half-hour of unexplained waiting, the plane drove

to an exit ramp and allowed its passengers to dis-
embark.

They were unexpected at customs and had to
wait for an inspector. When the uniformed official
arrived, he walked past the valises lined up at the
customs counter, marking each perfunctorily with a
piece of chalk. He questioned only the pretty girls,
and not about cigarettes or liquor.

"Cal, hey, Cal Kennelly," the bald-headed
man heard someone shouting. The name was a
relic from his Roman seminary days. At the age of
twenty-two, Thomas Kennelly had started to lose
his hair, and "*calvo*," the Italian word for "bald,"
or "Cal" for short, became his nickname among
friends and enemies alike.

For some strange reason, his old name sounded
good to him. Hearing it now, after so many years,
reminded him of the place. He was in Rome and
things would be different here.

The man shouting was Jake Whelan. He walked
to the tall red-haired priest standing behind the
customs barrier. "Jake, you old son of a gun, you
didn't have to come out here to get me."

"I know, but I came anyway. Let's hurry. I left my
car at the taxi stand. We'll catch up on the way in."

The priest handed him one of his valises and
they started off. He was surprised to see Jake here.
They had been classmates, but not really friends,
when they were seminarians together at the North
American College in Rome. Perhaps the rector had
sent him as a one man welcoming committee, or
perhaps he had come to survey the ruin first hand?
No, I must stop thinking that way, he admonished
himself. This was not Cape Forneau. Everyone here
does not dislike me. The people in Rome don't even
know about that.

The taxi drivers cursed mildly under their
breath as they saw the two black-suited men climb
into the blue Fiat 125 parked in their yellow-lined
preserve, but the Fiat quickly outdistanced their

insults. The car sped past the tall bulky statue of Leonardo, the founder of flight, and was soon on the main road to Rome.

"So, Cal, what have you been up to? Geez, I haven't seen you since, hell, since 1956, our last year at the College."

"I know. Thirteen years is a lot. I've been busy."

"Like what?"

"I was in a parish for just over a year after the College, then I went to work as secretary for Bishop Foley from Cape Forneau."

"Yeah."

"And I was with him till last year when he got sent to Chicago as archbishop."

"What was that like, working for him? Is he as hard-assed as people say?"

"A lot of that is sour grapes. You know, when you're in charge you step on some toes. What about you? How long have you been back in Rome?"

"Back? Hell, I practically never left. I was at a parish in Rockville Center for two years after ordination. Then here for post-grad work in moral theology at the Gregorian, and after I got my doctorate, the College needed a moral man, so I put in a good word for myself, and that was it. I've been at the College, holding moral seminars, ever since. I stay in Italy any longer, I'll be an honorary wop, but hell, I like it here. What about you? You're a monsignor, now, right? Pretty young for that, aren't you?"

"Bishop Foley did that to me. It's a long story."

"You'd be the last guy I figured for pastor-in-residence."

"Yeah?" Monsignor Kennelly paused. What did Jake know?

"I mean, it doesn't sound like you were a pastor in Cape Forneau."

Remember, Kennelly told himself. Give measured answers. Weigh your words. Do not react to everything in anger.

"Not exactly, but chancery work is very pastoral. You can learn a lot from dealing with the problems in different parishes, and I handled some pretty hairy cases. You know Charbonnier?"

"That guy that's been saying the old Latin mass at drive-ins and over the radio?"

"He's from Cape Forneau. I did the brief for the Curia on that case."

"The Congregation for Clergy censured him, didn't they?" Jake Whelan asked.

"Cardinal Rooney went easy on him, actually. But the word around is that Rooney misses the old mass himself."

"I see you haven't changed much."

"No?"

"Still an ecclesiastical gossip."

"Did you come out here to welcome me or ambush me?"

"No offense meant. Hell, I'm probably an ecclesiastical gossip myself. It's hard to live in Rome and not be."

"No offense taken. It's just that I think I've changed. Since I was a student here in Rome. I mean, I hope so."

Meters became kilometers as the priests' car sped over the bends in the Tiber, through the aqueduct-crossed farmland and towards the heart of Rome.

"What are those shacks up against the city walls, there? I don't remember those," Kennelly asked.

"Those? They're called '*baracche*,' like our barracks, but it really means 'sheds.' They're just lean-to's, put up by the poor folks who come to Rome from the south. They can't afford regular housing," Jake Whelan said.

"People live in those?" he asked.

"Yeah, whole families."

"*Ciao, ragazzi, ci vediamo sabato per la partita,*" the two American seminarians said good-bye and told the teen-age boys of the *Squadra di Sant' Ivaldo* soccer team that they would see them on Saturday for their game.

Sal Caputo and Ray Giordano were students for the priesthood at the North American College on the Janiculum Hill in Rome. Sal was already a deacon, in his fourth year of studies before priestly ordination, and Ray was in his second year. They were both from the Brooklyn diocese, in fact, from the same parish, St. Rocco's.

"*Don Flavio, dobbiamo tornare al collegio,*" Ray Giordano said to the scruffy Italian parish priest, Don Flavio, who had put the *squadra* together, letting him know that they had to get back to the seminary.

But Sal Caputo quickly added what they had already told the boys, that they would be back on Saturday for the *squadra's* next game.

Don Flavio was grateful to the two American seminarians for their work at *Sant' Ivaldo's*, helping to organize, train and referee the *squadra's* soccer games, and doing almost anything else he asked. He had his hands full just performing the basic tasks necessary to keep his poor parish afloat in the seedy outskirts of Rome.

Most of the parish was a shanty town, ramshackle dwellings with no plumbing, built of scraps of lumber and corrugated metal, inhabited by Italian peasants who had come to the big city looking for work that was not available in their home villages. The people were devout and filled the parish church on Sundays, but the offering basket was never very full. Just getting team jerseys for the soccer *squadra* had been a struggle, but, at the last minute, someone had come through with the final 40,000 lire to pay the bill.

Sal and Ray had to take two busses to return to the North American College, and, with good connections, the trip took almost an hour.

On the way back, standing in the middle of a

crowded Roman bus, Ray asked Sal, "How'd you ever meet Don Flavio? I mean, this is the remotest place in Rome."

Sal said, "You know Squiggs Andalucci at St. Rocco's?"

"That fat guy with his shirt always sticking out who ushers every Sunday?"

"Yeah, him. Don Flavio's his second cousin. Squiggs gave him my name and told him where I lived. One day, my first year in Rome, Don Flavio shows up at the College, out of the blue, asking for me. I been coming here ever since, and since you got here, I been bringing you because, you know, I feel responsible for you."

"Right. I still don't know how I let you talk me into babysitting these *scagnozzi*."

"You enjoy it, but doesn't your year have a class trip to Assisi this week-end? How you gonna be at the *squadra's* game Saturday?"

"My class? Who wants to spend time with those idiots? I'll be at the game."

"It wouldn't be you're short of money for the trip 'cause you used it for something else?"

"Sal, what's it to you? You my mother or something?"

"You pretend to be such a hard ass. Why'n't you admit it was you gave Don Flavio the money for the team's jerseys?"

"I don't know what you're talking about, and neither do you, so why'n't you shut up?"

Soon Jake Whelan's car was on the Via del Gianicolo, turning into the grounds of the North American College, perched on its hill, overlooking the Vatican on one side and the city of Rome on the other.

Monsignor Kennelly had half-expected a greeting party at the entrance to the College, but there was none. Only a few seminarians, dressed in their street clothes, passed them as they entered the large glass doors of the College.

"Hey, Jake," one of them greeted Whelan.

"Hey, Tim, off for another day on the town?"

"Nah, just escaping the cooking. Want to come? We found this cheap little osteria in Trastevere."

"Thanks, but I have to get Monsignor Kennelly here settled in. Would you guys like to meet the new pastor in residence?"

"Sure. How you doing, Monsignor?"

The newly arrived priest had a small epiphany. This was Rome, not Cape Forneau, and he needed things to be different here. "Not Monsignor, guys. Just Cal, Cal Kennelly."

"How are you, Cal? Where are you from?"

"Cape Forneau, Louisiana. You?"

"Joe Denzer, Rocksburg."

"Tim Ostrowski, Monsignor, uh, Cal. Altoona-Johnstown."

"Ollie Mosby, Yonkers."

"Nice to meet you all."

The two priests entered the second pair of large glass doors, walking over the College seal and motto imbedded in the pavement *"Firmum est cor meum*—My heart is true," and waited for the elevator.

"Fellows can leave the College grounds pretty much whenever they like?" Kennelly asked.

"Pretty much. They're supposed to be back at a reasonable hour, but the only real rule is that they can't spend overnight away."

"And they can pretty much wear what they want?"

"Yep. It's a helluva lot different than the old cam walks in our cassocks and clerical hats. The College has changed since our time, Cal, but for the better, I think. I know you were okay with the old system, but a lot of the guys weren't."

"Gee, I don't think ..." Kennelly wanted to say that he wasn't that way, not anymore, but that would take too much explaining. Better to let things be, at least for now, he thought.

On the elevator Jake Whelan said, "Everyone's probably in the Red Room before *pranzo*. We'll stop there so you can say your hellos."

On the refectory floor, they walked past stilted paintings of American prelates in their formal robes, looking unemotionally out through the glass curtain walls at the star-crowned fountain in the courtyard. Jake Whelan started for a large, padded red leather door when Kennelly said, "Is the chapel on this floor?"

Jake pointed and said, "Sure, straight down there at the end of this hallway."

"You go ahead, Jake. I'll be right there."

Monsignor Kennelly walked past the student cafeteria and the wall of bulletin boards to the chapel. The large wooden doors swung wide and he found himself in the darkened reaches of the chapel. He was the only one there. He knelt in the last pew.

Behind the main altar there was a mosaic of Mary, larger than life and surrounded by dancing angels, that gave a warmth to the place that he had not expected. The baroque chapel at the old college on the Via dell' Umilta, where he had lived as a student, had always felt so cold.

"Lord," he thought as he knelt there, "I am going to need your help on this one. It's make or break. So much of my priesthood has been a waste. I want it to change. I want to change. Give me the grace I will need for that. Please. Amen."

When Cal Kennelly got to the Red Room, he found clumps of men in black suits, standing and sitting, holding cocktail glasses and discoursing. Jake Whelan led him to a group in one corner, where a tall, slender man with reddish gray hair and an unhealthy yellow look to his skin was standing, fingering a gold chain hanging across his chest with one hand and holding a drink in the other.

"Bishop Guelph, Monsignor Kennelly's here," Jake said

"Monsignor, how good to see you!" the bishop

said as he embraced the bald-headed man, balancing his cocktail glass so as not to spill it. "How was your flight?"

"Fine, Bishop. Thanks."

"You must be tired, but join us for a drink while I introduce you to the rest of the faculty. Then, after lunch, you can settle into your suite."

"About my suite, Your Excellency," Cal Kennelly began before he realized that he had made a terrible mistake. Nobody said "Your Excellency" in the informal Church any more. Since the Vatican Council, bishops were simply "Bishop." He had tried so hard to remember, and now his anxiety had brought back his old sycophancy.

Overriding his nerves, Cal Kennelly plowed ahead. This was too important a part of his plans. "I'd really like to live with the deacon class, Bishop, the fellows I'll be teaching."

"But there are no faculty suites available on that floor, Monsignor."

"Perhaps I could live in a student room."

"A student room?" That was a curveball and Bishop Guelph did not expect curveballs from Bishop Foley's boy.

"Yes, Bishop. I feel it will help me get to know the fellows better, keep a closer eye on things."

"Well, that might be arranged, Monsignor," he said, and before he caught any more curveballs, the bishop led him around the room to meet the other faculty members.

Five weeks later, on an October evening, Sal Caputo and Ray Giordano were walking around the ballfield of the American College, as their stomachs grudgingly tried to digest another seminary meal.

Ahead of them, out of earshot, walked the topic of their conversation, Cal Kennelly, surrounded by a group of men from the fourth year deacon class, the students he was teaching as pastor-in-residence.

"Is that Baldy Kennelly guy for real?" asked Ray.

"What do you mean?" Sal replied.

"Look at him. He's got on a pair of Italian jeans that look like he poured himself into them, his Roman collar, he's got that pinned over a black tee-shirt, and all of a sudden the little bit of hair he has around his bald pate has frizzed out. What is he, a priest or an elf?"

"I don't think he's an elf, Ray. He's just trying to fit in."

"Fit in with what? The only person who looks like that around here is him."

"How'd you like to be a middle-aged guy dropped into a group of men in their early and mid-twenties? He's trying to act younger. Besides, a real Christian would feel sorry for him. Those jeans can't be too comfortable."

"Hey, I didn't buy them."

"Joe Denzer was in his room the other day, and all he has are two small suitcases full of clericals and underwear, plus some Italian clothes he bought here at Standa."

"Standa. That's a dime store."

"Poverty is simplicity, Ray."

"Poverty, my eye! It's a grab for attention. If he was really poor, like the Gospels say, he'd keep it to himself. You know, the left hand wouldn't know about the right hand."

"I'm not even going to try to deal with the illogic of that," Sal Caputo said.

"How'd Denzer find out about Baldy's clothes, then, unless Baldy told him? Denzer's a bit nuts, like all the rest of those guys from Rocksburg, but I don't think he's started poking through people's underwear drawers yet."

"So?"

"Baldy had to tell him, right?"

"Maybe."

"The whole idea is absurd. Pastor-in-residence. Why'd we have to import a pastor from America when we've got three hundred parishes in Rome with pastors, most of them, like Don Flavio, who could use all the help they could get?"

"You know the answer to that. Most of the guys here don't speak Italian. What could they do in a Roman parish?"

"That's the real problem. What kind of human being are you if you can spend three, four years in a country and don't relate to the people?"

"Ray, we were lucky. We came over here knowing Italian. We spoke it at home."

"Maybe you did. I came over here speaking a dialect from Sicily that got me chased out of every Roman store and restaurant I went into. I had to study to learn real Italian. This whole pastor-in-residence thing is just another nutso scheme not to upset the American ghetto we've created up here."

"Ray, most of my class think Cal's doing a good job."

"If I had a whole week to get ready to teach three hours of class, I'd be good too."

"I don't mean the preparation. I mean the practicality of it. He's really giving us good advice."

"Like?"

"Our last class. We were talking about hearing confessions. Cal says that people telegraph the answers they want from you, just by the way they ask a question. But you have to watch that, because the normal human tendency is to tell people what you think they want to hear, and that would be wrong. You'd be miss-stating the moral law. He makes a lot of sense."

"You're pretty easy to impress, Sal."

"Ray, you wouldn't be impressed with Cal if a halo suddenly appeared above his head."

"If that happened, I'd check it out for the dime store label."

In the classroom adjoining the library on the refectory floor of the American College, Cal Kennelly was flipping a piece of chalk as he spoke to the deacon class.

"One of the things about the indissolubility of marriage that Church marriage courts don't emphasize, I mean they're aware of this, but don't advertise it, is how difficult the lack of a sacramental bond is to prove. Any logician will tell you that proving that something is not the case is considered impossible. In our marriage courts, though, we ask people seeking an annulment of their 'marriage'" the balding priest held the chalk and made quotation marks with his fingers, "to do exactly that, to prove a negative, to prove that their marriage was not sacramentally valid."

"Cal," Joe Denzer lifted his hand to speak, "what if the person who's in that situation decides in good conscience that proving it is just too difficult, and he more or less annuls the marriage himself?"

"What have you been reading, Joe?" Cal Kennelly smiled at the deacon. "So you probably know, some priests back home are telling people to do just that. When they are convinced that a marriage was never a valid sacrament, but for some reason, like the refusal of the former spouse to give testimony, it could never be proven, they're telling people to give themselves a good conscience annulment without going through the Church marriage courts."

"What do you think about that?" Tim Ostrowski asked.

"What do I think?" Cal Kennelly repeated. "That depends on who's listening. I wouldn't want the fellows down the hill to hear me say that I liked the idea," he tilted his head toward the Vatican, "but realistically I know that a lot of priests back home are doing it. My own opinion...."

The bell rang and Cal Kennelly stopped speaking. This was the signal for notebooks to slam and chairs to screech and class was over for the day.

In the hall outside the classroom, Joe Denzer asked Cal Kennelly if he would like a short walk before supper. They took the elevator to the ground floor and soon were out of the College gate on their way up the Via del Gianicolo. They walked as far as the coffee bar just past the church of Sant'Onofrio and stood overlooking the tiled roofs of Trastevere as they each sipped an *aperitivo*.

"Cal, you never did say what you felt about that last point," Joe Denzer began.

"I was going to say that my own feeling was that it could go either way. I see the logic of not trying to prove the unprovable and just letting an honest, informed conscience make a decision. But I also see the need for the Church to have rules and to ask its members to keep those rules."

"Even when living with the rules could mean a life of misery?"

"Well, Joe, I'm not going to come out in favor of misery."

"You know what I mean, Cal. Most people who have been denied annulments accept that judgment, even with the pain it causes them. They're in second marriages and think that they're living in sin."

"They should be told there is another option, Joe. I already said that. No good priest could defend keeping them in the dark about their rights of conscience."

"Shouldn't the Church be telling them that then, instead of just, 'Sorry, your annulment is denied'?"

"The Church does tell them, Joe. Maybe not officially, but you'll tell them, I will, so will most of the guys in class, and we are the Church."

A year ago, even six months ago, Cal Kennelly thought, I would never have believed those words, let alone been able to say them. But he so wanted them to be true. He wanted his new life to fit him. Divorced and remarried Catholics weren't the only ones the official Church had disappointed. And if those words aren't true, he pondered, what do I do?

A small group of deacons was crowded into the priest's room, scattered over the bed, desk, reading chair, closet and floor. A weak desk lamp lit the room, giving the group a conspiratorial cast, high-lighting faces and shading bodies in the darkness. The room hung heavy with the cold dampness of the Roman winter about to begin that mid-November evening, but the bottle of Chianti in a straw-bottomed flask that was being passed around added some warmth.

"Let me pose a hypothetical," Cal Kennelly said. "In our theology of marriage, the priest is just there to witness the ceremony. The ministers are the bride and groom. The parties marry themselves, right?"

Joe Denzer, sloped into a corner, back against the wall, legs splayed on the floor, said, "That's what they taught us in sacramental theology."

"So think about this. What if two homosexuals decide to confer the sacrament on themselves?" Cal Kennelly asked. "Could you stop them?"

"I sure as hell wouldn't witness it," Sal Caputo, who was leaning against the closet, replied.

"What if you just happened to be there? I mean, what if you were at a gathering of homosexuals and suddenly two of them get up and exchange vows in front of you and the group?" Cal Kennelly asked.

"Cal, how likely is that to happen?" Sal said.

"I was involved in something very much like that, Sal. It happens."

"And?"

"And nothing turned out good for anybody involved. It was a sad case."

"Look, Cal," Ollie Mosby said. "These folks can't have it both ways. They want the approval of the Church, and they want a lifestyle that the

Church condemns, but they can't have both."

"But do they need you sacramentally? Couldn't they just administer the sacrament to themselves?" Cal Kennelly asked. "It's not that absurd. Think about it."

"C'mon, Cal. Thomas Aquinas settled that a long time ago, about the proper matter for the sacraments, which in matrimony is a willing and able man and woman, and not two men, or two women." Joe Denzer said.

"Maybe we have to stop looking at Thomas Aquinas for all our answers," Cal said. "This is the twentieth century, not the thirteenth."

"Two guys ask Father D'Annunzio to marry them at St. Rocco's, he'd run them out the building," Sal Caputo said. "Thomas Aquinas is still relevant in Brooklyn."

In the fading light of the December evening, Sal Caputo and Ray Giordano were pacing the asphalt walkway that lined the ball field at the American College. With an alpine chill rolling down from the north, there were not too many others who dared the outdoors after dinner.

"Ray," Sal said, "did it ever occur to you that you're the only guy in the College who still wears a cassock to meals."

"So? The second bus was late getting back from *Sant' Ivaldo*'s, and this was quicker than a shirt and tie."

"So, guys talk. My friends keep asking me if you know this is 1969 and not 1069."

"Friends? What friends do you have?"

"If I told you, you'd go to their rooms and terrorize them."

"It was probably Denzer, that putz. Whenever he sees me in this thing, he scowls."

"I've hardly talked to Denzer in weeks. Every time I turn around, he's with Cal."

"That's a pair, Kennelly and Denzer."

The conversation paused for a half-turn around the field. Then Ray Giordano said, "I hear Baldy wants the Church to marry homos these days."

"Where'd you hear that?"

"Oh, around. Baldy's late night bull sessions are the talk of the College. I even hear a certain deacon from Brooklyn is known to attend."

"Sometimes," Sal admitted.

"So does Baldy think the Church should ignore centuries of its own teachings or what?"

"Cal was only talking pastorally, about how you'd handle that type of a situation. Besides, I set him straight. I told him what Father D'Annunzio would do back at St. Rocco's."

"You set him straight? Who's the pastor in residence here, you or him?"

"Cal's not too good on answers, Ray. Mostly he just asks questions and gets us talking. But that's good. It stretches our minds without giving us any pre-conceived notions."

"That's what the Church is, Sal. It's a whole bunch of pre-conceived notions. We call it the Deposit of Faith, remember?"

"Excuse me, Paul the Sixth."

"I mean, this grab Baldy's making for relevancy. It has all you fourth years guys fooled. Fashionable Cal Kennelly, who believes the Catholic Church should do whatever it takes to give the world an orgasm. Bullshit."

The chapel of St. Peter's Chair, in the apse of St. Peter's Basilica, was filled with family and friends of the deacon class the December morning of the ordination ceremony.

Bishop Guelph stood below the huge baroque reliquary which held the wooden remains of the legendary chair of Peter, the apostle. Above the chair, shone the Holy Spirit in the ecru, ivory, brown and yellow stained glass window that lit the apse.

The bishop called forward those who sought

priestly ordination. Resplendent in their flowing white albs, the deacon class rose, approached the altar, and promised their youth, their enthusiasm and their lives to Christ and His Church.

In recollection of so many bishops before him, in a line that history could trace unbroken to Peter and his brother Andrew, to Matthew and Zebedee's sons, to Bartholomew, James, Philip, Simon and Jude, and to Thomas the Doubter, Bishop Guelph touched his outstretched hands to the deacons' heads and imparted to them the Holy Spirit, the power to forgive sins and to make Christ present in bread and wine.

In a new part of the ceremony, begun in the four years since the end of the Vatican Council, the bishop invited all other priests in attendance to impose their hands on the newly-ordained, signifying their common priesthood. Forward they came, priests visiting from America, gaping at their first glimpse of St. Peter's, pastors who had fostered the vocations of altar boys, friends who had given youngsters a glimpse of the joys of the priesthood. And the faculty of the College, joined by their newest member, Monsignor Thomas "Cal" Kennelly, dressed in a borrowed red-piped cassock and lace surplice for the occasion.

Together these priests trouped onto the altar and one by one walked past the kneeling *ordinati*, just made priests themselves, imposing their hands on each one. Cal Kennelly knew these men now, and had become close friends with some of them. The ceremony gave him a special happiness. It was becoming enjoyable to be a priest again. He felt almost re-ordained himself, as if he were being allowed by a forgiving God to recapture the lost joy of his own priesthood, the joy that Cape Forneau, the years with Bishop Foley, and his own ambition had stolen away. Then he came unexpectedly to Joe Denzer kneeling before him. Smiling, he pressed his hands heavily on Joe

Denzer's head, with the full weight of his five foot seven frame.

The grey telephone buzzed insistently at the end of the empty first floor hallway of the North American College. This first week of the New Year 1970, many of the deacon class were still away on their after-ordination trips with their families visiting from America.

"Will someone get that damned thing?" a voice yelled.

"Why don't you?"

"Hey, Denzer. Where the hell's Denzer? It's for you."

"Coming."

"He's coming. Hold on."

"Hello. This is Joe Denzer."

"Hi, Joe. Mike Krebs here. Sorry I got to Rome too late for the ceremony, but congratulations on your ordination."

"Mike Krebs? Are you in Rome?"

"Yep. Over at the Medaglia d'Oro Hotel, behind the Vatican. Can I buy a new priest lunch?"

They met at La Carbonara, and got a table on the second floor, near one of the windows. Outside, the Campo de' Fiori, swept and hosed clean from the daily morning market, was almost empty in the January cold.

"When did you get into town, Mike?"

"The group from St. Greg's got here just over a week before Christmas. I guess we missed the ordinations by a couple days. How was it?"

"Great, it really was. I never realized how I would feel that day. You study, you pray, you plan and all, but nothing got me ready for the feelings. It was pretty over-powering."

"And your folks?"

"My mom was floating on air, and my dad, Dad doesn't show his emotions too much, but I think I caught him wiping a tear from his eye."

"How long were they here?"

"They came a week before ordination, and then, right after, we took a week's vacation together in London. That's all the time Dad could get away from his law firm right now, but it was great."

"You looking forward to Rocksburg?"

"Better believe it. I have a small committee of about twenty or so planning my first American mass at St. Anne's. You'll be there, I hope."

"Sure."

"How's the tour going? Rome's a great town, isn't it?"

"You know Corny Sheehan, don't you? He's managed to make Rome seem completely uninteresting and unappetizing."

"That's too bad. I thought he was retired."

"He should be, but Don Himmelreich just lets the old boy keep going on," Mike Krebs said.

"Himmelreich does the best he can, I guess," Joe Denzer said. "Being rector at St. Greg's can't be an easy job."

"Yeah, I'm sure the fellow's pretty frustrated by now. Say, the rumor in Rocksburg is that you'll be joining him, as vice-rector of the seminary when you get back."

"The heck I will. I want to be in a parish."

"Relax, Joe. I was just joking. Actually Himmelreich has talked to me about the job. That's the official reason I came on this trip, to feel my way back into seminary life. Besides, living with Sparky Larkin at St. Teresa's is driving me batty. They say he practically drove his last assistant, Tony Capresi, out of the priesthood."

"I heard Tony had left. Bill Tuigg told me."

"Do you see much of Tuigg and the Cardinal?"

"Bill, I see around once a month; the Cardinal, less so. Bill was shook-up about Capresi. I guess they were old friends from the college sem, or something. I don't think Bill blames Sparky Larkin, though. He told me Capresi left to get married."

"Maybe, but that was later. Larkin just made his life miserable. He's trying to do the same thing with me, but I'll outlast the old bastard. Compared to life with Sparky Larkin, being vice-rector at St. Gregory's would be a piece of cake."

"Well, better you than me."

"That had you worried, huh? Sorry about that."

"I really do want parish work."

Changing the subject, Mike Krebs said, "I hear there's a guy at your place, name of Kennelly."

"He's the new pastor-in-residence. You know him?"

"Only by reputation. He did a good job on a friend of mine. You ever hear me mention Bobby Schweiger? He was with me at Josephinum, four years of college and four years of major seminary. He was from Cape Forneau."

"That's Cal's diocese."

"Cal?"

"That's his name, Cal Kennelly."

"How euphonious. But this guy's name isn't Calvin. It's Tom, Monsignor Thomas Kennelly. He's from Cape Forneau, though. He was Bishop Foley's secretary there. That's how he ruined Bobby Schweiger."

"How?"

"Schweiger was a great guy, a great priest, one of the sweetest, kindest people you'd want to meet, full of that Southern charm, you know. Too sweet, really. People were always taking advantage of him. Priests are set-ups to be taken advantage of anyway."

"What happened to Schweiger? How was Cal involved?"

"Bobby got mixed up with 'Dignity.' You know what that is?"

"Only from the National Catholic Reporter. Some kind of support group for Catholic homosexuals."

"I'm glad to hear NCR reaches Rome."

"We're not that cut-off from the States, Mike."

"Anyhow, Bobby got talked into going to some Dignity meetings by the parish organist. The organist was very, very fruit-tay. But that was Bobby, anything for anybody, so he starts going and it's all very quiet and all, until one meeting, two guys get up and exchange 'wedding vows.' Bobby didn't even know they were going to do it, but he was there. Then word gets out that a priest witnessed a homosexual wedding, and the proverbial shit hit the indoor air-conditioning. Bishop Foley was so apoplectic, he wouldn't even see Bobby, so he had his henchman, Kennelly, do it.

"I saw Bobby the day after all this happened and he could hardly talk about it. He was going through Rocksburg on his way to the nut-house, and he stopped to see me. The poor guy was stuttering. He never had a stutter in his life, and when he wasn't stuttering, he was crying. Kennelly really ripped him, accused him of being a closet queer. Told him he must be mentally unbalanced to do what he did. Never gave Bobby a chance to explain. Never even wanted to know what happened. He just revoked his assignment and all his priestly faculties in the name of the bishop, pending a psychological evaluation. Then he told him that he had to go to that treatment center for priests up in Rhode Island."

"Didn't the truth come out there?"

"Are you kidding? Those places are pre-disposed to find you need their help. If they say you're sane, you go home, and they lose all their fees. They told Bobby he had 'homosexual tendencies,' and needed treatment for at least a year. It killed him. Last I heard, he had disappeared, ran away to Toronto or some place. His family disowned him, his priesthood was ruined. All because of this Kennelly character."

"That doesn't sound like the guy I know."

"Ask him about Bobby Schweiger. See if the name strikes a bell."

Spring came on Rome quickly that year. Days of winter drizzle had lulled the city into inattention and, then, suddenly, unquestionably, spring. Young parents with their children in strollers walked along the Pincian Hill again. Old women shed their woolens for cottony dresses, still dark in color, but more suited for the warmer weather. The corner coffee bars were filled with the habitual men, playing the soccer lotteries and cursing their neighbors' good luck. Children rediscovered the piazzas and made each one into a noisy playground, their shouts competing with the rush of water from the baroque fountains.

On the quiet of the Janiculum hill, Father Joe Denzer sat in his room, looking at the note he had pulled from his mailbox. "See me. Please. Cal."

He did not know how he would handle this. After that lunchtime talk with Mike Krebs, he had been inclined to disbelieve his friend from Rocksburg. But he liked Mike, and Mike, in his own way, had been one of the many people who had encouraged him in his own vocation.

The problem was that Mike's wasn't the only story about Cal. The College was full of stories, about everything, like every other closed community in the world, but increasingly there were stories about Cal, disquieting stories.

Finally, Joe decided to take the whole thing to Bill Tuigg, secretary to Cardinal Rooney, and a priest from his own diocese of Rocksburg. Bill was the wonder of the American College. During the Vatican Council, he had been a student at the College. Bishop Rooney of Rocksburg had tapped him then for special help, since his own priest secretary did not speak Italian, or know his way around Rome, or care to be away from Rocksburg for that matter.

So in place of his provincial assistant, who

eventually came to be left in Rocksburg for conciliar sessions, Bishop Rooney had leaned on the seminarian, who spoke Italian and French, knew all the best Roman restaurants, and enjoyed eating there as much as Bishop Rooney did.

After Tuigg's ordination, Bishop Rooney had sent his old secretary off as pastor to a wealthy suburban parish and given his job to Bill Tuigg. Later that year, when Pope Paul VI made Rooney a cardinal, and called him to Rome to serve in the Curia, Tuigg came with him. Such a rapid return to the Eternal City in such a high position had become a legend at the College.

Joe Denzer knew Tuigg, however, as a level-headed realist who saw things clearly enough to make the best of a troublesome situation. Right now, he needed someone like that.

They met during siesta time in the cardinal's apartment overlooking Vatican City. Bill Tuigg looked tired, as if he could use the rest he was missing to talk to Joe Denzer.

"Bill, do you know Cal Kennelly?"

"I've met him, Joe. I don't know him."

"His reputation, then?"

"I'm sure he's a good man for the job. Bishop Guelph wouldn't have any incompetents on his staff."

"I don't mean now at the College. I mean in Cape Forneau, before."

"Is something the matter, Joe?"

"I don't know. There are stories on the hill. You know how the College is, though. There are always stories."

"About?"

"Cal. That he never spent a day in a parish. That he was a real s.o.b. as Foley's secretary. That he ruined people for his own ambition. That he's here in Rome now to have another go at the big time, to wangle a Roman appointment because he can't go back to his own diocese."

"Sounds like a pretty busy rumor mill you fellows have up there."

"I'm sure the place hasn't changed much since you left, Bill."

"And what can I do?"

"Are the stories true?"

"Joe, how would I know that? And what difference would it make?"

"Bill, I'm not sure how you know half the things you do. But I'm not here to gossip about Cal. I admire the guy. He's my friend. This whole last year of study for the priesthood has been better, in a way, because of Cal. And now, I don't know, if it was all a fraud, if what I've learned was built on sand, what does that mean for my own priesthood?"

Joe Denzer's voice quavered as he spoke. Bill Tuigg looked at him, thinking of how to respond, and he saw in him a small part of himself, the solitary student in Rome, fastening on friendships to support his loneliness and to enable his perseverance.

He chose his words carefully. "Joe, it's a mistake ever to pin our priesthood on one person. They're have been bad priests in the history of the Church. There will be more. There aren't too many idols without clay feet. Our strength has to come from our own personal relationship with the Lord, from our own prayer life and devotion. Christ is the polestar, no one else."

"So are the stories true?"

"Not entirely."

"But they're not all wrong, are they, Bill?"

"I think I've said enough, Joe."

In the weeks since then, Joe Denzer had been avoiding Cal Kennelly, but he could not any more. He guessed that he owed Kennelly an explanation, and he thought Kennelly certainly owed him one. That "Please" in the note, standing all by itself, seemed to be a cry for help or understanding.

A lonely cry. He went to Cal Kennelly's room.

"Hello, Cal."

"Hi, Joe. Come on in."

"You wanted to see me?"

"Yeah. I've missed you in class lately."

"I haven't been going, Cal."

"Lectures go through May, even though you've been ordained, Joe."

"You're not going to report me, are you Cal. I mean, that wouldn't be in character, would it?"

"In character?"

"For your Roman holiday."

"I don't know what you mean, Joe."

"I have this friend, Cal, a priest from Rocksburg. He was over here about a month ago, and he told me to ask you if you knew Bob Schweiger, a priest from Cape Forneau. The guy's gone now, went crazy or something. Do you know him?"

"Oh," was all Cal Kennelly said. His face faded to grey and the plastic Roman collar he had pinned to the top of his black T-shirt seemed to droop pathetically around his skinny neck.

"I was afraid this would happen," Cal Kennelly said quietly.

"How many other classroom examples were people whose lives you ruined, Cal? What did you do, take every wrong thing you ever did and rewrite it with you as the hero?"

"You learn from your mistakes, Joe."

Joe Denzer laughed. "Mistakes? From what I've heard you were doing exactly what you wanted to do."

"But I know now it was wrong. And I've paid for it, Joe."

"Paid? How? You're in the catbird's seat."

"Joe, I'm only now putting my life back together. You don't know what it's like to go almost right from the College to the bishop's office. That's what Bishop Foley did to me. I was young. I liked being close to the power, and Foley sensed that. He used

me. Every job that he didn't want to handle went to
me. People would call the chancery about this or that
new outrage, demanding to see him. Then when the
time came, he would be indisposed and send me,
with exact instructions on how to handle everything.

"I enjoyed it at first, having older priests and
people begging for my help, but I finally realized
that I wasn't a secretary—I was a hatchet man.

"He kept dangling the appointment of chancellor in front of me, but he never came through.
Instead, two years ago, he made me a monsignor,
the youngest in the diocese. That was fine until the
pope picked him for Chicago.

"Our chancellor, Norb Rhinehalter, was named
bishop and the first thing he did was call me into
his office and tell me he would not need me as
his secretary. He asked what parish I would like
and he named a few. They all had pastors already.
None of them was open. I asked what he meant.
He said I would be going as an assistant pastor. I
told him I was a monsignor. He said he knew that,
but I was under the age requirement to be a pastor,
and he didn't want to waive it. He made a big deal
about not showing any favorites. So that was it. I
was going to be an assistant pastor. Can you imagine? A monsignor-assistant. I would have been the
laughing stock of the diocese."

"Why didn't you go with Foley to Chicago?"

"I begged Foley to take me, to have me incardinated in Chicago before his move was official, but
he wouldn't. I was used goods, and he didn't want
to take me with him. He wanted to start fresh, he
said.

"I went to see him, though, in Chicago, after
Rhinehalter humiliated me. I was in his office
crying. I begged him to do something for me. And
he did. He sits on the board at the College, and the
pastor-in-residence was open, so he pushed Bishop
Guelph to take me."

"So that's how you got here," Joe Denzer said.

"That's how I got here, Joe," Cal Kennelly said, "but that's not why I'm here. I'm here to change what went before. I know it doesn't work, now, that ambition in the priesthood is a sure road to failure. Can't you understand?"

"Sure. Look, about class, I'll try to come more often."

"And the others?"

"What?"

"How many other people know about Bob Schweiger?"

"No one, Cal. I haven't talked about this and I won't. There are some other stories, but I don't know how true they are or where they come from."

"What other stories, Joe?"

"I don't know, Cal. Stories. But don't worry. They're not about you. They're about that other guy, the one you left back in Cape Forneau."

Joe Denzer turned and departed Cal Kennelly's room. As Monsignor Kennelly closed the door, he realized that he was still a fugitive, that he would always be a fugitive, but from the only person that he could not escape. And then he made a reluctant, but familiar choice.

May is a beautiful month in Rome. The heat of summer has not yet arrived. The tourists are still in the travel agencies, planning their summer assault on the Eternal City. The backpackers are still in the sporting goods stores, looking for the largest possible backpack. And Rome still belongs to the Romans, a cool and pleasant town on the Tiber.

On such a May evening, Sal Caputo and Ray Giordano found themselves again walking around the ballfield behind the American College. A friendly breeze from the Tyrrhenian Sea fluted the edges of the sash on Ray Giordano's cassock.

"When are you ever going to stop wearing that thing?" Sal asked. "Doesn't it make you hot?"

"Hot? This cassock is the coolest thing in the

world. This time of year, I don't wear anything underneath it, and it fits loose," Ray Giordano said, shaking the sides of his cassock.

"You're kidding."

"No. Don Flavio has me and some guys from the *squadra* repainting the oratory. I got back here in paint-covered clothes, running late as usual, so I tore everything off and threw this on just in time for *cena*."

"I'm sorry I haven't been at *Sant' Ivaldo's* lately. I've been busy getting ready to go back home."

"Don't worry, Sal. Nobody missed you. So how's all the arrangements for your first American mass?"

"Everything's set. St. Rocco's on Sunday, July 19th. Reception in the church hall. The parish ladies are pitching in to make the cookies and canapes. All those Thursdays my mother went to Rosary Guild are finally paying off. You sure you don't want to come back for it, Ray?"

"Spend a summer in Brooklyn instead of touring Greece? Besides, it's your show. If I went back for it, who'd pay any attention to you?"

"You are such a phony. You're not going to Greece. I saw your name on the Biafra missions list," Sal Caputo said.

"I wrote my folks I'm gonna be in Greece, and I don't want them worried, so you need to shut up about that," Ray Giordano said.

"Left hand, right hand?"

"Maybe. You have any idea where you'll be assigned back home?"

"I'd kind of like to pick up a doctorate in canon law."

"Canon law? You mean you'd like to come back to Rome?"

"Yeah. Back to study at the post-grad house on the Via dell'Umilta."

"Good. So you'll be with your old friend, Baldy Kennelly."

"What?"

"Don't tell me you don't know?" Ray Giordano

asked. "Baldy's been appointed the new rector at the post-grad house. The story is Baldy's going to be made a bishop, too."

"Where did you hear that?"

"Never mind. It's true."

"So Cal grabbed something after all. I'll be a son of a bitch."

"You already were a son of a bitch, Sal. What you are now is a stupid son of a bitch. I told you nine months ago Kennelly was a fraud. In between those late night relevancy sessions in his room, he must have been out kissing some heavy Curia butt."

"You could have fooled me."

"Sal, Mother Goose could have fooled you. How are you ever gonna survive in Brooklyn without me?"

VI

The Noonday Devil

"My point," Barney Ramage said.

"You aimed for that crack on purpose," Arthur Darner said as the little black ball bounced at an odd angle, off the handball court and onto the parking lot of the vacant convent building.

"I'll get it," Barney Ramage said as he ran after the errant sphere.

The handball courts at St. Gregory's Seminary had been built back in 1935. After more than thirty years, the concrete had settled and separated, and the courts were famous for their unevenness. Monsignor Donald Himmelreich, the seminary rector, had put handball court repairs on the annual budget every year, but it was always at the bottom of the list, and was inevitably displaced by more urgent demands.

As Barney was about to grab the ball, it took one last arc and bounced down a window well of the convent building.

"Get it," Arthur Darner shouted at his fellow seminarian.

"I can't," Barney Ramage said. "The window's open. It fell into the basement."

"You have a spare."

"That was the spare. I'm going after it."

"We're not allowed in there."

"Why not? Did you ever think about that? There hasn't been a nun around here for years."

In the decades before the Second Vatican Council, there had been a convent full of nuns at St. Gregory's Seminary, whose duties had been to cook and clean for the priests and seminarians, but then the Council opened the convent doors for those devoted women to perform more socially valuable tasks, and for the last years the building had been vacant.

"You know they say that place is haunted." Arthur Darner replied.

During the Spanish Flu of 1918, which had hit St. Gregory's Seminary particularly hard, the basement of the convent building had been used as a makeshift morgue, where the bodies of the dead priests, seminarians and nuns, enjoying a commonality in death that they never had in life, were kept until they could be buried. Seminarians who walked near the convent building at night swore that they could hear cries and whimpers coming from the basement.

"Balderdash," Barney said. "We have an hour of free time left, and that's the only ball we have. I'm going to get it. Are you coming?"

"Why's it take two of us to get one tiny ball?" Arthur grumbled.

"Coward," Barney said.

Embarrassed, Arthur Darner trudged along.

The old convent door was wedged shut, though not locked. The electricity was off in the building, but there was enough daylight streaming in from the huge double hung windows that the two seminarians could see where they were going.

They went down the dust-filled stairwell.

"It should be over here," Barney Ramage said, pushing open the first basement door they came to.

Inside was a sea of ceramic. The subterranean

room was filled with rows of ancient sinks, toilets and urinals, carefully piled one on top of the other, whiteness wall to wall, floor to ceiling. It looked like the treasure trove of a mad porcelain collector.

"This stuff must be from that remodeling job on the old jakes," Arthur Darner said. "Remember that story Cardinal Rooney told us in Rome about when Himmelreich remodeled the bathrooms here?"

"How're we going to get past all this stuff to the window?" Barney Ramage asked.

"We're not, is how. There's too much to climb over," Arthur Darner said. "Besides, I have a better idea."

Fred Gacious was justifiably pissed. During recreation time, while Fred had been in the seminary library, some character had taken the desk chair from his room and replaced it with a toilet. The commode had been put right in front of his desk and was obviously meant for him to sit on while he studied.

Fred tried to move the porcelain appliance but it was awkwardly heavy, and besides, he thought, it had an odor.

At dinner that night in the seminary refectory, Fred sat at his regular table, with the fellows he thought were his friends. He knew the culprit had to be one of them, or probably two, given the weight and size of the toilet.

"Who's the wise guys?" Fred asked the table in general.

"What are you talking about?" Larry Lombardy asked. Larry had been in the minor seminary with Fred and was inured to Fred's whining tone.

"You know," Fred said. "You probably all know. Who was in on it?"

"Know what, Fred?" Arthur Darner asked.

"In on what, Fred?" Barney Ramage asked.

"Some wise guys took the desk chair from my room and put a toilet there instead."

"Why would anybody do that?" Arthur Darner asked.

"I just want my desk chair back, is all. How am I supposed to study without a desk chair?"

"Study? Who does that?" Barney Ramage said. "Anybody here ever study?"

"You know there's a moral theology exam Friday," Fred Gacious said.

"Think of the time you'll save, though, Fred, having a jakes right in your room," Larry Lombardy said.

"It's not hooked up, you idiot," Fred said.

Fred Gacious had trouble sleeping that night. He could study in the library, but he had to sleep in his room, and the presence of the translocated toilet troubled him too much for that. Something had to be done.

The next morning, at breakfast, Barney Ramage asked him how the throne in his room was doing.

"I guess whoever did it thinks it's funny," Fred said, "but Himmelreich won't."

"You going to tell the rector about a practical joke?" Barney Ramage asked.

Fred understood the implication. If he went to Monsignor Himmelreich, he would be a snitch, the worst thing in common life that you could be. He would have joined the side of the oppressors over the oppressed. He would be a quisling.

So for days, Fred Gacious endured the toilet in his room, and for days at meals, he complained to his fellow students, in the hope that his appeals to their better natures would have an effect. All to no avail. If anything, his protests made the on-going prank even more enjoyable.

The culprits left him no choice. He would have to go to the top about the toilet.

The rector's study was just off the entry way of McCulligan Hall, the main dormitory building at St. Gregory's, named for a long dead bishop of

Rocksburg. Fred Gacious knocked sheepishly on
the rector's door, but he got no response.

Inside, Monsignor Donald Himmelreich was
lost in thought. He had been reading Jacques Maritain's latest book, *The Peasant of the Garonne*, and
had been struck by a particular passage. "To think
of the admirable abnegation of a contemporary
biblical scholar is enough to make one's head spin,"
Maritain had written. "He kills himself with work,
he gives his life's blood, only to find himself passé
in two years."

Admirable abnegation—that described his
life rather well. He remembered that the Italians
translated *"abnegazione"* as self-denial. How much
of himself had he been denying lately? He was a
fine scripture scholar, with a doctorate from the
Biblicum in Rome. He had been sent there to study
as a very young priest, just two years ordained,
and he had loved the experience. Rome had been
enchanting as it cleaned itself up after the Second
World War. The bright Italian sun illuminated his
days. Each Roman piazza was a treat, each fountain
throwing water into the air, an unexpected thrill.

In those years, the Biblicum was burgeoning
with talent from around the Catholic world, liberat-
ed to study scripture by Pius XII's encyclical, *Divino
Afflante Spiritu*, which endorsed Protestant critical
methods of reading the biblical texts. He felt chal-
lenged by his talented professors and he worked
hard. His doctoral dissertation had been about the
Apostles' growing understanding of Jesus's role as
Messiah and Son of God. It had been published as
a book, *What the Apostles Knew*, by Orbis Press and
had sold through three printings.

Full of promise, he came back to work at St.
Gregory's Seminary where he taught and wrote
articles for biblical journals for ten years, until John
Rooney, then bishop of Rocksburg, had appointed
him to be the rector of St. Gregory's.

He had not wanted the job because he knew

it probably meant the end of his scholarship, but Rooney had been persuasive, appealing to his sense of duty as a priest. "Remember, Don," the bishop had said, "we need to go where the Lord sends us," conflating, of course, his will with the Lord's. Rooney also named him a monsignor at the same time that he made him rector, a rare honor for a priest so young, who had never even been a pastor. That had been almost ten years ago. And, to his anticipated regret, he had spent those years fretting, fretting about inadequate professors and immature students. And worrying about bills, bills for heating oil, bills for electricity, bills for food, bills for gasoline, bills for books, bills for toilet paper, bills.

He had become discontent with his life. He was a priest and he could not imagine himself being anything except a priest, but what did he do that was anywhere near priestly? The daily seminary mass had become routine, and his office prayers often got put off until the end of the day, and frequently, put off entirely. He was a priest who barely had time to pray, a scripture scholar who had no time for scholarship.

He would rather be anywhere, doing anything, than be rector of St. Gregory's. He loved to read, but he scarcely had any time to read. This afternoon was the first time in an age that he had been able to pick up a book, and in the first dozen pages, he found the famous author dismissing his life. *What the Apostles Knew* had been out of print for five years. You didn't have to be dead to be passé. Old Jacques Maritain knew what he was writing about.

He put the book down and looked out his study window. Now that he had some time to read, he was not even sure that he wanted to. He was not sure what he wanted to do. He was tired of St. Gregory's and tired of his job as rector. He felt such a sense of emptiness, neither hot nor cold, just ... nothing. His spirit was vexed, and he did not know why.

He should talk to somebody, but who? He

hadn't had time to speak to his spiritual director in months, and Bishop John Rooney, who had made him rector, had been taken from Rocksburg to become a cardinal in Rome.

The new bishop, Marty Phelan, was a decent man, but not a scholar, far from a scholar. What would he understand about a scholar who had no time for his books? And could he even call himself a scholar anymore? With the press of administrative duties, he had not been able to teach for the last five years. He hadn't published a scholarly article for an unconscionable time. He felt so vacant and blank.

Then came the knock on his door. That was something else he was weary of, the constant demands of his charges. Why were such needy men attracted to the seminary? He felt like a nanny, not a rector, and certainly not a priest and scripture scholar. Before he could decide to say "Come in," the person at the door began knocking more insistently. He had better get up and answer it.

"Fred, what do you want?" His question was pointed at Fred Gacious, who was standing there in the doorway. He hit the "you" a bit too forcefully, driving the seminarian a step or two back into the hallway.

"Monsignor," Fred Gacious flushed. "Sorry to bother you." Fred began to have second thoughts about his decision to tattle to the rector, but then he remembered the toilet in his room and the havoc it was wreaking with his life, so he hurried on. "Do you have a few minutes?"

"I was reading, Fred, but I guess so. What's this about?" He led him into his study and pointed to a chair.

"I didn't want to bother you with this, Monsignor, but I'm afraid I have to. I've asked the guys and they're no help."

Bruskly, Monsignor Himmelreich said, "Do you want to let me in on the secret, Fred? I have no idea what you are talking about."

"I'm talking about the toilet, Monsignor, the toilet in my room."

"Fred, why is there a toilet in your room?"

"Monsignor, I don't know. I didn't put it there."

"Who did?"

"I don't know that either."

"How did it get there?"

"Monsignor, I don't know. Tuesday, I came back to my room after studying in the library for a while, and it was there, in front of my desk. They took my desk chair, and they left the toilet there. I mean, I don't even have a decent place to sit down, you know, unless I use the toilet."

"There's your bed, Fred. You could sit on your bed."

"But my typewriter and all my books, they're on my desk. Besides, with that toilet in my room, I can barely sleep nights."

"Fred, this is Friday. If this happened Tuesday, why'd you wait so long?"

"I was hoping whoever put it there, after they got my goat, maybe they would take it back."

"And that hasn't happened."

"Well, no, or I wouldn't be here."

"Fred, let me look into it. I'll see what I can do."

"Can't you just have the maintenance man move it, Monsignor?"

"Fred, the last time I asked the maintenance man to move something that wasn't in his job description, I had to pay six months of disability, and I didn't have a maintenance man for six months either. I do have the seminary budget to consider."

Later that day, Monsignor Himmelreich took a walk past the cracked concrete of the handball courts to the old convent building. He shook his head, wishing he could afford to do something about the uneven pavement, but he knew that he couldn't.

Inside the old convent building, he saw footprints in the dust on the stairwell. It looked like two sets. In the basement, the door to the room where he was storing the old fixtures from his bathroom remodeling project was open. He looked around for damage, but saw none. The thieves had at least been careful.

That evening, in the seminary refectory, Monsignor Himmelreich asked for quiet when the meal was over.

"It looks like we are training some of you here at St. Gregory's to be interior decorators instead of priests," he began. "I am referring to the gentlemen who moved some furniture out of the basement of the old convent building and used it to redecorate a student's room. I am not going to waste my time trying to figure out who you are. I will only say one word. I want the furniture moved back and I want the chair that was taken out of the student's room restored. Do that by the start of Grand Silence tonight and all will be forgotten. Oh, and one more thing, you had better not damage the goods when you move it. I have plans for those toilets."

The seminary students, who were terrorized at first by the angry tone in the rector's voice, began laughing at this last pronouncement, and when he realized what he had said, Monsignor Himmelreich smiled too, especially because he had found a way to move the toilet that would not cost him anything.

Fred Gacious was not surprised when he saw Arthur Darner and Barney Ramage carrying his desk chair into his room. "I should have guessed it was you two," he said.

"And we should have guessed you would go running to Himmelreich, you snitch," Barney Ramage said.

"I didn't go running. I waited for three days, till I couldn't take it anymore. That's not my fault."

"Here's your chair," Arthur Darner said. "Just let us take Himmelreich's precious toilet and get out of here."

"Say, what do you think his plans are for the toilet?" Fred Gacious said in an attempt to mollify them. Even though he had been their victim, he did not want them to be angry with him.

"Why'n't you go ask him, Fred," Barney Ramage said, "now that you're best pals?"

As a matter of fact, in the press of his other duties, Monsignor Himmelreich had almost forgotten about the ancient toilets, sinks, and urinals in the basement of the old convent building. He had asked Al Mingotti of Mingotti Construction, the firm who did the bathroom remodeling, to haul them away at the end of the job, but when Al Mingotti pointed out that hauling had not been in his contract and would cost an extra two thousand dollars, Monsignor Himmelreich balked. He checked around for a second-hand buyer, but found none. He was too parsimonious to simply have the fixtures junked, and since he had all that free storage space in the basement of the convent building, there the porcelain fixtures had remained, an investment waiting to find their value.

Monsignor Himmelreich was sitting at his desk the next day, going over the last year's heating bills. He was trying to understand why, with fewer seminarians than the year before and fewer dormitory rooms being used, the heating bills had gone up. He knew that the old boiler in McCulligan Hall was hard to regulate and that the seminarians sometimes opened their windows in the middle of winter because the heat it threw off was so stifling, but that only made the boiler over-function, use more oil and churn out more heat. He would have to make a rule against that, he thought, and then he held his head in his hands and knew that he was going to lose his mind. A rule against opening windows? Had his life come to that?

Then the telephone rang and he heard a distant

voice over the line.

"Don?"

"Yes."

"John Rooney here. How are you?"

"Your Eminence," he said. "I'm fine. How are things in Rome?"

"Too much Italian food and wine, but that's another story. Old Bishop Weihnachten in Greenview has handed in his resignation. It's not public yet, but he has. Are you interested?"

"Maybe, your Eminence. I don't know. I think. Maybe."

"Of course you are. You must be dying a slow death at St. Gregory's. I never meant to keep you there so long, but there really was no one ..."

"I know, your Eminence."

"I am sorry about that, Don. Listen, I can't promise anything, but the Apostolic Delegate is an old friend and I am sure he would like my advice. Can I mention your name?"

Don Himmelreich thought to himself, anything would be better than where I am now, doing what I am doing.

"You must be tired after so many years at St. Greg's, Don," Cardinal Rooney said. "It's time to move on. Greenview's right next to Rocksburg and its last two bishops were Rocksburg priests. With all the Germans there, you'd be a good fit. Shall I talk to the Delegate?"

Another phone call, two days later. It was his classmate, Mike Burlip, pastor of St. Joachim's parish in Ravenna, a wealthy Rocksburg suburb.

"Don, you know Archbishop Luigi LaMonde, the Apostolic Delegate? He has relatives in my parish, a niece and her husband."

"No, I didn't know that, Mike."

"Yeah, the husband got transferred over here from Italy somewheres. He works for that Italian company that makes those huge printing presses out by the airport. Nice guy, good donor, Enrico Something-arelli. Anyhow his wife is LaMonde sister's girl, so every now and then old Luigi drives up here from D.C. to get some home-style Italian cooking from his niece."

Don Himmelreich wondered when Mike would get to the point.

"So he just called me to say he's dropping by this Sunday, and he wants to concelebrate the 11 o'clock mass here at St. Joachim's."

"That's very nice for you, Mike."

"No, he doesn't want to concelebrate with me. He asked me special to call and invite you, buddy. So what's up?"

"I don't know, Mike. I never met the man. I don't know him from Adam."

"Well, I'm happy to pass the message along and invite you. Usually he comes, says a quiet early mass, and wants no fuss. You must be in line for something big, fella."

"Listen, Mike, I accept, but," he hesitated before he lied again, "I don't know any more about this than you do."

That Sunday morning, when he woke up, Don Himmelreich felt very strange. He had gone to sleep thinking about meeting the Apostolic Delegate and wanting to make a good impression, and now he had a strange lack of sensation on one side of his face.

He checked himself in his bathroom mirror. The left side of his mouth had collapsed. He tried to close his lips, but he couldn't. There was a permanent gap and his teeth showed through. His left eyelid was a bit droopy too.

He felt no pain. Maybe he had lain too heavily on the left side of his face while he slept? It had to be something minor, but he looked odd to himself in the mirror. It would probably wear off in a few minutes or so, he thought. Besides, he had to get ready for the drive to St. Joachim's and mass with the Apostolic Delegate.

In his car on the way to St. Joachim's, he realized that he was drooling out of the left side of his mouth. Since he could not close his lips, he could not hold his saliva. What, he thought, would the Delegate think of a drooling candidate for bishop of Greenview?

What the Apostolic Delegate thought, when he saw Monsignor Himmelreich, in the sacristy of St. Joachim's, as they vested for mass, was that the man was drunk. What else could explain his contorted expression and his slurred speech?

The Delegate's English was quite good, and when Monsignor Himmelreich had greeted him with a slow, strung-out, almost tortured, "Goood Moorning, your Esshellency," he thought that the man had more than diction problems.

As the Mass went on, and as Monsignor Himmelreich continued to mispronounce the words from the missal, the Delegate became convinced. How could anybody be drunk at eleven o'clock in the morning unless they were a serious alcoholic?

The Delegate knew that alcoholism was a persistent problem with the American clergy, especially the Irish ones. Himmelreich was not an Irish name, though. Himmelreich was a good German name. But these Americans are mongrels, the Delegate thought. One could have a German name and still be ninety percent Irish.

How could his friend John Rooney have recommended *quest' ubriaco*, this drunk? Maybe some recent problems had led this Himmelreich to alcohol. In any event, he was happy that he had had taken the trouble to meet the man personally. There were already enough bibulous bishops in the United States. The country did not need another one.

"Bell's palsy," his doctor said, after examining him for a few minutes. "It's a weakness of the muscles on one side of your face. It comes on unexpectedly, usually overnight, and goes away just as quickly. We think maybe a virus causes it. Anyway, I wouldn't worry about it. It'll probably be gone in a few weeks."

And to Don Himmelreich's relief, it was. He woke up one morning and his face was the same as it had always been. He wanted to call the Delegate and tell him, "You need to see me again, the normal me," but how could he do that?

Weeks and then months went by and he heard nothing about a move to Greenview. His daily routine was listless. He performed every task lethargically. He felt like he was living in limbo. He was tired of his job at St. Gregory's, tired of the minutiae of administration, tired of the seminarians, tired of the faculty. Sometimes he felt that he wanted to climb out of his own skin. He felt so oppressed by his duties, by his life. What enemy was doing this to him? Why did he feel so plagued? Thoughts of removal to Greenview and a new career as bishop were the only thing standing between him and insanity.

Finally it was announced that an older auxiliary bishop from Philadelphia was being sent to Greenview as its next bishop. When he heard the news, Don Himmelreich felt light-headed. He wandered over to the seminary chapel and knelt in a dark corner, where he could see the flickering red vigil candle at the tabernacle, announcing the presence of Christ.

Unexpectedly, he felt like a burden had been lifted from his soul, a burden of indecision, indetermination and drift. He recalled Christ's prayer from scripture, "Not my will, but thine be done," and he believed such things to be true. He thought for a moment of the nuns who used to live and work at St. Gregory's for over a century, caring for the priests and seminarians in selfless devotion. They had given everything up to the Lord's will in lives of loving servitude, never enjoying any prestige, any recognition. Could he do any less?

It was not the Lord's will that he leave St. Gregory's, so he had better bend his back to the task. He went about his work with an uncanny eeriness, and somehow things were not half as bad as he had thought them to be. The infinite void he had felt in his life was filled by another Infinite. The seminarians with all of their foibles could be a source of light-heartedness, the faculty could be a source of true intellectual challenge, and for some reason, even the seminary bills seemed lower and easier to manage.

It is amazing, he thought, what being content with the Lord's will did for your point of view. He found time to pray that he thought he did not have. He found time to read that had previously escaped him.

He knew for certain that he was in God's place for him when he got a telephone call from Al Mingotti from Mingotti Construction. "You still trying to unload those old toilets and sinks, Monsignor?"

"Yes, Al, I am."

"Well, then, have I got a deal for you. I just heard about an oyster farm down on the Chesapeake that's looking to use old porcelain to create some artificial oyster beds. Turns out baby oysters love to nest on porcelain. I could get you five, maybe six thousand for your junk."

"How much did these oyster farmers offer you for my junk, Al?"

"I can't trick a trickster, can I, Monsignor? They promised ten thousand, including delivery."

"Tell you what, Al. Give me eight and they're yours."

"Deal, Monsignor. I'll send a few trucks over next Monday."

Don Himmelreich was smiling as he put down the telephone. He finally had the money to repair the handball courts. Maybe he could find time to play a game or two himself.

VII

Stained Glass

"What do you see up there, Nick? Is it the same as the rest?"

"I'm afraid so, Father Larkin," the man from the diocesan property office said. "The lead joints are corroded. That's why you're getting the water and the wind in. These windows are in bad shape, all of them."

Nick D'Angelo, building inspector for the Diocese of Rocksburg, was standing on a ladder that Sparky Larkin was holding against the inside wall of St. Teresa's church. Sparky, the pastor of St. Teresa's, had finally called the diocese for help after years of complaint from his parishioners that the parish church was drafty and damp.

The crisis began with the Tooley wedding. Francis X. Tooley was the wealthiest man in the parish, perhaps the wealthiest man in all of Rocksburg. His grandfather got his start selling canaries to the coal mines that underlie the Rocksburg countryside, and his father, who had a scientific bent, used the profits to develop more sophisticated means of testing air safety deep inside the earth. Since there were many mines around Rocksburg, the Tooleys had made a lot of money.

Francis X. Tooley's oldest daughter was being married in St. Teresa's and it was quite the occasion. Francis X. had invited all of his business friends, many of them Protestant and Jewish, to the wedding and he wanted the affair to be perfect.

There had been a few small problems. Francis X., an ardent Notre Dame graduate, had asked the parish organist to play the Notre Dame fight song when his daughter carried her wedding bouquet to the Blessed Mother's altar, instead of the traditional *Ave Maria*. Weren't they both songs to the Blessed Mother, after all?

The organist had refused because a football song was not liturgical, but then Francis X. Tooley had talked to Sparky Larkin and Sparky had laid it on the line to the organist. Either play what Francis X. Tooley says or find another job. The organist, an unmarried man who was the sole support of an aging mother, had quickly seen the liturgical value of the Notre Dame fight song.

The wedding day had been drizzly to start with, and during the ceremony a sudden thunderstorm had blown up. Through the chinks and cracks in the stained glass windows at St. Teresa's, the rain had poured in on the invited guests in their tuxedos and designer dresses. The high point in the ceremony occurred when one wiseacre, seated next to a leaky window, raised his umbrella inside the church to keep himself and his wife from getting wet.

Sparky had tried to wave the umbrella down from the altar, but the man was not a parishioner and he did not understand why the priest on the altar was wildly flailing his arms at him. Only when Sparky realized that he was not getting through to the man, and that he was making a spectacle of himself, did he stop his flapping. By that time, everybody in the church was staring at the crazy man on the altar, and the bride had started to cry.

After the ceremony, Francis X. Tooley had come

back to the sacristy to give the priest his offering for his daughter's wedding mass. He said, when he handed Sparky the envelope, "Maybe you ought to use this money to plug the holes in some of those windows, Father," in a tone that did not sound like he was joking.

"It's a shame about the weather, Frank," Sparky Larkin had said in an attempt to calm him. "Every bride expects her wedding day to be a sunny one."

"Father, a dry day would have been appreciated, at least inside," Francis X. Tooley said, as he stomped off.

Sparky Larkin opened the envelope and looked in. A check for a measly five hundred dollars. What a cheapskate. Tooley earned that much in an hour.

But Sparky Larkin had taken the hint. The following Monday he called the building inspector from the diocese to have a look at his windows. And now he was hearing the verdict. Corroded, all of them.

"What it is, Father," Nick D'Angelo was saying as he climbed, huffing, down from the ladder, "is that they must have used some impure lead as a binder, and most of it has crumbled. I'm not sure what's holding all of those pieces of stained glass together. That's why you're getting the wind and the rain in. They all have to be releaded and resealed."

"How much will that cost, Nick? Do you know?"

Nick D'Angelo rubbed his chin. "They just had it done over at St. Basil's, windows about the size of these. Hunt Studios was low bidder. Cost them five, six thousand a window."

Sparky Larkin winced. There were six windows in the nave and four in the transept. He did the math quickly in his head.

"That's fifty or sixty thousand dollars," he said.

"What it is, Father," the inspector said, "is that

they have to remove each window entirely, board up the opening, take the windows to their studio where they redo the whole thing, then bring them back and re-install them. What you get is practically a new window, but it costs."

"Where am I supposed to get that kind of money? The parish doesn't have it."

"Father, I can't help you with that. All I know is, these windows won't last too long the way they are."

"What do you think I should do?"

"Father, I'd get the Hunt people out here right away. Let them give you a bid at least. See what they say."

Tim Hunt came himself when Sparky Larkin called. Followed fretfully by Sparky Larkin, he walked around the church for a few minutes and then he said, "Fifty thousand."

"Wait a second," Sparky Larkin said. "You only just got here."

"You won't get a cheaper bid, Father. Or a better one."

"I need a cheaper bid. This parish can't afford fifty thousand dollars."

"Father, that's my bare bones bid. I could hold you up for sixty, but I won't. Fifty's my lowest."

"I'll need to think about that," Sparky Larkin said. "Maybe talk to the chancery. I don't have that kind of money."

"Sure, Father. You let me know," Tim Hunt said as he left. "But you won't get a better bid."

Sparky Larkin went back to his rectory and called the chancery. He was put through to Monsignor Henry DaSilva, vicar general and chancellor of the diocese.

"Henry, I got a problem," Sparky rushed into the heart of the matter. "I got to repair ten stained glass windows. Need to borrow fifty thou."

"From where, Father?"

"From the diocese. You know, the parish loans program."

"Do you have half of it?"

"I don't have any of it."

"You know the rules, Father. In order to borrow money from the loans program, for a capital project, the parish has to have, on deposit, half of the amount the project will require."

"Now that's a dumb rule, Henry. If I had half the money, I would hardly need to borrow anything, would I?"

"It's the rule, Father."

"Well, it's a dumb rule. I got the rain coming in my church. Last weekend, some twit put up his umbrella right inside the building. This is an emergency, Henry. Don't you have any exceptions for emergencies?"

"Are the windows in danger of collapse?" Monsignor Henry DaSilva asked.

"Not right now, but ..."

"Then we don't have an emergency, do we? Tell you what, Father, why don't you hit your athletic fund. See what's there. Maybe you could afford it after all."

"What are you talking about, Henry?"

"I'm sorry, Father. Maybe you don't call it that. What do you call it? The bingo account? The men's guild account? You know, all the money that you don't report to the diocese so you don't pay the diocesan tax. All you old-time pastors have slush funds. What do you call yours?"

"I have no idea what you are talking about. And I must tell you, Henry, that I am greatly disappointed in you. You are a very cynical and distrusting person."

Sparky Larkin was shaking as he hung up the receiver. How did that bastard know, he wondered.

Upon becoming pastor of St. Teresa's parish over a dozen years ago, Sparky Larkin had paid a visit to the local bank to learn about the parish accounts. It was all as he had expected. There was a general parish account, a separate account for the school, another one for the convent, and one for the parish cemetery. The only wrinkle was a "lyceum" account, which held just under fifty dollars. That account was not on the parish register.

When Sparky Larkin asked the bank manager what it was, the man just shrugged his shoulders.

"I don't know, Father. I think it was some kind of men's club that used to run a bowling alley in the church basement. But that was a long time ago. That account has been inactive for years."

"That's good to know," Sparky Larkin had said at the time, and, on his way back to the rectory that day, he began to make plans for the "lyceum" account. In the beginning, it was where he stashed the extra income that had come the parish's way, unexpected gifts and legacies. But then, when the diocese got selfish and raised the tax that it levied on Sunday collections, Sparky began siphoning off collection revenue into the "lyceum" account as well. The diocese was never the wiser, and in a matter of years, Sparky Larkin had over one hundred thousand dollars in his lyceum account, that he could do with as he wished, free from diocesan oversight.

It was his rainy day money; not really his, but the parish's. For Sparky would never make personal use of parish funds. And he had no need to, since the parish already took care of most of his needs, from his car expenses to his annual golfing vacation in Myrtle Beach.

But how did DaSilva know? It had to be a guess, just a lucky guess. That sallow-skinned dago doesn't have a thing on me, Sparky Larkin thought. He was just generalizing.

But it bothered Sparky Larkin enough that he brought the subject up at the next forty hours celebration he attended, at Annunciation parish in Burke's Glen, where his classmate, Jerry Donnelly, was pastor.

The excellent meal that the women's guild had cooked for the visiting priests was a pleasant memory as Jerry Donnelly and his invited priest friends finished their after dinner brandies and cigars in the rectory dining room.

"Has DaSilva been bugging any of you guys about your athletic funds?" Sparky Larkin asked the assembled pastors.

The group of priests shook their heads. No one said anything.

"Ah, come on, don't give me that. I called for a loan the other day, cause the windows in my church are leaking rain, and all I got was this routine about the secret funds I'm supposed to have. He says the chancery knows that all us pastors have them, so we don't pay the diocesan tax."

Jerry Donnelly said, "He's never asked me anything like that, Sparky. How about you guys?" he nodded at the other pastors.

They all stared blankly at the question.

"Are you saying that you don't have slush funds, or that DaSilva just never asked you about them?" Sparky Larkin asked.

"We're saying that we'd rather take the Fifth Amendment on both, Sparky," Carl Kalina, pastor of Visitation of the Blessed Virgin Mary in Little Poland, answered.

"Okay, so you don't want to talk about it. I can take a hint," Sparky Larkin said. "Criminees, you guys aren't much help."

The discussion quickly turned to another topic. That day, in the mail, all of the pastors in the Rocksburg diocese had received questionnaires from Archbishop Luigi LaMonde, the Apostolic Delegate in Washington D.C., asking about possible candidates for an auxiliary bishop to assist Martin Phelan, Rocksburg's new bishop, who had been appointed to succeed Bishop John Rooney, called off to Rome to be a cardinal.

"If we get an auxiliary bishop, I think it should

be someone who's already a senior pastor here in Rocksburg," Jerry Donnelly said. "That's what I'm going to tell him. Someone with good pastoral sense who knows the diocese. What do you guys think?"

"You're right, Jerry. We need a pastor. Marty Phelan's a good man. At least he's from Rocksburg, but he's spent practically his whole life in the chancery. We need somebody who's been out in the field," Dave Bairn, pastor of St. Timothy's in Allenvale, said.

"I would agree with that," Carl Kalina added. "I think almost anybody in this group would be qualified."

"Well, no offense, Carl, but I think he should be Irish," Sparky Larkin said. "After all, most of the faithful in this diocese are Irish, and bishops should be from the people. You dagos already control the whole Vatican. Leave us the United States for criminees."

"Relax, Sparky. I wasn't nominating myself," Carl Kalina said.

"Nothing against you, Carl," Sparky Larkin said. "God knows we've been friends long enough."

"Sure, Sparky. We've been friends long enough."

At the end, as he was seeing his guests to the door, Jerry Donnelly whispered to Sparky Larkin, "The truth is, Sparky, I'm putting your name in my letter to the Delegate. I know a few other guys who are, too."

On the way home, in his car, Sparky was delighted at the thought. It was possible. God knows, the Holy Spirit had chosen less deserving men than him to be bishops in the Church. Look at all those heretic bishops in the early centuries. And this wasn't even bishop, it was just auxiliary, but it was the title and the honors and all. Yes, he could certainly see it, Bishop Larkin. Yes, it had a certain ring to it, Bishop Larkin. By the time he reached his rectory, he was planning his episcopal ordination ceremony, who he would invite to the banquet afterwards and who he wouldn't.

His euphoria continued into his mid-morning mass the next day. He could feel the bishop's mitre on his head as he went about the ritual of the mass. And the Holy Spirit must have been visiting, because it was then, during his mass, that Sparky had the inspiration about the windows.

The stained glass windows at St. Teresa's were all triptychs, made up of a large central section portraying some biblical theme, with narrower panels on either side in geometric designs. At the time they had first been installed, back when the church was built in 1920, the people who donated the windows had been allowed to have their names painted on the white, lower section of the two side panels.

Typically, the first side panel at the bottom would say, "Gift of" or "In Memory of," and the lower panel on the other side would have the name of the person or family. This arrangement had left wide blank spaces of white glass at the bottom of each large central section of the windows, the parts with the scriptural scenes above.

And that was Sparky Larkin's idea. Why not ask for additional donors to pay for the repair cost for each window, and then let them put their names in the blank space at the bottom of the middle panels? It could say, "Restored by the kindness of" and then the donor's name. Hell, somebody in the parish might even pay for one to say, "Restored in honor of Rev. Terrence Larkin." That would only be right.

What a great idea, Sparky Larkin mused, as he continued with his mass. Why, for the cost of a gallon of paint, I could pay for the entire restoration job, maybe even make a profit. Sparky, you are a genius, he thought. You deserve to be bishop, for that idea if nothing else. With your financial acumen, you'll have the diocesan budget balanced in no time, maybe even be able to lower the diocesan tax on parish collections. The other pastors would like that.

Sparky Larkin announced the idea in his parish bulletin the very next Sunday. "Be a benefactor of St. Teresa's Parish," the notice said, "and have your generosity memorialized in stained glass. For only $6,000.00, payable in installments, you can have your family name become a permanent part of St. Teresa's Church. Details available at the rectory. See Father Larkin."

Sparky had four of the windows sold before Francis X. Tooley heard about it. He went to see Sparky right away.

"My father paid for one of those windows," he said, "and two of the others were bought by his sisters, my maiden aunts, God rest them."

"Gee, Frank, that was very generous of them way back then," Sparky Larkin said. "Maybe you'd like to continue the family tradition and pay to have those three windows restored yourself. Only cost you eighteen thousand. A pittance to someone whom God has blessed as generously as you. It'd look nice to have your name up there with those of your dear departed father and aunts, don't you think?"

"Father Larkin, you're missing my point. I don't want anyone else's names on those windows. It's not right. It insults the memory of the dead who already paid for them, God rest them."

"Frank, first you ask me to do something about the windows, and now that I am, you think it's a bad idea."

"It's a cockamamie idea. Where'd you ever think you could sell those windows twice?" Francis X. Tooley said.

"Now wait a minute, Frank. I'm the pastor here, and if I want to have those windows painted all over with black paint, that's my right. Canon law gives me that right. I just thought this was a very good way to pay for the work, work that you suggested be done. Besides, I announced the project already and I can't go back on it. And I already have pledges for twenty-four thousand dollars."

"Who pledged?" Francis X. Tooley asked. "Who's paying to have their names on my family's windows?"

"I'm not sure you have the right to that information, Frank. Now, if you were to become a donor, I think maybe it'd be appropriate for me to share that information with you. How about it?"

"You never give up, do you? I'm not going to donate a penny for windows that my family already bought fifty years ago. The Tooleys didn't get where they are today by paying for the same things twice."

"Frank, you're just being stubborn. Why'n't you go home and think about it? Talk to Mildred. See what she says. We could put her name up there with yours. I'm sure, when you're calmed down, you'll agree it's a good idea."

"Father Larkin, if you go through with this, I will withhold all financial support from this parish."

"You know, Frank, when we had that little tiff with the organist, I checked on your records. You're good for about five thou a year to this parish. Now, for five thou a year, you can humiliate the organist. I'll let you do that. But it takes a lot more than that to buy me."

"You haven't heard the end of this, Father," Francis X. Tooley fumed as he turned on his heel and left the rectory.

What a nerve, Sparky Larkin thought to himself. He thinks with all his money he can run this parish. Well, he needs to learn that the Church isn't for sale, not to anyone. And, besides, what kind of name is "Tooley" anyhow? I've heard of "O'Toole," and even a stray "Toole" here and there, but who the hell ever heard of "Tooley"?

The following day, Sparky Larkin got a telephone call from the Rocksburg chancery. It was Monsignor DaSilva.

"Father Larkin," he began. "I hear that we have a little problem with the stained glass windows at St. Teresa's."

"Henry, tell me something I don't know. I called you two weeks ago to borrow money for my leaky windows from the parish loans program. You turned me down, remember?"

"That's not the problem I'm talking about, Father. I hear that you have an ad in your bulletin, and have even accepted donations to restore the windows."

"That's right. What's wrong with that? You guys been talking to Tooley? Did that pompous ass call down there?"

"As a matter of fact, Mr. Tooley did talk with Bishop Phelan."

"And?"

"The bishop asked me to look into it. Father, it's no secret that the bishop has been after Mr. Tooley for some time now for a major donation, a million dollars, to the new diocesan foundation."

"If you can get the money out of that cheapskate, go ahead. The fellow was too cheap to give me eighteen thousand dollars to restore his own family's windows, and eighteen thou is peanuts compared to a million."

"That's the problem, Father. Mr. Tooley had already informally agreed to the bishop's request, but then he called yesterday and said that he was having second thoughts. The bishop asked why and Mr. Tooley said that he wasn't sure that he could trust the Church to treat a gift properly. The bishop asked him what he meant, and Mr. Tooley told him about you changing the memorials on the stained glass windows at St. Teresa's."

"Oh, I see," Sparky Larkin said. "Blackmail.

Well, I hope that Marty Phelan is bishop enough to tell Mr. Francis X. Tooley what he can do with his blackmail money. What does Tooley think, that he runs the whole diocese with his money? It's parish trusteeism all over again, Henry. It's worse than parish trusteeism. It's lay investiture."

"Father," Monsignor DaSilva said, "that is a very harsh characterization."

"It's history, Henry. We let the lay people have that kind of power and pretty soon they'll be wanting to elect their bishops and the pope, too. Next, they'll be wanting to hold a referendum on the Ten Commandments, and they wouldn't approve but one or two of them. Is that the kind of Church you and Marty Phelan want here in Rocksburg, Henry?"

"Don't get carried away, Father. Both Bishop Phelan and I both think that Mr. Tooley has a legitimate point."

"And what might that be?" Sparky Larkin asked.

"It's in the Code of Canon Law, Father. It says, once the Church accepts a gift with a condition attached to it, it must honor that condition."

"Yeah. So?"

"The original memorials honoring the donors of your windows are a kind of condition, Father. The donors were evidently told, when they made their gifts back in 1920, that their names would be inscribed on the windows. They were never told that you were saving space for additional names fifty years later."

"Okay. So what?"

"Once the Church makes a promise like that to solicit a gift, Father, it can't change things later on. You can't put someone else's name on a gift that was already given."

"Is that in the Code of Canon Law, Henry, just like that?"

"Not exactly, Father," Monsignor DaSilva

replied. "The Code's not that specific. It requires an interpretation."

"And whose interpretation is this?"

"Well, it's mine. But Bishop Phelan agrees."

"So what are you telling me?"

"You can't put anyone else's names on your windows. The canon law won't allow it."

"Why is it, in this diocese, that whenever a pastor has a good idea, the canon law won't allow it? The law's a killer, Henry. The law's a killer."

"But it is the law, Father."

"Listen, if you guys aren't going to let me do this, what about my loan?"

"You know the rule, Father. If it's not a structural emergency, you have to have half the project amount on hand before the parish loans program can advance you the other half."

"It's a dumb rule, Henry," Sparky Larkin said as he banged down the receiver.

Damn that DaSilva, Sparky Larkin thought. That's what comes of putting canon lawyers in high places. Wouldn't it be sweet if I do get that appointment as auxiliary bishop? The first thing that I'll do is to convince Marty Phelan to fire that greaseball.

And if they won't help me with the windows, fine. Let them all fall down for all I care.

The next week one of them did. A fierce evening storm took out the bottom half of the central panel of the window depicting the Blessed Mother's Assumption into heaven, and with the bottom gone, the rest of the window collapsed.

When the janitor called him early the next morning, Sparky Larkin went over to inspect the damage. It was total. The window was in shards, with pieces of stained glass lying inside and outside the church. He had his emergency.

He put a call into Monsignor Henry DaSilva's office. Now he could borrow the whole fifty thou, he thought, without touching his rainy day money in the "lyceum" account. The secretary answered the telephone, "Rocksburg Chancery, Bishop DaSilva's office."

"What did you say?" Sparky Larkin gulped.

"I said, 'Rocksburg Chancery, Bishop DaSilva's office.'" the secretary repeated.

"Since when?" Sparky Larkin asked.

"It was just announced by the Apostolic Delegate in Washington. Monsignor DaSilva is the new auxiliary bishop of Rocksburg. Didn't you hear the news? It was on the radio this morning. I think it's wonderful."

Sparky Larkin's throat clutched in anguish as he managed a congratulatory grunt before he hung up the telephone.

VIII

Friends No More

"Monsignore, Monsignore, venga subito." Bishop Guelph heard one of the cleaning men calling him from the hallway, telling him to come quickly.

The rector of the North American College in Rome was sitting at the desk in his apartment on the fourth floor of the College, sweltering in the heat of a Roman August afternoon, and wondering how he had let himself be the only administrator available to babysit the empty College at the tail-end of summer.

It was a subaltern's duty. In the summer, the College was a hostel, housing those few seminarians who happened to be passing through Rome on their summer travels. There was nothing to do except suffer the heat and ride herd over the maintenance staff.

Next summer, he vowed to himself, this will be the vice-rector's duty. Then he heard the voice calling.

It was Sandro, one of the young Italian workers. The bishop knew him to be a very excitable type. His arms, in his light grey *personale* coat, were flailing the air, and he kept saying *"Monsignore, Monsignore,"* and *"che peccato,"* what a shame.

"*Tranquillo*, calm down, Sandro," the bishop said to him in Italian, "and tell me *che cosa c'e*, what's going on?"

"*Padre Brennan e un altro padre stanno scopando*," the young worker said.

"*Piano, per favore. Sandro*," the bishop asked him to speak more slowly.

The bishop's Italian was quite good, but he had never heard the word *scopando* before, and he didn't understand the man. It was probably slang or some crazy Roman dialect, he thought.

"*Monsignore*, Sandro continued in Italian, "I was cleaning the hallway. And in Father Brennan's room, with another father, they are ..." and then he made a gesture inserting his right index finger back and forth into a ring made of the fingers of his left hand.

"Where, Sandro?"

"On the first floor, *Monsignore*, on the hospital side."

The bishop followed the worker down the main hallway to the elevator and then onto the first floor wing of the College facing *Bambino Gesu* hospital. Near the end of the floor, the door marked "Brennan" was open a crack, enough for anyone passing the deserted hallway, or cleaning it, as Sandro had been doing, to see that two naked men were inside, in bed together.

The bishop stood there for a half-second, long enough to determine what was going on and who was involved. He told Sandro to leave and then, realizing that he had no choice, banged on the door. He waited a few minutes, before Peter Brennan, in a bathrobe, opened it.

"Yes, bishop," Peter said, his voice tremulous.

"Both of you, dressed and downstairs, in ten minutes."

On his way to his office, Bishop Guelph pondered what he would do. Damn this hot summer, he thought. Next year somebody else will do this duty.

He thought of the two young men he had just seen together. They were both handsome and athletically built, Peter Brennan, a black Irishman, and the man who was with him, Mark Merolac, another fourth year deacon, with bright blue Slavic eyes and a head of shocking blonde hair. Either one of them would have been attractive to a hundred women. Perhaps, he thought, that's why they were attracted to each other.

When the two of them came into his office, wearing their black clerical suits and their Roman collars, Bishop Guelph told them to sit down. He looked at them both for a minute and then said, "How long has this been going on?"

"What do you mean, bishop?" Peter Brennan said.

"Don't be cute, Pete," the bishop cut him off. "I have eyes to see."

"We were just wrestling, bishop," Mark Merolac said. "It was just some rough-housing."

"In bed, with your clothes off? Give me credit for some sense," the bishop said.

"Bishop," Peter Brennan said, "I don't think you know what you saw."

"Are you denying it?" the bishop said.

"Bishop," Mark Merolac said, "Maybe it looks suspicious, but would you condemn us for a suspicion? We promise this won't happen again."

"Mark, I know what I saw. And I wasn't the only one. I don't police the hallways, for goodness sake. Sandro saw you when he was dusting the corridor. He came and told me, and by now every worker in the College knows. At the end of the summer, when the other students return, they'll find out, because there are a few students, you know, the Italian Americans and the ones that speak Italian, who like to gossip with the workers."

The two deacons looked at each other, their faces fallen.

"Now," the bishop said, "I want some straight

answers. How long has this been going on?"

"This was the first time, Bishop, honest," Peter Brennan said. "We were just rough-housing, like Mark said, and I guess it went too far."

"We've never done anything like this before, Bishop, I swear," Mark Merolac said.

"Has either of you ever had a relationship with anyone else here at the College?"

"No, Bishop," they both answered quickly, one speaking on top of the other.

"Or with anybody else, at your home seminaries, on vacation, over the summer?"

They both shook their heads "no."

"Quite honestly, gentlemen, that's a little hard to swallow. But if that's what you say, then that's what you say. I will contact each of your bishops, back home, tell them what has happened, and ask for their guidance. You are both on the ordination lists for this December. I don't know what your bishops will do. I'll let you know," Bishop Guelph said, dismissing them with a wave of his hand and a distinct tone of disdain in his voice.

"And," he said as they were about to leave his office, "don't let me see the two of you together again. I mean never in the same place at the same time. I don't care if it's St. Peter's Basilica. I don't want you talking to each other. I don't want you seeing each other. I don't even want you waving at each other. Is that clear?"

Then Bishop Guelph rang Eugenia Buzzati, his Italian secretary, and asked her to get him a list of chancery telephone numbers in the United States.

He called the bishop of Sheboygan first. They had been friends and classmates thirty years ago at the College and it would be the easier call.

"John, this is Andy Guelph here," he said when he got John Dowd, bishop of Sheboygan, on the line.

"Andy, how are you? Where are you?"

"I'm in Rome, John, at the College."

"In August? I bet it's hotter than hell there, Andy."

"Yes, John, it is. Thank you for reminding me. John, we have a problem."

"What is it, Andy? Your budget need some adjusting? Say the word. I'm good for an extra five thou for alma mater."

"No, it's not that, John. It's one of your seminarians, a deacon, Peter Brennan."

"Is he hurt? Has there been an accident?"

"No, John, he's not hurt. There's no easy way to say this. I just caught him in bed with another member of the deacon class."

"Ah, shit," the bishop of Sheboygan said from across the Atlantic.

"My sentiments too, John. The thing is, what do you want me to do about it?"

"Put him on the first plane home, Andy. Help him pack his damn bags if you have to. Tell him he has an appointment to see me in the chancery, let's see, this is Tuesday, make it this Thursday morning at 10 a.m. Okay?"

"Fine, John. I'll do that right now."

Bishop Guelph called the TWA manager in Rome and made a reservation for that evening's flight. Then he called a cab. Then he walked upstairs to Peter Brennan's room and told him.

The deacon seemed to take it well. He only asked if he could tell Mark Merolac good-bye.

"No, I don't think so, Pete," the bishop said. "The less contact the two of you have, the better. Besides you only have a half hour to pack before your taxi gets here. Your ticket will be at the TWA counter at the airport." Then he turned and walked away.

As he was going down the hall to the elevator, the bishop could hear Peter Brennan flinging items into his suitcases and, he thought, sobbing as he packed.

The next telephone call was to Sean O'Kelly,

the bishop of Santa Anna in California. Bishop Guelph did not know him that well. He had talked with him a few times at bishops' conferences in the States, but that was the extent of their contact. He knew the man was Irish born and trained, one of the F.B.I's—foreign born Irish—that the California dioceses had needed so badly in the twenties and thirties when they were just getting started.

"Bishop O'Kelly," Bishop Guelph said when he came on the line, "this is Bishop Guelph at the American College in Rome. I'm calling about Mark Merolac, one of your seminarians."

"What kind of trouble is he in?" Bishop O'Kelly said.

"How did you get that idea, Bishop?"

"The rector of the North American College would not be calling me about him for anything else, now would he?"

"No, bishop."

"So then?"

"Here's the problem. Mark has admitted to having relations with another member of the deacon class here at the College."

"Jesus, Mary and Joseph," Bishop O'Kelly said. "And what are you going to do about it?"

"That's why I'm calling you, Bishop, for your guidance."

"My guidance? I'm not the rector of the bloody seminary, am I, man? What are you going to do about it?"

"Bishop O'Kelly, the man's a deacon. He's already incardinated in your diocese. What do you want me to do?"

"What did you do the last time this happened?"

"Bishop O'Kelly, this is not a regular occurrence. I have no idea what they did the last time this happened, if there was a last time."

"So what do you recommend then?"

"The bishop of the other party, the other party involved with your seminarian, has ordered him home."

"And do you know what he'll do with him then, at home?"

"No, I don't Bishop."

"So that's not very good advice, is it?"

"I guess not, Bishop."

"Fine. Let's just leave things be until I've had a chance to mull on it and talk to some of my people around here."

"And in the meantime?"

"In the meantime the bugger is a student there, isn't he? I mean he has classes to go to and so forth?"

"Classes at the Gregorian University don't start until the second week of October. That's five weeks from now."

"Are you fellows still up the hill from the Jesuits?"

"Yes, Bishop, we are."

"Then tell my fellow to find a good Jesuit and do the Ignatian exercises, all of them, before the university starts. That'll keep him out of trouble for a month."

"What about the ordination list, Bishop? Mark is on the list to be ordained a priest this December with the rest of his class."

"Bishop Guelph, it seems to me that you are very good at telling me the problems and not very good at telling me the answers. I said let me think on it. I'll be back to you," he said, and then, abruptly, he hung up.

The rector was flabbergasted. Why, he wondered, did the Vatican ever make a foreign born Irishman the head of an American diocese? He had no idea what he was to do with Mark Merolac, short of telling him that he was to spend the next thirty days on silent retreat, doing the spiritual exercises of St. Ignatius Loyola.

He walked up to Merolac's room and told him his bishop's instructions. The deacon's reaction was complete confusion. "Is that my punishment?" he asked. "Will it be all right after that? Can I stay at the College?"

"Your bishop was very non-committal, Mark, except that he wanted you to do the Ignatian exercises. Perhaps you should contact him when your thirty days are over."

"But how can I stay? You said that everyone will know," Mark Merolac said.

"Sandro doesn't really know who he saw, Mark. The *personale* don't know most student names. He told me Brennan, I'm sure, because he saw the name on the door. He never mentioned you by name, and now that Peter's gone, it might just blow over."

"Peter's gone?" Mark Merolac asked.

"Yes, he's in a cab on his way to the airport. Those were his bishop's instructions."

"Why didn't you, I mean, why didn't somebody tell me?"

"What for, Mark?"

"We were friends. To say good-bye is all."

"Write him a letter. You'll have plenty of spare time on your retreat to write letters," Bishop Guelph said as he turned to walk away.

Mark Merolac made his thirty day retreat at a small Jesuit house in Castelgandolfo in the Alban hills south of Rome. His director was a gaunt and dry old priest who drove his charge unsparingly. When the retreat was over, Mark Merolac felt as if he had atoned for a lifetime of sins that he had yet to commit.

He had had no word of the outside world for thirty days. No television, no radio, no magazines, no newspapers. He was carrying a briefcase full of letters, to his family, to some special friends, and four to Peter. He mailed them at the Vatican Post Office in St. Peter's Square on his way back to the College from the bus station.

The College was full of returning students and new men. He felt odd when he saw them, as if he knew some secret of the universe that they did not share, only the secret was about him, that he and Peter were lovers and that Peter had been sent home because of it. The thought increased the sense of apartness, of strangeness that he had felt ever since he had been told that Peter was gone.

He went to see Bishop Guelph, to find out if there had been any news from his bishop.

"I haven't heard a peep," Bishop Guelph said.

"Does that mean I'm still on the ordination list? I should go to classes and all?"

"I guess so, Mark. I haven't heard anything to the contrary," Bishop Guelph replied.

"Do you think anyone here knows, bishop?"

"Mark, I can't tell you what people know."

"Because I would die if people were talking."

"Mark, if there's any talk, it will be about Peter. I told you, Sandro never mentioned your name."

"But lots of students know that Peter and I are friends. What if they ask me why he's not here?"

"Lots of dioceses have a full year internship now before priestly ordination. Peter wasn't the only member of the deacon class called home."

"But he didn't get called home for that."

"No one knows that, Mark, unless you tell them. Just because you were friends doesn't mean that you know all the details of his life."

"And the other priests on the faculty?" Mark Merolac asked.

"Mark, I have not told them either. Until this matter is settled by your bishop, I think I owe you that confidentiality."

"Thank you, Bishop."

On his way back to his room, Mark stopped on the ground floor to check his mailbox. Peter had been gone over a month now and there was still no letter from him. Why hadn't Peter written, Mark Merolac wondered. Maybe he will when he gets my letters. I hope he will.

Classes started at the Gregorian University that

Tuesday with an opening day mass at St. Ignatius, celebrated by the Rector and the Jesuit faculty. The mass was a disorganized affair, as most Italian liturgies usually were, and many in the seminarian audience moved around, got up, stretched their legs or went outside, to the portico, for a cigarette during the ceremony.

Mark Merolac, vested as a deacon for the mass, had helped to distribute communion to the student body. Putting on an alb and stole again made him feel good, as if things were somehow returning to normal, now that classes were starting, but then, on the way back to the College, after Mass, he found himself alone. There were groups of students from the College strolling ahead of him, and some behind, but no one sought him out to walk or talk with him.

Crossing the Principe Amedeo bridge over the Tiber, watching the late morning sun shining on the statue of St. Michael sheathing his sword atop Castel Sant' Angelo, he remembered that last year he had walked back from the opening mass with Peter.

They had lunched at a small trattoria in Trastevere and then had climbed a long pair of steps at the far end of the Janiculum, and there, in the gardens of the Villa Doria Pamphilii, on the back of the hill, away from the city, they had made love in the grass that warm October day.

He really missed Peter, and he wondered if Peter felt the same. On self-pilot, he walked up the hill to the College. He stopped in at the mail room, found a letter from his mom and read it as he headed for his room on the first floor. He took the elevator up, and as he got off, looked down the long hospital corridor towards Peter's old room. A tall dark-haired fellow was just going into it. Peter, he thought, Peter's here. His bishop has sent him back for the start of classes. Thank you, Lord! He flew down the hall, his heart racing.

"Peter, Peter," he said as he flung himself into the room. Sal Caputo and Ray Giordano, a fourth year deacon and a second year seminarian from Brooklyn, were there trying to take the bed apart. They looked up at him as if he were insane. Immediately he realized his error.

From the back, he had mistaken Giordano for Peter. How could he have made such a stupid mistake? Giordano looked nothing like Peter.

"Oh," he said, trying to recover. "I thought you were Peter."

"Are you nuts, Merolac?" Ray Giordano said. "Brennan's not here this year. Don't you know that?"

"Sure I know. I just thought, for a minute, that he was back."

"Mark," Sal Caputo said to his classmate, a bit more patiently, "Pete's doing a pastoral year in Sheboygan, isn't he? How could he be here?"

"I know, Sal. You're right. You're absolutely right. I just forgot. But why are you in his room?"

"This room isn't assigned this year," Sal Caputo said, "so we're going to use it for our diocese. You know, kind of like a rec room. We're going to put in a couch, a table, some chairs and a refrigerator."

"Oh," said Mark Merolac. "Does Bishop Guelph know?"

"Does Bishop Guelph know?" Ray Giordano repeated in a mincing voice. "What's he gonna do, tell us we can't use an empty room?"

"I don't know, I just thought ..."

"Hey Merolac, you want to hang around here, give us a hand. Otherwise, go put on your make-up for lunch," Ray Giordano said.

Mark Merolac was stunned. Make-up? What was Giordano talking about, make-up? He turned quietly and walked down the hall towards his own room.

As they continued taking the bed off its rails,

Sal Caputo said to Ray Giordano, "Ray, you got to get custody of your mouth."

"I'm sorry, Sal. You're right. I'm sorry. But that guy gives me the willies. Did j'ever see the way he looks at people, as if they were a piece of meat or something?"

"No."

"That's cause you're not cute like me."

"Ray, the only one who thinks you're cute is your mother," Sal Caputo said as they continued to try to lift the bed rails out of the headboard.

"You know," Ray Giordano said, "I heard from the *personale* that Guelph caught Brennan in bed with someone this summer. I wonder if it was Merolac?"

"Ray, the Italian workers think anyone who wants to be a priest is queer. That's just another one of their stories."

"No, I heard this from Sandro. You know I like to joke around with him, talking Roman dialect. I don't think he'd lie. I bet it was Merolac."

"Stupid rumors is all it is. And you know what, let's get this mattress off before we rupture ourselves with this bed."

Mark Merolac went to his room to lie down. Make-up? He had never used make-up, except that bronzing stick he got at a cosmetics store near the Piazza di Spagna, when his tan started to peel a bit at the end of last summer. Make-up. What did Giordano know?

The bell sounded for lunch. Mark Merolac went down to the refectory and looked for a congenial table to sit at. He saw one table, near the windows, full of people he didn't recognize. They must be new men, he thought, the first year theologians. He sat beside a short fellow with blondish-brown hair, worn over his ears in sort of a page boy, without any part. He had vivid hazel eyes and his girlish hair and dimples made him look kind of cute, Mark Merolac thought. He introduced himself.

"I'm Tom Bumbaucher," his new acquaintance replied.

"Where are you from, Tommy?"

"Rocksburg."

"So you're from Joe Denzer's diocese?"

"Yeah."

"What's that place Denzer's always talking about, your home seminary? St. Gregory's, right? With some crazy Kraut rector. Boy, Denzer has a million stories about that place. Is that where you're from?"

"I did my college seminary there," Tom Bumbaucher replied. Just then an older, balding priest asked if the seat beside Mark was taken. It was Cal Kennelly, the newly arrived pastor in residence.

That was the last chance that Mark got to talk to Tom Bumbaucher. Cal Kennelly was desperately trying to make friends with all of the students at the College and he monopolized the conversation at table.

After the meal, Cal Kennelly asked if anyone wanted to go for a walk around the ballfield. Tom Bumbaucher said that he would go along and Mark Merolac decided that he would, too.

"Where'd you do your deacon work last summer, Mark?" Cal Kennelly asked as they strolled the cobbled walk that bound the athletic field.

"I was at the American Army base at Garmisch, near Munich. It was the closest I could come to a real American parish."

"Was it a good experience for you?" Cal Kennelly asked.

"I think so. The base chaplain was good to work with, and the American families were just great."

"Were you there all summer?"

"Eight weeks, then I was back here for a while doing a thirty day retreat before classes started."

"I'm impressed," Cal Kennelly said.

"Thirty days?" Tom Bumbaucher asked. "The longest retreat we ever did at St. Gregory's was three days, and I could hardly keep quiet that long. Is thirty days normal here?"

"Don't worry, Tommy," Mark Merolac said, resting his hand on the younger man's shoulder. "It's not part of the program. It's just that ordination is a serious step, and I wanted to make sure that I was ready for it."

Strolling a few yards behind Cal Kennelly's group were Sal Caputo and Ray Giordano.

"It looks like Merolac made some new friends. Who's the kid that looks like the Infant of Prague?" Ray Giordano said.

"His name is Bummer or Baumbartner or something. He's Joe Denzer's diocesan," Sal Caputo said.

"Another guy from Rocksburg? God, the College is crawling with them. Pretty soon they'll have us guys from Brooklyn outnumbered, Sal." He grabbed Sal and hugged him. "You'll have to protect me."

Sal Caputo pushed him away and said, "Stop hugging me. It's embarrassing."

Laughing loudly, Ray Giordano let the other seminarian go.

Mark Merolac heard "hugging" and "embarrassing," and Ray Giordano laughing, and he wondered if they were talking about him, when he had put his arm over Tommy Bumbaucher's shoulder.

"You were pretty hard on Mark this morning, Ray," Sal Caputo said. "Where's your Christian charity?"

"I know, Sal, but that guy just creeps me out."

"That crack about using make-up was out of line. You think he's a fairy?"

Ahead of them, Mark Merolac thought he heard the words "make-up" and "fairy," but he kept on talking to Cal Kennelly and Tom Bumbaucher.

"Sal, the guy's always tanned, even in winter time. Now you tell me how he does that."

"He has a sun lamp in his room. I know that."

"Yeah, sure, and I guess that's where he gets his blond hair, too."

"Mark says that his hair always turns more blond in the summer. It's the sun."

"Well that sun shines out of a bottle. I think he uses peroxide. You can see his dark roots."

Mark Merolac overheard the words "peroxide" and "dark roots" and he felt a bit faint. He wondered if Tommy Bumbaucher and Cal Kennelly had heard it too. As they completed the turn near the covered veranda and the door to the College, he said he would see them and went to his room.

Is this how this year will be, he thought, lying on the bed in his room, will I die a little death every day? But how do I even know they were talking about me? Peter said I always did that, that I always thought people were talking about me when they weren't. I'm too self-conscious, he said. Gosh, I wish he were here so I could ask him what to do. Peter would know what to do.

It would be easier, he thought, if I knew where I stood, if my bishop would write and say I could be ordained, or if Peter would write at least. Why hasn't Peter written?

Every day, as soon as he got back from classes at the Gregorian, he ran to check the mailroom on the ground floor, but the time went by and there was no letter from Peter.

He went to see Bishop Guelph almost daily for news from his bishop, but time after time the answer was the same. Bishop Guelph had not heard from Bishop O'Kelly, not a "peep," as he liked to say.

"When do you think he'll let me know, Bishop?" Mark Merolac asked after weeks of episcopal silence.

"I have no idea, Mark," Bishop Guelph said. "You could call him or write yourself, you know."

"You don't think he'd let me get close to ordination and then pull me, do you? I mean, here it is the start of November. Ordination's next month. He wouldn't do that, would he? Everybody would know something was wrong if he pulled me now."

"Mark, I have no idea what your bishop might do, and right now no news is good news. The dimissorial letters for permission to ordain aren't due until the end of the month. Either he sends your letter or he doesn't. I wouldn't worry until then."

It was almost as if waiting without knowing was its own punishment. Just like my bishop, he thought.

The only good thing in his life was the friendship that he was forming with Tommy Bumbaucher. The second week of class Mark had suggested that they go to see the Villa Borghese museum together that Thursday, a free day from classes on the Gregorian schedule, and after that they spent every Thursday together. Tommy would pick the sights in Rome that he wanted to see, and Mark would be his guide. They would stay out the entire day, buying slices of pizza for lunch, and at night looking for an inexpensive neighborhood osteria, with cheap food and good wine.

Aside from Thursdays, Mark was careful not to spend too much time with Tommy because he didn't want the fellows at the College to talk and he knew that Bishop Guelph still had his eye on him. Sometimes they ate at the same table in the refectory, but that was by chance. Mark never looked for Tommy to sit with. Well, almost never.

One Thursday, the week before Thanksgiving, Tom Bumbaucher happened to mention that the day after the holiday was his birthday. It got Mark to thinking. He wanted to do something special for Tommy to let him know what he thought of him.

He wasn't sure if he should do something hokey or get a really nice present. For a while he considered buying him a little Infant of Prague statue. Somehow the fellows at the College had taken to calling Tommy the Infant of Prague. Mark

Merolac thought that that big mouth from Brooklyn, Ray Giordano, was behind it. But people said it to Tommy's face, and he only laughed. A small statue of the Infant of Prague from one of those religious goods stores on the Via dei Cestari, over near the Pantheon, might be a nice gift, he thought. Kind of funny, but meaningful too.

Or maybe I should get something more serious. Tommy doesn't have many nice clothes. Maybe he would appreciate an Italian knit shirt with a silk tie to go with it. Of course, that would be expensive, but at least Tommy would know how I feel.

He went to Battistoni's on the Via Condotti for the shirt and he got the tie nearby at his favorite tie shop, Giofer, on the Via Frattina.

Thanksgiving at the American College in Rome is quite a special feast. The Italian kitchen staff experiments for weeks making pumpkin pies. Turkeys and canned cranberry sauce are purchased in bulk and shipped from the PX at Gaeta, the large American naval base near Naples where some of the seminarians did pastoral work on weekends.

The whole endeavor is meant to recreate as closely as possible an American Thanksgiving meal for two hundred seminarians and their guests four thousand miles away from home. Aside from dinner at the American Ambassador's, it is the hottest ticket in town that day. Ecclesiastics and seminarians from all over Rome cozy up to the American seminarians and faculty for weeks in the hope of getting one of the rare invitations that are issued for this meal.

That year, Mario, the chief cook, and his staff outdid themselves. The pumpkin pies that in years past had been flat and tasteless were excellent. The turkey was crisp and moist. The only odd note was a first course of fettucine al burro, but the Italians did not know how to serve a festive meal that began without pasta.

The celebration lasted until late afternoon and

then broke up into hour long parties in various rooms throughout the College, where seminarians from the same diocese usually congregated with their guests to share Sambuca and Aurum and other after dinner liquori and digestivi.

Mark Merolac was celebrating with the other men from his diocese, but his thoughts drifted off to another Thanksgiving evening, three years before, his first year at the College. He had been invited to a party by Lou Asaya, a fourth year man from Los Angeles. The room was smoke-filled, and he knew that at least one of the smells was not tobacco. He thought that he heard someone say that the good stuff came from this guy in Trastevere, and when he was passed a joint, he inhaled more deeply than he should have.

He had ended up in Lou Asaya's room, inhibitions shed, and wrapped in the sheets of Lou's bed.

"Let's go easy," Mark Merolac said. "I'm kind of new."

"Really. I wouldn't have guessed," Lou Asaya said.

"Why?"

"The way you've been looking at me ever since you got here. It was practically an invitation."

"I didn't realize ..."

"Sure you didn't."

But Lou Asaya was ordained that year and had gone home to Los Angeles. Lou had let it slip that he had been together a few times with Peter Brennan, another student in Mark's year from Sheboygan, and Mark and Peter became fast friends soon after Lou Asaya's departure. Lou still wrote him from time to time, and he knew that when he was back home in Santa Anna he could easily drive the 200 miles to Lou's parish in Los Angeles. But that wasn't now.

Later that night, when he thought nobody would see, Mark Merolac went to Tommy Bumbaucher's room with his birthday gift. He had wrapped it all up with a bow and a card. He knocked on Tommy's door. There was no answer. He knocked again, and then tried the door. It was open. Tommy was asleep inside.

Mark tiptoed in. He looked at Tommy in his bed, his tousled hair splayed out at odd angles on his pillowcase. He wanted to smooth it back, to round it to his head and stroke his cheek and tell him how much he liked him, but he had left the door open, and he thought that he could hear someone coming down the hallway. He quickly left the room, closing the door behind him.

It was Ray Giordano in the hallway, singing some dumb Italian pop song about sugar this and sugar that.

The following night Ray and Sal Caputo were sitting at the same table in the student refectory for the evening meal. While they were waiting for the *personale* to bring the first dish, Ray Giordano impatiently took a bread roll from the basket on the table, tore it apart, doused it with olive oil and ate it piece by piece.

"If my mama could see me now," he said, "she'd be proud of her little dago boy."

"Knock it off, Ray. Nobody eats peasant food in Brooklyn anymore."

"You rich people don't, but us poor people still do. Can I help it your dad's a fireman and mine only works for the sanitation?"

Sal Caputo said to the rest of the table, "He's kidding."

"Don't worry, Sal," Joe Denzer, Sal's classmate who was sitting at the same table, said. "Nobody takes him seriously."

"Who asked you, Denzer?" Ray Giordano said. "If I were you, I'd worry about my own backyard before I criticized anyone else."

"What's that supposed to mean, Giordano?"

"The Infant of Prague," Ray Giordano said.

"Tom Bumbaucher?"

"That's what I said, the cute little fellow from your diocese with the Jackie Kennedy haircut."

"What about him?"

"Why'n't you ask him what Mark Merolac was doing coming out of his room late last night?"

Joe Denzer thought that Giordano didn't know what he was talking about, but he still promised himself to ask Tom Bumbaucher about Mark Merolac the next time he saw him.

The story was a simple one, Tom Bumbaucher explained. Mark had offered to show him a few places around town on Thursdays when there were no classes. He and Joe Denzer were talking the next day in Joe's room when Tom came to borrow a set of Joe's notes for Father Latourelle's course on revelation.

"He hasn't done anything funny, has he?" Joe Denzer asked.

"Kind of. He gave me a birthday present the other day."

"It was your birthday? I didn't know. Happy birthday."

"It was a shirt and a tie. I think it must have cost him a fortune. It was from over near the Spanish Steps. I don't know why he did it."

"Was that why he was in your room the other night?"

"I guess. I mean, I was asleep. I didn't even know he was there till I woke up next day and saw the present all wrapped up."

"Tom, I don't think that's healthy. Fellows in the seminary just don't give each other expensive gifts, especially fellows they barely know."

"Joe, I didn't ask him."

"Tom, I think your size, and the way you look, they make people think of you as a youngster. I hope Mark's not taking advantage of you or anything."

"Taking advantage of what, Joe?"

"Of you, like I said. Unless you …?"

"What?"

"Look, Tom, at St. Greg's, we were three years apart, so I don't really know you that well, but I mean you're not ... I mean, do you find Mark, uh ...?"

"Are you asking if I like other guys? Cause if you are, the answer is no, I'm not that way."

"Good. Whew. Okay. Whew. But this thing with Mark. You really should call it off. I mean, those Thursday outings should stop, and I think you should return his gifts."

"Joe, he's a sensitive guy. I don't want to hurt him. The way he talks, his year is already ruined because that friend of his from Sheboygan got called home for a pastoral year."

"Tom, if you think it would help, I'll tell him. He's my classmate."

"Could you do that, Joe? That'd be great. Let me get the stuff."

When Joe Denzer walked into Mark Merolac's room that afternoon, holding the presents rewrapped in the familiar paper, Mark knew something was wrong.

"Tom Bumbaucher asked me to give these back to you, Mark," Joe Denzer said.

"What's the matter, Joe, he couldn't face me himself?"

"Mark, let's not make anything of this. I've had a talk with Tom, and presents like this just make him feel uneasy. He wanted me to ask you to give him some space. Okay?"

"Okay. Thanks. You did your duty."

"Sure. I'll see ya."

Alone in his room, Mark Merolac threw himself onto his bed, tears of hurt pride and loss burning his eyes.

Why do these things always happen to me, he thought. Why can't I just have a normal life, with friends who like me as much as I like them? And why, after two and a half months, after all the letters I've sent, why hasn't Peter written?

I can't take it, he thought. I just can't take any more. They call this place a seminary and we're all supposed to be such great Christians and love one another, but nobody here cares for me. Nobody.

He put on his jacket and left the College grounds. He needed to take a walk through the city. Rome was such an alluring place, narrow alleys opening onto spacious piazzas, decorated with fountains and statues, the riotous noise of children at play or tradesmen hawking their wares filling the air. The city almost always cheered him.

There was a bar that he knew about, just off the south end of the Piazza Navona. Word was it was heavy trade, and there were always a few motorcycles parked outside, but maybe just today. Gosh, I miss Peter so much.

He met a very charming, middle-aged man there, a fellow with greying hair on his temples and a pleasant accent on his English. They had started out speaking Italian over their drinks, but Mark Merolac was not very good at it, and soon the man suggested that they try English. They did not exchange names or even tell each other where they were from. Mark Merolac thought there was something Germanic about the man.

They left the bar together and went to a small fleabag hotel across the Corso Vittorio, just off the Campo de' Fiori.

As they were entering the hotel, a gang of Roman street kids kicking a soccer ball around eyed them and started bantering about the *finocchi*, but the two ignored them as they made their way inside.

The man was not Peter, but he was gentle and experienced. Throughout their lovemaking, Mark had the suspicion that the man was a priest, but he did not have the courage to ask. When they were done, the man said that perhaps they should leave separately, it would be less noticeable. He bent down and kissed Mark on the forehead and then he was gone.

The same gang of street kids was still kicking their soccer ball around as Mark left the hotel. He was not paying much attention to them, though, and he failed to duck when an errant ball came at his head.

It caught him above the left eye and really hurt. For a while he had to lean against the building to get his balance. He put his right hand up to his forehead and it came away bloody.

An older man who had been watching the kids yelled at them and then he came over to see if Mark was all right, but Mark couldn't really understand the rush of Italian that the man threw at him, so he waved him off. He thought he heard the boys tell the man something about *finocchi* again. He knew what that meant—queer—and he just wanted to get out of there.

He hurried back to the College and looked for the infirmarian to help him bandage his eye. With a gauze strip patched over his cut, he went back to his room. There was a note on his door. It was from Bishop Guelph. "I looked for you all day. Please see me."

He's heard, Mark Merolac thought. He's heard from Bishop O'Kelly about my ordination.

Mark Merolac ran down to the bishop's office on the ground floor. Mrs. Buzzati, the bishop's secretary, was there, but she told him that the bishop was not feeling well and had left for the day. He hurried to the bishop's suite on the fourth floor, but the door was locked and no one answered the bell.

He decided to try the Red Room. It was an hour before dinner. Maybe the faculty had started their cocktails. The door to the Red Room was padded and covered in red leather. There was no bell to sound, and no one would hear a knock on the padding. After pacing back and forth about what to do, Mark decided just to open the door and walk in.

There were a few priests making drinks in the kitchen on the left as Mark entered. They looked at him like an interloper. No one smiled or looked pleased to see him.

The portly vice-rector, Monsignor Phil Rogers from Syracuse, came up to him, as if to impede his advance into this restricted faculty preserve.

"Mark, you know students aren't supposed to be in here. Is something wrong?"

"I have to see Bishop Guelph," Mark said.

"He's not here."

"Where is he?"

"Let's go outside, Mark," Monsignor Phil Rogers said, and he held the Red Door open for the seminarian to join him in the corridor.

"Now what's the problem, Mark?" the Vice-Rector asked as they stood outside the room.

"I need to see Bishop Guelph," Mark Merolac said.

"That's impossible, Mark. The bishop left late this afternoon for Fiesole. He's Bishop Ragnoli's guest there for a few days. He really needs the rest."

"Monsignor Rogers, I absolutely have to talk with him. He has an important message for me."

"Mark, I know the bishop looked for you all afternoon. I'm sorry you missed him, but I don't see how I could get in touch with him now."

"Don't you know where he is? Don't they have a phone there? You could call, couldn't you?"

"Mark, the bishop has gone away for a rest. His kidney stones are acting up again, and I really don't want to trouble him unless this is some kind of an emergency."

"But it is. It is an emergency."

"What kind of an emergency, Mark?"

"It's private. I mean it's confidential."

"Mark, I've been in this business a long time, and I've never heard of a confidential emergency."

"I wish I could tell you, Monsignor."

"Mark, are you sure this can't wait until the bishop gets back?"

"When will that be, Monsignor?"

"He'll be back tomorrow or the day after. It depends on how fast the water up there does the trick."

"I can't wait till then, Monsignor. I'll go crazy. You have to let me talk to him now."

"Mark, the bishop went over all the urgent matters on his desk before he left, and your name wasn't among them."

"The bishop would want to talk to me. Can't we just call him? That's not much, just a phone call."

Monsignor Rogers looked hesitant. He pondered for a few moments and then he said, "Come up to my suite."

In the second floor vice-rector's rooms, Monsignor Rogers checked a telephone number scrawled on a pad beside his telephone and called it. Mark Merolac could hear the number ringing.

"*Pronto*," Monsignor Rogers said and then he identified himself and asked for Bishop Guelph.

Mark Merolac watched the Monsignor as he heard the news from the other end. The older man frowned and then he said, "*Si, si. Allora, quando tornanno, gli dica che ha telefonato il Monsignore Rogers nel riguardo di Mark Merolac e se lui potrebbe richiamarmi.*" Then he put the receiver down.

"You heard that Mark. They are out to dinner. I left a message for him to call when he gets back. That's the best I can do."

"Sure," Mark Merolac said. "Thanks, Monsignor."

Dinner that night was another disaster. He thought he saw Tommy Bumbaucher purposely avoid him as the seminarians decided where they would sit. He ended up at a table with a mixed bag of first and second year men who mostly ignored him.

Afterwards in his room, he tried not to worry as he undressed to go to sleep. Peter always said

I worried too much. Maybe Bishop Guelph wants to see me about something else. Maybe it's not even about my ordination. Who knows? Think of what Peter would say, "Try not to worry." He said it over and over to himself and, lullaby-like, the repeated phrase and memories of Peter helped him overtake an elusive sleep.

The next day, when he got back from classes at the Gregorian, the first thing that Mark Merolac did was to search out the Vice-Rector. He caught Monsignor Rogers on his way into the Red Room before lunch.

"Did you talk to Bishop Guelph?" he asked.

"Mark. Yes. The bishop called this morning. But the connection was so poor, I could barely hear him. I'm pretty sure he said he had good news. He had heard from Bishop O'Kelly, he said."

"But what? What exactly did he hear from Bishop O'Kelly?"

"Relax, Mark. Like I said, good news."

"No, but it could be something else. Are you sure he said my ordination was okay?"

"Why wouldn't it be? Is there something else I should know here?"

"Monsignor, you have to call again. I need to talk to him."

"Mark, this is getting a little unreasonable. You asked me to call the bishop. I did. The bishop called back. He said good news. What more do you want?"

"I want an answer. I want a goddam answer. Am I being ordained this December or not?"

"Mark, I'm not your classmate and I don't care for the profanity."

"Monsignor, I'm sorry, but this has me really tense. I have to talk to Bishop Guelph."

"The bishop will be back tomorrow. Whatever it is that's worrying you, you'll have your answer then."

Monsignor Rogers entered the Red Room and closed the door behind him. Mark Merolac stood there in silence, staring at the padded red leather door. He could not believe the insensitivity of the man.

Mark wandered into the student refectory. He was about to take an isolated seat when he saw another seminarian opening an airmail envelope. He had forgotten the mail. He had been in such a hurry to talk to Monsignor Rogers that he had forgotten to check the mail room on his way back from the university. He hurried downstairs. Maybe there would finally be a letter from Peter. He really needed to hear from Peter. Wouldn't it be great if there was a letter today, when he needed to hear from Peter the most?

There were a few letters in his box. One he recognized from the pastor he had worked with in Garmisch. The other one was from home. God bless Mom, he thought, she writes practically every other day. There, on the bottom was a third envelope.

Mark Merolac's hand trembled as he picked it up. It was Peter's handwriting.

Peter had written. Peter had written.

He tore the envelope open and started reading.

"Mark," he wrote, not "Dear Mark" or anything, just "Mark."

"Your constant letters are embarrassing me and you must stop writing. I have had quite a few long talks with Bishop Dowd. He has been really kind to me and he trusts me. He had me psychologically evaluated when I came home, and he assigned me to live in a parish with one of our senior pastors. The pastor is a tough old bird, but fair. The psychological testing wasn't easy, but I did okay, and I'm doing well at the parish, or so my pastor tells the bishop.

"The point of all this is that Bishop Dowd has decided to ordain me after all. That is really generous of him, and I could never express my thanks to him enough. He is truly a kind and courageous man.

"I promised the bishop that I would write you,

187

though. We really cannot have any more contact, Mark. That means letters and everything. The bishop made me promise that, and that is a reasonable thing for him to ask. We can be friends no more. I hope that you will understand and honor my request.

"Yours truly, Peter."

"Yours truly," Mark thought, what kind of crap was that? Not even "Sincerely" or "Affectionately" or "Your pal"?

And what did he mean, "friends no more"? Was that all they had been, friends? The word itself was a lie. They had been lovers, not friends.

This is devastating, Mark Merolac thought. Just when I needed Peter the most, just when I thought that he had come through for me, it all turns out to be a tease, just a tease. Peter never cared for me. The first chance he got, he threw me aside. Well, I hope he's happy, Mark Merolac thought as he wiped a stray tear from his eye.

He had no appetite to return to the refectory. He went to his room, slammed Peter's letter into his top dresser drawer, took off his black seminarian's suit and changed into his street clothes. He needed to get the College out of his system and get a good breath of Rome into his lungs. The city would be his solace.

He walked down the Janiculum Hill and crossed the Ponte Principe Amedeo. He went across the Lungotevere and the Corso Vittorio into the back streets. The chestnut men were out on the corners. He smelled the burning orange coals that he could see through the nail-pinched plate where the chestnuts lay. He let the smoke spiral ahead of him as he found the Via del Governo Vecchio. The narrow street was full of the smells of Rome, the roasting chestnuts, the scent of bread baking in a wood oven, the strong aroma of expresso brewing. The jumble of fragrances always made him feel so alive.

He walked past the old furniture stores, past

the shops of chests and cupboards and chairs inside. Sometimes the back curtain of the shop was pulled back and there was the carpenter, working a plane or hammer, hunching to get the work just right.

He stopped in a *Vini ed Olii* and bought a bottle of Montepulciano. As he walked, he sipped it from inside its paper wrapping. When, he thought to himself, will the Italians discover paper bags?

The wine was strong and good and it made him feel outgoing. He walked past the art shops, saluting the people in the paintings that seemed to stare back at him, in one, a lady wearing the gown of an earlier era; in another, hanging above her, a gentleman of stern visage dressed in a fine, well-tailored military coat. A ruffle of lace lined the lady's neck and the soft pink of her bosom was peeking through. Who knows, thought Mark, perhaps they will meet some day? He lifted his bottle and gestured to the lady and then to the gentleman, caught in their separate frames for all time.

Wandering through more back streets, he returned to the Lungotevere and Bernini's bridge, lined with statutes of angels holding the instruments of Christ's torture and death. He was thinking perhaps that he should head back to the College. He looked left to see the way. The late afternoon clouds over the Janiculum were thick and bulbous and no light was falling through. Community mass would be soon, but no, he thought as he walked away from the bridge. Rome was its own liturgy. The leaves had all fallen from the huge plane trees lining the Tiber. Red of an early evening, a wafer sun hung in their bare boughs. There were mounds of leaves lying beneath them, and even though he was twenty-five years old, he kicked them, the brown ones, the yellow ones and the gold.

He stopped every once in a while to gaze back. The vision in his left eye was still blurry and partially obscured by the gauze patch that the infirmarian had taped over his cut. But the view was spectacular, his favorite one of Rome, the Castel Sant'Angelo on the right, St. Peter's to the left, and the Tiber below. Van Wittel had painted it best and he loved the painting. The leaves crinkled beneath him still.

What would it mean to lose this, he wondered, when Bishop Guelph would tell him, as he knew he would, that Bishop O'Kelly was pulling him, that he would not be ordained, that he wasn't even a seminarian any more for the Santa Anna diocese? That he was being sent home?

What would Rome be like when it was only a memory? He wished that he had learned Italian better. If he had, maybe he could stay, get a job in a travel agency or some other business that serviced Americans. But how? He wanted to be a priest. He needed to be a priest.

Maybe he could find the man he had made love to yesterday, he thought. He seemed to know his way around the city. Maybe he could help me.

Wouldn't it be funny, he thought, if he was some curial big shot, a monsignor or bishop high up in one of the Vatican Congregations that ran the Church? A guy like that could probably find me some diocese somewhere that would let me be ordained. Too bad I didn't get his name.

It wasn't fair. Life wasn't fair. Peter is being ordained, why not me? As if I'm the first guy who wasn't straight that wanted to be a priest? And Peter. At least now I know how much I meant to Peter. Not a whole helluva lot.

He finished his bottle of wine and dropped it in the gutter. He suddenly realized how tired he was. He was not anxious to get back to the College but he did not know where else to go. The last thing that he wanted to see now was a bunch of seminarians, all happily proceeding towards the ordination that would never be his.

He so much wanted to be a priest. He had done all the right things. He had studied hard. He had a good prayer life. He had done well at his summer assignments. He assisted at masses as a deacon. He knew that some of the other things he did, people might look down on, or think were wrong. But if he could be a priest, if he could be that one very good thing, then the other things that he did could not be as wrong as people said.

If they even were wrong. He had known from his earliest memories that he liked other boys more than girls. God had made him that way. Could God have made a mistake? How could the things that his nature made him do be wrong?

He trudged up the Janiculum and into the College gate. At the *portiniere*, a group of seminarians was leaving as he entered. He saw Tommy Bumbaucher and Joe Denzer among them and realized that it was a group from Rocksburg. Tommy looked so angelic, with his long hair crowning his androgynous face. Mark Merolac wanted to tell him how much he had meant to him. He went over to Tommy and reached out to him.

Tommy evaded his touch and hurried away, mumbling something about catching up with his friends. He watched as Tommy rejoined the crowd and thought he heard him say something about him. Then came a brief burst of laughter. That's the way it will be from now on, Mark Merolac thought. As soon as they find out I'm not being ordained. People will look at me and they will know why and they will laugh.

He went to his room and from his closet took out a half bottle of Sambuca, left over from a night last spring when he and Peter had been on the roof of the College, looking down on the city and kissing in the dark.

With the bottle, he climbed the stairs to the fifth floor and from there up to the terrazzo roof of the College where he and Peter had sat that

May evening that now seemed so long ago.

He perched on the parapet that edged the roof and studied the city below, stretching from the illuminated statutes on the facade of St. John Lateran in the south, past the neon signs at the railway station, to the shining monument of Victor Emmanuel and the curved roof of the Pantheon in the city center and around to St. Peter's on his left.

It truly was a beautiful city. In the night air, with its rooftops and monuments giving off a mellow glow, and the traffic a distant din, it seemed enchanted, a magic place in a magic land. He had been so happy here, with Peter.

He drank directly from the Sambuca bottle. It tasted sweet, but burned when it reached his stomach. He pulled another long swig and thought to himself that this was going to be a lousy drunk. Too much Sambuca always gave him a terrible headache.

He had almost finished the bottle when he bent over to put it down. But the vision in his left eye was still hazy and he put the bottle down unevenly. The bottle tumbled and started to roll. He reached for it, before it dropped off the parapet, but he missed, and, losing his balance, he fell himself instead.

He screamed as he plunged into the empty air, six stories above the earth.

He was dead of fright halfway down, but his body imploded upon contact with the macadam parking lot and that resolved any doubt.

Students in the College heard his scream and alerted the first faculty member they found, Monsignor Rogers, the Vice-Rector. He hurried to the body with his anointing oils, thinking all the while to himself, "Shit, what am I going to tell Bishop Guelph about this one?"

The bishop was back from Fiesole by the time the Italian officials released the body. They had kept it for a day, according to Italian law, lying on a marble slab in the charity hospital down the hill from the College, with an electric buzzer-like device in its hand, so that, in case a medical mistake had been made and the corpse was not really dead, it could wake up and summon assistance. Mark Merolac was beyond such help.

The following week, in his office, Bishop Guelph was assembling Mark Merolac's personal effects to mail back to his family. He had packed all of the dead seminarian's notes and personal papers. All but the letter from Peter Brennan, which he had burned in the sink in his private bathroom. The last item that he placed in the large cardboard box was the dimissorial letter that had just arrived from Bishop O'Kelly, giving him permission to ordain Mark Merolac a priest for the diocese of Santa Anna that coming December 11th in St. Peter's Basilica. He thought that Mark's family would want to have that.

IX

Deserving of All My Love

The waves along the South Carolina shore were long and frothy green. On the beach, there was no shade and no breeze and the flat white sand glimmered in the heat.

It was late hurricane season and even though the nearest tropical disturbance was somewhere off the coast of Cuba, few people came mid-October to the shore, but the water was still warm and the sun was blistering.

The man and the woman, lying in their swimsuits on the dark army blanket, were looking at the waves and the sky.

"Where do you want to eat tonight?" the man asked.

"How about that big white stucco place on the beach road, the Moorish one?" the woman said.

"Moorish?" the man said. "What's Moorish about white stucco? I thought it looked sort of Spanish."

"How about we settle on Mediterranean and call it a draw," the woman said.

"Sure, fine," the man said and turned face down on the blanket.

They were quiet for a while. Thundering surf and the squawk of gulls filled the air.

"Look, I'm not upset about last night, if that's what you're thinking," the woman said.

"I wouldn't blame you," the man said.

"Those things happen every now and then," the woman said.

"It's the first time it ever happened to me," the man said.

"Really?" the woman said. "I thought you were new at this."

"I am. You know I am. You're the first. But those things aren't supposed to happen when you're twenty-six. It's an old man's problem."

"It can be anybody's problem. It happened to Joe a few times and he's only two years older than you. And my first husband, Tommy, whenever he was drunk, which was most of the time, he was el limpo. That's Spanish, by the way."

"I bet it never happened on your honeymoon," the man said.

"No, as a matter of fact, it didn't," the woman said. "Is that what this is supposed to be, our honeymoon?"

"Sure. I thought," the man said.

"Because I thought a honeymoon was after you get married," the woman said.

"We will. You know we will," the man said. "As soon as you get divorced from Joe and have your annulment and as soon as I get permission from the Church."

"How long will that take?" the woman asked.

"I don't know," the man answered. "I wrote my petition and mailed it to Rome before we left Rocksburg. I sent it to Cardinal Rooney for his help."

"Do you think he will?" the woman asked.

"His secretary is ... was a good friend. We were in the seminary together. He'll help me if he can," the man said.

"But it could take a long time, couldn't it? I mean, the Vatican could take years to decide you're not a priest anymore. Will my Church annulment from Joe take that long? The first one didn't," the woman said.

"Your first marriage was invalid because of a prior bond. That's a paper case. An annulment from Joe could take a year or more," the man said.

"So when will it be?" the woman asked.

"You'll probably hear from the Rocksburg marriage tribunal before I hear from Rome."

"But when will that be?"

"Connie, please."

"Why does it have to be in the Church with all their rules? Why can't we just go to a justice of the peace as soon as I have my divorce from Joe?"

"Look, Connie, I left the priesthood. I didn't leave the Church."

"And what if the Church says I can't have you?" the woman asked.

"Don't borrow any grief. We'll deal with that if it happens," the man said.

"But I want to know, Tony. Would you marry me if the Church said you couldn't?"

"Connie, we talked about that last night."

"And you didn't answer me then, either," the woman said, sitting up on the blanket.

"I was upset last night," the man said.

"It was probably just stress. We both need to relax and it'll be okay," the woman said.

"Sure," the man said.

"Let's try now," the woman said and she slid her hand along the blanket under his belly and into his swim trunks. The man did not turn over.

"Not here," he said.

"Why not? There's no one around," the woman said.

"It's just not the right place," the man said.

"The right place? Where's that, Tony? My basement floor was good enough the first time."

The man thought, it was hard to believe that they had been lovers for only a month. His life had changed so much that it seemed much longer than that.

They were both crazy about their cars. He had a brand new 1968 Chevy Impala, an ordination gift from his parents, and she and her husband, Joe, had scrounged to buy a vintage Corvette convertible. They used to wash them together in her driveway, across the street from his rectory, while her husband was at work.

One day, for no reason, they began splashing soap suds at each other, but Connie had picked up the hose and they both ended up sopping wet, standing in her driveway, dripping on each other, giggling and hugging in fits of laughter.

"I can't go back to the rectory like this," he had said. "Sparky Larkin will call the bishop for sure."

"Go inside," she pointed to the steps along the driveway that led down to her basement. "Just throw your stuff in the dryer. It'll be okay in half an hour. I'll clean up out here."

He went down the concrete stairs and pushed the basement door open. He took his clothes off and wrung them out over the laundry tub before he put them in the dryer and turned it on. He looked around for something to wear and settled on a bath towel from the shelf above the washer. He pulled the towel down and wrapped it around his waist.

Connie came in. "What about my things?" she asked. "Why didn't you wait for me?"

Then she opened the dryer door and began taking off her wet clothes and throwing them in.

It happened very quickly. Both of them seemed to fall into each other, almost instinctively. When they were done, lying there in a crumple of towels on the concrete floor, with the dryer thumping away in the background, he ran his finger along the profile of her face and said, "Why did we do that?"

"Because we've both been wanting to, for a long time," she said.

"How did you know?" he asked.

"You are not the most difficult person to read, Tony. Those cow-brown eyes of yours give you away every time."

"What happens next?" he asked.

She folded him in her arms and said, "I don't know about you, but I'd like to try it again."

"And Joe?"

"Joe's at the university. He won't be home for hours," she said.

After that day, they found every minute they could to be together. An academic conference that Connie's husband went to in Cleveland gave them two precious days. Tony told his pastor that he was going on retreat, and he and Connie had spent the time at a lakeside cabin in Maryland.

At the end of those two days they decided that they would leave Rocksburg forever. Tony would resign his priesthood and Connie would ask Joe for a divorce.

They ran off together in his Impala, chasing the escaping summer sun down the Atlantic coast, until they had run it to ground in South Carolina.

"Stop thinking," the woman said, throwing some sand on the man's back.

"What'd you do that for?" the man asked.

"You think too much," the woman said. "Relax and just go with the flow."

"I'd like to know where the flow is going first."

"We're the flow, Tony. Just us, together," the woman said.

"Sure," the man said.

"Are you having second thoughts?" the woman asked.

"No, of course not. It's just that, I don't know, Connie. I studied to be a priest for twelve years, from when I was fourteen. Nothing got me ready to make love on the seashore with a beautiful woman. I keep thinking of my mom, my dad, my friends. They really wanted me to be a priest," the man said.

"What do you want, Tony?" the woman asked.

"You. Us. Us together." He rolled over, leaned up and kissed her.

"Sure about that?" the woman said at the end of their kiss.

"Yes, sure," the man said."

"Cause I lose you sometimes, Tony. You drift off and I wonder where you are, what you're thinking about, why you're not thinking of me," the woman said.

"Connie, that's screwy. It sounds like you're jealous of my thoughts."

"Why's it screwy? Why can't I be jealous of every part of you that's not mine?"

"I am yours," the man said.

"Then let's get married as soon as I get my divorce," the woman said.

"Connie, what's the harm of waiting till the Church says it's okay? We're young. We have the time."

"Where's your guarantee, Tony?"

"My what?"

"Your guarantee that we have all the time in the world. There are no guarantees, Tony. I want to marry you now, as soon as we can. I don't understand why you won't."

"Because I don't know, Connie. Because ..."

"Tell me, Tony."

"What?"

"Because maybe you think it's wrong, you and me."

"I don't."

"Then what was last night all about?"

"What are you talking about? You said sometimes ..."

"I hear you, Tony. You may think you're whispering, but I hear you."

"Hear what?"

"Every time, after we make love at night, even last night when nothing happened, before you fall asleep, you say an act of contrition. What are you telling God you're sorry for, Tony? What sins do you think we're committing?"

"You can't be serious, Connie. That's just a habit. I've been saying that prayer at nighttime since I was a little kid. It's like 'Now I lay me.' It doesn't mean anything."

"I wonder, Tony. I wonder if you'll ever be all mine. I'm afraid that one day, who knows, a year from now, three years from now, you'll wake up and say, 'It's been fun, Connie, but I'm going back to my true love, back to the Church.'"

"Connie, I've already asked to be released from the priesthood."

"And you could never go back?"

"I wouldn't want to."

"But you could."

"I guess, theoretically. I mean, the sacrament of orders, when a man becomes a priest, the Church says that lasts forever."

"That's what I thought." She pulled her knees up and put her head down between them.

"Connie, please don't pout. I hate it when you get like that."

"It's just not fair, Tony. It's like there are two sets of rules here. When you leave the priesthood, it's the sacrifice of a lifetime. But I leave my home, my husband, my car, everything I have, and it's what? I don't know, a woman in heat."

"Connie, don't say that. It's not true." He sat up and put his arm around her shoulders.

"Then marry me as soon as I get my divorce. We could always get married in the Church later on, after you hear from Rome and I get my annulment."

"Sure," the man finally said.

"Oh, that'll be fine, Tony. That'll be great."

She threw herself on him and pinned him to the blanket. The nimbus of the sun shone behind her head and almost blinded the man lying on his back.

He closed his eyes and held her tightly to himself as he thought, "I will be this woman's third husband."

X

Cursed

"Did they come today?" It was the first thing Francis X. Tooley said as he walked in the door to his home, before he took off his coat, before he put his briefcase down, before he kissed his wife hello.

"Yes," she answered. "Those electricians were here all day. They put flood lights at every corner of the house and under all the eaves, like you said. They even put lights up in the trees on the front lawn. This place will be lit up like a Christmas tree whenever you turn those things on. I don't know why you needed so many lights."

"It has to stop. I will not be made mock of," Francis X. Tooley replied.

"Frank, it's just a dog."

"Folks are laughing at me, Mildred, and I won't have it. No one puts one over on a Tooley and gets away with it. It was that way with my grandfather. It was that way with my father, and it will be that way with me, or I am not Francis X. Tooley."

What Francis X. was referring to was that, in recent weeks, the manicured lawn around his mansion, the lawn so finely kept that it put many of the living room carpets of Rocksburg to shame, was being vandalized by a dog. Once a perfectly even blue green of the finest Kentucky seed, clipped to a perfectly even height by his lawn man, it was now dotted in yellow and brown, and was even bald in some spots where the dog had struck.

It had become a daily ritual in the Tooley household. Every morning before showering or dressing, Francis X. hopped from his bed and tromped his baronial lawn in his pajamas, bathrobe and sturdy slippers, looking for the offending matter. And most mornings he found it, under one of the two majestic oaks that shaded the front of his mansion or alongside one of the manicured flower beds. The droppings were so huge that, at first, Francis X. Tooley thought that a horse must have wandered onto his lawn. But there were no horses in Rocksburg anymore.

It had to be a dog, a very large dog. Discovering who the animal was had become an obsession with him. The vandal always came at night. During the day, there were no suspicious dogs to be seen. He had put his gardener, his lawn man and even the cook on the look-out, and they swore to him at the end of each day that no dogs had been on the property. No, the miscreant was a creature of the night, a sneak-thief, without the courage to travel by day.

He had started keeping watch from his bedroom window at night, and one late evening he had come close to catching the criminal. He saw a shadow on the lawn from the street lamp, but, by the time he got to the front door, he heard a low whistle. There was a huge German shepherd on a leash, loping away with a stumpy figure behind him, and he thought that he knew who it was. That was the night that he had decided to have the lights installed.

"It's that crazy Larkin. I know it," he told his wife the next day. "I just want to catch him at it. That was his stupid dog Rex I saw, I'm sure."

"Frank, why would our parish priest want to

do anything to hurt you? You're one of his biggest givers every week in the collection basket."

"Mildred, that man has been angry with me ever since I told the bishop about his cockamamie scheme to sell the stained-glass windows at St. Teresa's twice, the ones with my family's names on them."

"It seems like such a fuss over a little bit of grass."

"That's where you're wrong, Mildred. It's the Tooley family name at stake here."

"There's no use talking to you about that, Frank. I just hope that you know what you're doing."

"Trust me on this one, Mildred."

As twilight ended and merged into the darkness of evening, Francis X. sat fully dressed at his open bedroom window, next to the large master switch that controlled all his new floodlights. Ten o'clock, then eleven, then midnight came, but he was patient. He was almost nodding off to sleep when he heard a noise, looked out and saw a large animal on his front lawn. Then he heard a voice.

"There you are fellow, your favorite outhouse. Go ahead now."

It was just as he had thought, there was some evil human behind the dog, egging him on, and it sounded like Larkin.

With a great twinge of delight, Francis X. Tooley threw the master switch and suddenly his mansion and lawn were bathed in daylight. And there, beneath the large oak that stood next to the long concrete driveway that wound its way up to the house from the sidewalk, was a strange sight. A large crouching German shepherd suddenly sprang up and began racing around the tree, pulling the man on his leash, who seemed to be dancing around after him. Man and dog were hopping around the tree, the man making strange sing-song noises. The whole scene looked like a witches' sabbath. What strange ritual are they performing,

Francis X. wondered as they danced around his tree. He knew that pagan priests worshiped oak trees, but hadn't St. Boniface stopped all that?

What Francis X. Tooley did not know was that the lights installed by the zealous electricians in the oak tree had awakened two squirrels from their nest, and the poor confused creatures had scurried down the tree, one going one way, one another, and the German shepherd, delighted at having some animals to chase, had started running after them, zigging and zagging around the tree, barking loud enough to raise the dead, dragging his owner behind him. The man pulled on the leash, trying to restrain the dog, knowing that the noise would give them away, but in his travels around the tree, he had stepped in the animal's droppings with both feet, and began to wiggle them, first one foot, then another, to shake free the dog's deposits, simultaneously repeating in a loud whisper, "Whoa, Rex, whoa. Whoa, Rex, whoa. Be good, boy. Be quiet, boy. Whoa, boy, whoa."

It was a strange sight, and Francis X. could not imagine what was going on, but he did know that he had caught his culprit red-footed. It was Sparky Larkin and his German shepherd, Rex. The Tooley ingenuity had prevailed. By the time Tooley got to the front door, however, the vandals were long gone, as was most of the proof, carried away, evidently, on Sparky Larkin's shoes. He threw up his hands and turned to go back inside.

A City of Rocksburg emergency van, on its way back from the Divine Word Hospital, was driving by the Tooley home, and when the driver saw all of the lights on the expansive Tooley front lawn, and Francis X. Tooley standing there, shaking his arms, he thought that he should check it out. The driver knew that Tooley was a good friend of the mayor's, and, well, maybe a good turn to Tooley would not go unnoticed at City Hall.

The driver pulled up the driveway, parked,

rolled down his window and asked, "Everything all right, Mr. Tooley? Do you need any help?"

"Thanks, officer," Tooley replied. "I can take care of things myself, but thanks."

In a home across the street, Alice Manion was awakened by the lights and went to the window. Seeing the emergency vehicle, she said to her half asleep husband, Michael, "Something's wrong at the Tooley house. The lights are all on and there's an emergency van in the driveway. I wonder if old Tooley didn't have a stroke. The way his face is so red all the time, I'm sure he has high blood pressure."

"Come back to bed, dear. If the emergency folks are there, Tooley's in good hands," her husband said before he faded back to sleep.

Francis X. Tooley began to plot his revenge that night. He considered the possibilities. Should he call the bishop on Larkin again? He knew that he could get Larkin in a pile of trouble. He had just made the second installment of his million dollar pledge to the new diocesan foundation, ten thousand shares of Tooley Safety Products stock, worth a quarter of a million dollars, and the bishop was very fond of him at the moment. But going to the bishop might seem a bit heavy-handed, especially since he had already complained to the bishop about Sparky Larkin once when he had tried to re-sell the stained glass windows at St. Teresa's. No, better not to wear out that welcome. He might need the bishop for something more important one day.

He could confront Larkin in person, parade into the rectory one day with a bag-full of Rex's souvenirs that he could have his lawn man prepare, leave it there and tell Larkin that he was returning something that Larkin had misplaced at Tooley's house. That would be rich, but you could never predict what that wild man Larkin would do. Personal confrontations with him were best avoided.

No, something psychological would be better.

He would send Larkin the bill that he just got from his landscaping company for the repairs to his lawn, with a note, "I expect you to pay for the damage done by your dog." The bill had come to two hundred dollars. There was nothing Larkin hated more than to part with a dollar. He would be apoplectic. It was a great idea!

On that pleasant note, Francis X. Tooley went to sleep, with only a fleeting recollection of Larkin's odd dance around his oak tree troubling his thoughts. What had that strange man been doing?

The next day at his office he was signing his personal note to Sparky Larkin with the landscaper's bill attached when his secretary, Mrs. Connolly, came into his office without being buzzed for. That was an unusual occurrence and a sure sign that something was wrong,

"Mr. Fitzgerald is here to see you," she said. Bob Fitzgerald was the controller of Tooley Safety Products. He was so excited that he had followed Mrs. Connolly into the office.

"Something's wrong, Chief," the controller said by way of salutation.

Francis X. Tooley was truly concerned now. He knew that Bob Fitzgerald was an unflappable, button-down fellow. In all their years together, he had never known Fitzgerald to over-react.

Fitzgerald continued, "It's our stock, Chief. It opened this morning at twenty-five, but now it's down to twenty-two and still falling. I've been calling around to see what's happening, but I can't get any clear answer. Someone on the street must be putting out sell signals but I can't figure out who or why. This quarter's forecast are no different than last, and we are on track to meet them. I just don't know."

Francis X. Tooley felt his chest tighten. A healthy chunk of his fortune was in his own stock, and it was now suddenly worth twenty percent less than it was yesterday. For Francis X.

Tooley that was a loss of about twenty million dollars. Still he did not panic. The Tooleys never panicked.

"Look, Bob," he said. "There must be a reason. Drop everything to find out why. I'll make some calls of my own."

His broker had no idea, nor did his investment advisor or his banker. Bob Fitzgerald came up empty, too. The stock's plummet was unexplainable. His investment advisor told him to stay calm. These were the vagaries of the market. "Wait a few days, and it'll probably bounce right back up."

But the inexplicable loss was embarrassing and in the days that followed, Francis X. did not feel up to lunch at the Rocksburg Business Man's Club. He could not have taken the finger-pointing. His absence at his regular table was another source of concern for the business community.

In Tooley's world, nothing happened without a reason. If lightning struck, it was because somebody wanted it to. And so, on the third day, when his stock had not yet rebounded, and he could get no logical explanation for it, he began to look elsewhere for the cause. It was then that he remembered the odd dance that Sparky Larkin had done around the oak tree on his lawn at midnight. He thought, when he saw it, that it looked very strange, like some sort of Walpurgisnacht. That was it. That had to be it. It was the very next day that the Tooley stock began falling. That priest had cursed him. That dance around his oak tree at midnight, those weird incantations, that was it. That man had put some sort of priestly hex on him and now his stock was in free fall.

He had heard of priests who worked miracles through their prayers and holy lives. Half the saints were priests or monks whose holiness gave them great powers, like that Padre Pio fellow the Italians at St. Teresa's were always praying to. Of course,

Larkin was not so holy; no, quite the opposite, his powers must have a different source, one whose followers had for centuries worshiped him in the dark and at midnight, in forests and remote places, with weird dances and chants, the Evil One himself. Wasn't that exactly what he had seen Larkin doing? Yes, that was it. Larkin was in league with the devil, and had used this power to curse him. That was why the Tooley stock had inexplicably fallen in value.

Now that he knew the reason for his misfortune, he knew how to handle it. Another phone call to the diocesan chancery was in order.

Bishop Phelan wasn't in, so he got shuffled to Henry DaSilva, the auxiliary bishop and vicar general of the diocese. DaSilva was having trouble with Tooley's story.

"A priest of this diocese has cursed you? I can't believe it."

"All due respect, Bishop DaSilva, I know what I saw. It was midnight. He and his dog did a weird dance around my oak tree, reciting some sort of crazy words. The next day, Tooley stock starts falling. It's down again today. It's at twenty now and I want it to stop. You've got to order Father Larkin to remove his curse."

"Frank," Bishop DaSilva said, "you're a cradle Catholic, a devout man from a devout family. Surely you know that a Roman Catholic priest would not curse anybody."

"Bishop, all due respect, I am an educated man. I go to the movies. I saw that one, uh, *Becket*, where that Richard Burton, the archbishop of Canterbury, and all those monks, cursed that Peter O'Toole fellow, and O'Toole was the king of England. He did it out of a book, actually read the curse, 'Cast him out into the outer darkness, O Lord,' and all those monks threw lit candles down to the floor. It was all in the movie. Now are you telling me that didn't happen in Church history? Or that Larkin doesn't have that same book?"

"Frank, that's Hollywood. The Church doesn't act that way."

"Bishop DaSilva, begging your pardon, but you are taking things all too lightly. The new diocesan foundation that Bishop Phelan started holds twenty thousand shares of Tooley stock. You can't sell it for ten years because that's in the terms of my gift, and it used to be worth $500,000 dollars. Now it's worth $400,000 and falling. Your man Larkin has cost you a lot of money, too."

Bishop DaSilva grimaced. A report on the success of the diocesan foundation was being prepared to attract new donors. This sudden drop in its value would not look good.

"Okay, Frank," he finally said. "I will talk to Father Larkin and see what this is all about."

"Get him to remove the curse, Bishop. Remember, we're in this boat together."

Bishop DaSilva dreaded the phone call that he would have to make to Sparky Larkin. Telephone calls with Sparky were never easy.

"Father Larkin," he began, "I just got a very strange report from Mr. Tooley."

"What is that crybaby yapping about now, Henry? I swear I've never seen a grown man complain so much."

"I don't know how to say this, Father, except to repeat what he told me. He says that you put a curse on him."

"A curse? He's out of his mind. I mean, I don't like the pompous ass. He gives a niggling share of his fortune to the parish, and he thinks he has the right to run the place, but a curse? Never a curse, Henry. It would hardly be a Christian thing to do, much as Mr. Francis X. Tooley needs a come-uppance in the world."

"Father, he says he saw you the other night at midnight doing some kind of ritual dance with your dog around the oak tree in his front yard. He says you and the dog circled the tree several times,

211

dancing and reciting some strange chant. It sounds very suspicious, Father."

"He said WHAT?" Sparky screamed across the line. "And you, a bishop of this diocese believed him? What do you think I am, Henry, some kind of druid, some kind of whorelock? I'm ashamed of you, Henry, an auxiliary bishop of the diocese, believing such things about a fellow priest."

"He's been very generous to the diocese, Father."

"And that's another thing, Henry. He's more generous to the diocese than he is to his own parish where his own forefathers are buried. It's not right, Henry. I should have first call on his generosity, what there is of it."

"Father, I did not say that I believed Mr. Tooley. I just asked if you could explain his story."

"Henry, I can't explain what never happened. Why would I, a priest of God, do such a thing?"

"I don't know, Father. All I know is that I have a very angry Francis X. Tooley on my hands and a pile of Tooley stock in the diocesan foundation that has dropped drastically in value, all because of a curse he says you put on him."

"Oh, so that's it. It all comes down to money, doesn't it? And what does Marty Phelan say about this? Does he believe this nonsense?"

"Bishop Phelan is away right now, Sparky. You know he goes to the Jersey shore this time every year. I am afraid that you and I will have to work this one out."

"What are you suggesting that I do, Henry?"

"Would it hurt so much to go to Tooley's house and throw some holy water on the tree?"

"So you want me to give into this lunatic's fantasies?"

"There's nothing wrong with blessing nature, Father. Think of St. Francis. 'Be praised, O Lord, for Mother Earth.'" Without giving Sparky a chance to reply, Bishop DaSilva hung up.

An idea came to Sparky Larkin at what Bishop

DaSilva said, maybe even an inspiration. "That little greaseball may have half an idea there," he thought to himself as he began to plan his next steps.

The next day, the people on the street where Francis X. Tooley lived were confronted with a strange scene. A police car was driving slowly down the middle of the street, the light on the top of the car spinning and blinking, the siren on very low. Right behind the car, an altar boy in a cassock and surplice marched, holding a large procession-al crucifix. Beside him were two more altar boys, also in cassocks and surplices, carrying candles that were almost bigger than they were. They were followed by Sparky Larkin, in an alb, a stole, and a massive gold cope, swaying in the wind. Beside Sparky were another two altar boys, one carrying a holy water vessel and the other a censer on a long golden chain and an incense boat. It was an impres-sive scene. Catholics on the sidewalk felt compelled to stop and bless themselves as the group passed. Sparky acknowledged each of them with the sign of benediction.

The further the group processed, the more the crowd grew. Alerted by the siren, people came from their houses to observe the scene. When the troupe arrived at the Tooley home, led by the police car, priest and altar boys processed up the Tooley driveway. The crowd remained on the sidewalk. Francis X. and Mildred Tooley were waiting at the front door.

Sparky Larkin motioned to them to join him under the oak tree that had been the scene of the midnight debacle. The altar boys followed Sparky and lined up behind him. He then addressed the Tooleys in a ritual that he had cobbled together himself from the Sacramentary.

"We are here for the exorcism of the tree. Do you renounce Satan?" he said in a loud and stern voice that could be heard by the crowd on the sidewalk. In a stage whisper, he said, "We do."

The Tooleys dutifully replied, "We do."

"And all his works?" Sparky shouted. He started his stage whisper again, but the Tooleys got the point, and quickly replied, "We do."

"And all his empty promises?"

"We do."

"I am now prepared to exorcise this tree," Sparky continued, calling forward the two altar boys with the censer and incense boat. He sprinkled a good amount of incense from the boat onto the hot coal in the censer. Immediately huge plumes of fragrant smoke began to emerge. Sparky took hold of the chain from which the censer hung and solemnly walked around the tree, incensing every side of it. He handed the censer back to the altar boy and asked for the holy water.

He beckoned to the Tooley's to join him. He held Frank's hand and indicated to Frank that he should hold Mildred's. He then began walking all the way around the tree, the Tooley's in tow, every turn quicker than the previous one, while sprinkling the trunk with as much holy water as he could, and shouting in Latin, for effect, "*Exorcizio te, exorcizio te, exorcizio te.*"

He gave the holy water sprinkler back to the altar boy and bowed to the tree. Then he turned to the Tooleys and said, "That should do it. Those are pretty powerful words of exorcism." Then he whispered to Frank, "It's customary, for ceremonies like these, to give the altar boys a little something. I think forty dollars each should do it. It was a long walk from the church. My services, of course, since they are sacramental in nature, are absolutely free."

He stood there waiting and Francis X. realized that the priest wanted the money then and now. Opening his wallet, he counted out two hundred dollars and gave them to Sparky, who accepted the bills with a smile. Francis X. Tooley could not help but question why it was the exact same amount as the lawn services bill he had sent to Sparky earlier that week, and wondered if the altar boys would ever see that money.

Putting the money into his pocket, Sparky said, "Oh, and Frank, you can take care of the policemen yourself."

In the crowd, watching the whole affair from the sidewalk, was Michael Manion, a local businessman who had been on his way home for lunch. He was surprised to see Francis X. Tooley in the pink of health standing under the oak tree. As soon as he got back to his office he called his stockbroker.

"Is Tooley stock still at 20?"

"Give me a second," his broker replied. "Yeah. Still is."

"Buy a thousand on my account."

"Did you say 'buy'?"

"Yeah. Those rumors about old man Tooley having a stroke—they can't be true. I just saw him healthy as a horse running around an oak tree on his front lawn."

XI

Call in the Nuns

"Let me get it straight about my name. It really is Sister DeeDee. My dad taught Medieval Philosophy at the University of Rocksburg, and he was a huge St. Augustine fan. Augustine named his son 'Adeodatus'—'God's Gift,' in Latin, so my dad had to name me 'Adeodata,' the female version. I don't know how my mother let that happen.

"Thank God for Sister Mary Elizabeth in first grade. She said, 'No child should be burdened with that,' and from then on she said my name would be DeeDee. It was a modern abbreviation of Adeodata, she claimed.

"You can imagine how angry my dad was when he found out. So he hurries up to the school and he's going to talk to Sister Mary Elizabeth about this. He had no idea what he was in for. That lady was formidable. She wasn't assigned to teach first graders for twenty years because she was a pushover. So DeeDee I was, from then on.

"The name the novice mistress gave me when I entered the convent was Sister Mary George. Now I ask you, do I look like a George? Anyhow, as soon as the Vatican Council was over and the rules changed, I took DeeDee back.

"But I was telling you about this very strange experience. I think it was one of the weirdest things that ever happened to me. I mean, I don't know how I get myself into these things. I guess my biggest problem is, I don't say 'no' when I should.

"It's not like I don't have enough to do. You try teaching high school by day and studying for an MSW at night. It doesn't leave you a whole lot of time for a social life.

"But Cindy asked me and she's my friend. I guess it's because we're the two oldest women in class. All these young kids fresh out of college, studying to be social workers, and Cindy and I working on our second careers. I guess that's why we bonded so fast. We were best friends by the end of the second night.

"Of course, she was surprised when she found out that I was a nun, DeeDee Moriarity, SVD. Not too many people understand that's what the little cross pin on my lapel means. I mean, can you imagine going to the University of Rocksburg in a nun's get-up? Thank goodness we dropped all that garb as soon as the Vatican Council said we could.

"It didn't make any difference to Cindy, really, my being a nun. She was raised very Catholic herself. I mean, when I first told her, she 'Sister'd' me to death. So I said, 'Stop making me feel like I'm back with my ninth graders.' Just call me, 'DeeDee.' All my friends do.

"Cindy and I got along real well from the start. It was very supportive having someone my own age to talk to during breaks and after class. I mean, I tried it with the young chippies, but talk about living in a different world.

"And the guys in class. Well, for some reason, social work attracts a very strange type of male. Half of them wanted to do my hair, and the other half thought older women were easy game. It's one of the few times I missed the old habit. Those straitjackets we used to wear would have turned them off.

"By the middle of the semester, though, everyone knew that I was a nun, and that ended that. I
mean, it's not something I try to hide, in spite of the
secular clothes.

"But anyhow, towards the end of the first semester, Cindy starts telling me about her brother,
Joe, and how his wife left him. There are no kids,
but still he's very distraught about this and he's
very angry at the Church.

"I didn't understand that at first. I mean, at
first I thought Cindy was saying that he was angry
because the Church wouldn't give him an annulment and all. But no, I mean they wouldn't, but the
real reason he was so angry at the Church is—get
this—his wife picked a priest to run off with, and
the priest had been one of their best friends.

"Talk about being screwed by the Church.
Cindy was telling me that her brother's marriage
was outside the Church to start with. Then this new
priest comes to their parish and tells them he can
do everything, you know, he can straighten out the
whole mess and get them married in the Church.
So he does, only while he's doing it, he's falling in
love with Joe's wife. Connie, I think her name was.

"So anyhow, practically right after the ceremony, this Connie runs off with the priest who
married them. And Joe, Cindy's brother, is madder
than a hatter at the Church and this sneaky little
priest. He wants to kill him in fact.

"Well, who wouldn't? I mean, talk about cheap
tricks. If the priest wanted to run off with the woman, why didn't he do it before he married them? At
least then Cindy's brother wouldn't be stuck in a
Church marriage with a woman who wasn't there
anymore.

"One night, after I've heard this story maybe a
dozen times from Cindy, she says to me, 'DeeDee,
you have to talk to him.' I say, 'To who?' She says,
'To Joe, my brother.' I say, 'Why, you know, why
me?' It isn't like I don't have enough to do, what

with teaching during the day and going to school at night. I mean, isn't there someone at the parish he can talk to? What about the pastor? I ask.

"Then Cindy tells me that the pastor is this guy named Sparky Larkin. Well, enough said. This guy is famous in the whole diocese for being a lunk-head on wheels. He's probably driven more people away from the Church than he's baptized into it. So Joe doesn't want to talk to him. That's out of the question, and I can't blame him.

"And Cindy's worried. Her whole family is worried. Joe's very bitter. He's despondent. He's upset with the Church. So Cindy asks if I can talk to him.

"I say, 'Cindy, I like you. You're my friend, but I don't have my MSW yet. What do you expect me to do'?

"'Just talk to him' she says. 'He's bitter, very bitter. Let him know that the Church isn't to blame for this. Just help him see his way out of this mess. DeeDee,' she says to me, 'I'm terribly worried. I think he's pre-suicidal.'

"So that's it. This guy's screwed by one priest. His pastor is incompetent. He hates the Church and is about to kill himself. So Sister DeeDee to the rescue, right?

"Do you see how I get roped into these things? I mean, what choice did I have at that point? It's typical Church. Send in the nuns to straighten up the mess that the priests have made. So I tell Cindy, okay, I'll at least talk to him.

"Well, she thanks me like I just promised her and her whole family passage to America and she gives me her brother's phone number. I gave him a call at work the next day. He works at the university. And I agree to stop at his house on my way to class that night.

"Now his house—get this—is right across the street from St. Teresa's Church. I mean, how absurd can you get? Here's his parish, right across the street, practically looming over their house, he has a major problem with the Church, and he can't go to his pastor. Call in the nuns.

"This was winter time, and it's dark out early. I knock on the door and he answers it.

"'You're the nun?' he says.

"Cindy's friend, DeeDee. You're expecting me, right? We talked earlier today,' I say, so he lets me in, I take off my coat, and the way he looks at me, I wonder, am I dressed funny or something? There's this weird gleam in his eyes. But it's Cindy's brother, so I figure he must be okay.

"He had coffee ready, so we just sat down in the kitchen and talked. At first, I thought, well, he seems pretty normal. I mean, he's no movie star in the looks department, actually, he had a little potbelly and he wore his hair hippie-length, but he wasn't a turn off, either, except for the funny way he kept looking at me, but you know, I thought, maybe it's my imagination. Mostly I just listened. It's like they taught us in Intro to Counseling, be a sponge. Let the guy emote. Let him get it off his chest. Then intervene if you have to.

"The story was just like Cindy said, only worse. This priest wasn't just their friend. He lived in their house. Can you believe it? Sparky Larkin, the pastor, has some dog as big as a truck and this wimpy priest is afraid to go near it, so he runs away from the rectory and moves in with this couple. Can you imagine a nun doing that? Sorry, Mother, I hate your cat so I'm moving out of the convent. Wouldn't she just shake your wimple? I mean, you wouldn't get past the front door with that kind of nonsense in the convent. I tell you, it's a shame what priests get away with. But it's their Church, and we're just servants.

"So this guy lets this priest move in with him and his wife. Can you believe it? I mean, what a jerk. And it takes a good while for the diocese to do anything about it. Meanwhile, this priest is eating with them, sleeping with them, doing everything they do. Well, not everything, but almost.

"Joe's telling me all this, and he says, 'I can't believe he betrayed me. We were so good to him. Wait,' he says, 'wait, you won't believe this. We even took him on vacation with us. Come up here,' he says, 'come on up here and I'll show you.'

"So we go upstairs, and there, on the vanity in their bedroom, stuck between the frame and the mirror, are all sorts of pictures. He pulls down a couple.

"'Look at this,' he says, practically crying. 'This was at Cape May,' and he shows me this picture— three people in swimsuits on the promenade. 'We had someone take this for us. There's me, Connie in the middle and Tony on the end.'

"You wouldn't believe this picture. First of all, the woman is in a two piece that barely covers anything. They're all laughing at the camera, and these two guys both have their arms around this woman's waist. I'm thinking, what a schmuck you are, fellow. Can you imagine, taking another man on vacation with you and letting him hold onto your wife like that, all the while you're smiling at the camera like this is nice and normal? Give me a break. I mean, this guy had a terminal case of the dumbs.

"But wait, that's not all. He starts taking other pictures down from the mirror. 'Look at this,' he says. 'This was Connie's twenty-fifth birthday.' There's his wife, leaning over her cake to blow out the candles, and I mean, really leaning over, everything was hanging out, and behind her, with an arm on each of her shoulders, is this Tony character.

"'Where were you when this picture was taken?' I ask.

"'Oh, I took it, ' he says.

"Didn't you think something was wrong? I mean, look at the way he's holding her.'

"'Well, I didn't think anything of it at the time,' he says.

"I can't believe what this guy is telling me. I

mean, I just looked at him. What could I even say at that point?

"'Wait,' he says, 'you haven't seen it all.' Then he gets this photo album out from the night table and he sits down on the bed.

"'Come here,' he says, 'these are our wedding pictures.' So I sit down beside him while he flips through this album. There's this Tony guy on the altar, in his chasuble, looking so angelic, you know, the way priests look when they know everybody's watching them, but there's a distinct glint in his eyes. He's not looking at the camera. He's not looking out towards the people. He's looking at the wife.

"And there's more. I mean, this priest was in as many pictures as the bride and groom. There's even two or three of him, in his Roman collar, dancing with the bride at the reception.

"Now this is very strange, right? So I say, 'Gee, this priest is in a lot of your wedding pictures,' and Joe says, 'After he did all the work, you know, straightening out Connie's first marriage so that we could get married in the Church, it was like he was a part of us. I just never thought.'

"'Sure, you just never thought,' I say. 'You let him go away on vacation with you, let him take center stage at your wedding, let him live with you. For God's sake, didn't that seem a little bit odd to you?'

"'No,' he says, 'I trusted him,' then he starts taking off his shoes and socks.

"'Well, you obviously trusted the wrong man,' I say, wondering to myself, what is this nut doing now with the shoes and the socks?

"'But he was a priest,' he says.

"'Priests are like anyone else,' I say. 'Some you can trust and some you can't.'

"'I guess I just caught on too late,' he says and he starts unbuttoning his shirt and then he gets up and turns down the bed covers. Meanwhile I'm just sitting there, looking at him, thinking, is this guy weird or what? I mean, he's obviously one of the most passive guys on earth. He stood there and watched this priest steal his wife out from under his nose. Now, I'm talking to him, and he's acting like he wants to go to sleep in the middle of the conversation.

"Then he looks over at me. 'Aren't you going to get ready?' he says.

"'Ready for what?' I say.

"'For what the Church sent you here for,' he says. 'Aren't you going to, uh, you know, get in the sack with me?'

"'What?' I say. 'Who gave you that idea?' I say. I was shocked.

"'Cindy said you were coming to make things right with the Church,' he says. 'I haven't had a woman for over a year now. That priest stole my wife. The Church owes me.'

"'And you think they sent me here as a replacement?' I say. By now, I'm inching my way to the door.

"'Well, why else are you here?' he says.

"'Look, buddy,' I say. 'Things don't work that way. I think I better be going. G'bye,' I say and I fly down those stairs like a bat from hell, grab my coat, and I'm out the front door before he can turn around.

"Can you imagine what that looney tunes thought? That I was some kind of temple prostitute sent over there by, who knows, probably the pope, in order to make up for his being out a wife. What a nut case! No wonder his wife left him. I mean, there's something wrong there, terribly wrong. The fellow has toys in his attic. Let me tell you, I got out of there just in the nick of time. I haven't been saving it thirty-five years just to lose it because some priest took this guy's wife. I mean, nuns have been making sacrifices for centuries to cover up for the sins of the clergy, but that would have been beyond the call of duty.

"I never did tell Cindy exactly what happened. I just told her that her brother needs professional help. Which he does."

XII

Priests Without People

The largest item in the upstairs library at St. Teresa's rectory was the bar that the pastor, Sparky Larkin, had bought from a catalog discount store. Its vinyl padded front and Formica top clashed with the room's leather chairs and rich walnut trim and wainscotting, but what the hey, Sparky Larkin had thought when he bought it, a bar is a place where you spill things. Who needs a high class bar?

Although Sparky still referred to it as a library, and it had bookshelves, two walls full of them, the room was bereft of books. At one time, under Sparky's predecessor at St. Teresa's, a bookish and learned man, the shelves had bulged with the most recent treatises on philosophy, theology and sacred scripture.

But George Sennot had died young, and the bishop had sent Sparky Larkin to replace him. One of the first things Sparky did was to empty the shelves and fill them with his athletic trophies and sports magazines. The books had been packed in boxes and disposed of.

Monsignor Don Himmelreich, rector of St. Gregory's Seminary in Rocksburg, was livid when he found out. He went to Sparky's rectory and confronted him.

"Where are my books?" he said.

"Your books?" Sparky had answered. "Who said they were your books?"

"There was a will, you idiot. Did it ever occur to you that George Sennot left a will? All his books were left to the seminary library."

"Look, Don, those books were on parish property. I'm the pastor now. Check your canon law. If they're on parish property, I had a right to dispose of them."

"No you didn't. You have broken that man's will. He promised those books to me and he put it in his will."

"Criminees, Don. If they were so damn important, why'n't you come for them sooner? Sennot's been dead more than a month now."

"I thought they were safe here. I never thought another priest would throw out the best collection of theology books in the diocese. I didn't count on the biggest Philistine since Goliath getting his hands on those books."

"Now stop right there, Don. I know what that means and I won't be insulted in my own rectory. If you came for the books, the books aren't here, so why'n't you just leave?"

"But where are they? Can't you at least tell me where they are? Who has them? Did you give them to the St. Vincent de Paul Society? Maybe I can get them back."

"The Goodwill has them, Don, not the St. Vincent de Paul."

"The Goodwill?" Don Himmelreich was crushed. "You gave them to the Methodists? You couldn't even call St. Vincent de Paul to take a dead priest's belongings?"

"Yes, I could have," Sparky Larkin spit out, "but I didn't, because in this diocese the Goodwill makes pick-ups and the St. Vincent de Paul don't. So the Goodwill got 'em, okay?"

"I'll go there. I'll go there and ask for them back.

Surely they'll understand. There was a will. Those books are mine."

"Bring some money with you, Don. They paid me for the books and things."

"You sold them? For how much?"

"Three hundred bucks, the whole kit and ka-boodle."

"Three hundred dollars? Those books were worth thousands."'

"Good, then you won't mind parting with a couple hundred to get them back, will you? Good-bye, Don."

Under Sparky's reign, the bar, not the tomes in the bookcases, was the room's focus. It was where he hosted the visitors to his rectory, as long as they were priests. It was a well-established rule at St. Teresa's that laymen were not allowed upstairs and laywomen were barely tolerated inside the front door.

Today, on a warm Indian summer's afternoon in the fall of 1970, the bar was beclouded in cigar smoke, and the enclosed air of the room hung heavily with the sour odors of scotch and perspiration. Sparky Larkin was there with his guests after a hard-played round of golf.

"Hey," Sparky Larkin said as Jerry Donnelly started to crank open one of the cross-hatched, lead-ed library windows, "whaddaya doin' that for?"

"Sorry, Sparky, but I got to open a window. It stinks in here," Jerry Donnelly said.

"The air-conditioning's on," Sparky Larkin protested, waving his cigar in the air.

"The air-conditioning's not doing anything for your cigar or your b.o. or Rex. This room is rank," Jerry Donnelly said as he continued to crank.

Hearing his name, Rex, Sparky Larkin's over-weight German shepherd, got up from beside Sparky's chair and went over to Jerry Donnelly. He licked his hand.

"You should have showered like the rest of

us, before we left the country club, Sparky," Carl
Kalina said.

The other priest in the room, Joe Denzer, newly
returned from his seminary studies in Rome, was
observing his elders. He wondered if he was meant
to participate in this conversation.

Sparky Larkin, Jerry Donnelly and Carl Kalina
were classmates, all pastors of major parishes in the
Rocksburg diocese, in their mid-fifties. They had
been playing golf, on and off together, most warm
Wednesdays, for years. The other member of their
foursome floated, depending mostly on who was in
or out of Sparky's favor.

Today, Joe Denzer was the fourth invitee at
Sparky's insistence. The rumor was around in
Rocksburg that Joe was to be Sparky's new assistant pastor, and Sparky wanted to check him out
before he told the bishop okay. His last two assis-
tants had been real jerks. Tony Capresi, who hated
dogs and loved women, had run off with a parishioner. And Mike Krebs, who was still around, was a
constant thorn in Sparky's side.

Sparky believed that you saw a person's true
character in athletic competition, and so, once he
heard that he might be getting Joe Denzer as an
assistant at St. Teresa's, he had been anxious to get
him on the golf course. After his last two disasters,
he did not want another one.

"Why should I have showered there?" Sparky
said. "We were coming back to my rectory, weren't
we? I have plenty of showers here, don't I? Besides
I didn't bring a change of clothes to the course like
you fancy guys did."

"I told you the country club had a nice dressing room, not like the municipal course we usually
play, Sparky," Jerry Donnelly said.

Joe Denzer's heart sank. He put his drink down on
the floor beside his chair. He had brought a change of
clothes to the country club and had showered there.
He wondered if Sparky Larkin would hate him for it.

"You'll never change, will you, Sparky?" Carl Kalina said. "Even in the seminary, you never showered after gym. Sitting in front of you, in class after that, was enough to turn me green."

"So what? That's ancient history," Sparky Larkin said. "Besides, you dagos were never known for being that clean. Hey, Joe,'' Sparky drew Joe Denzer's attention, "you know the safest place to hide something in Italy? Underneath the soap, ha, ha. They never pick it up."

Rex left Jerry Donnelly and went over and sniffed at Joe Denzer. He licked at his shoes, and then stuck his long pink tongue into the drink glass that Joe Denzer had placed, unthinkingly, on the rug beside his chair.

"Of course, being Roman-trained, you probably knew that already," Sparky Larkin continued. "Tell me, Joe, how'd a good kid like you survive four years in dago-land?"

"You illiterate," Carl Kalina said. "You've known me for over thirty years and you still think I'm Italian just because my name ends with a vowel. It's 'Kalina' with a 'K', remember? There is no 'k' in Italian. It's Polish, not Italian."

"Who cares?" Sparky replied, drawing another long pull on his cigar and releasing the smoke from his mouth with great flourish.

"Look at this, would you? Isn't that your assistant pastor, Sparky?" Jerry Donnelly said, peering out the window he had just opened.

"Where?" Sparky Larkin said, rising from his chair.

"Out in the street there, holding that girl's hand."

"I'll be damned," Sparky Larkin said. "I told Krebs to stay away from her," he said as he ran from the room and down the steps. Barking loudly, Rex ran after him.

"Where's he going?" Joe Denzer asked.

"I think Krebs is in for it," Jerry Donnelly said.

They could hear the screen door of the rectory porch bang, and the loud baying of the dog. Sparky Larkin was screaming at his assistant pastor, Mike Krebs, on the street in front of the rectory.

For unending minutes the three priests in the library tried to pretend that this was not happening. Jerry Donnelly and Carl Kalina sipped at their drinks. Joe Denzer wondered what to do with his now that Rex had shared it.

They glanced around the room. Vacated of its books as the first act of Sparky's pastorate, the library looked a bit forlorn. On the shelves, sports magazines and newspapers, stacked horizontally, alternated between gold and silver lacquered trophies, men swinging golf clubs or lofting bowling balls.

"I told you to leave her alone. People in the parish are talkin'," they heard Sparky's voice through the open window.

"Look, get this through your thick mick skull, I was helping the lady across the street. That's all," Mike Krebs shouted.

"Whaddaya? Some fruity boy scout or somethin'?"

"I know it never occurred to you to be considerate to anyone, but some of us were brought up differently. We're polite to ladies and we help them when we walk them across the street."

"You weren't helpin' nothing. You were holdin' hands. I saw the whole thing."

"You're too plastered to know what you saw."

"I'm going to the bishop on this one, Krebs."

"Go ahead. Be my guest. Tell Marty Phelan you saw me escort a lady across the street, and that's a sign I'm not fit to be a priest. He'll throw you out of the chancery."

"Martin Phelan is a friend of mine and he'll do no such thing," Sparky Larkin said, all the while Rex danced and barked around Mike Krebs.

"Look, I'm tired hearing what good friends you

are with the bishop," Mike Krebs told Sparky. "You tell him whatever you want, but I'll be there too, to make a liar out of you. I'm no Tony Capresi. You're not going to drive me out of the priesthood."

Rex kept barking and nipping at Mike Krebs' ankles, but the priest ignored him.

"I didn't do nothin' to that Capry fellow. Guy was a skirt-chaser from the git-go. Nothin' to do with me."

"Larkin, I'm tired of you and your goddam dog. Get him the hell out of here before I poison him."

"Don't use your curbstone vulgarities with me, mister."

"I'll do worse than that if you and that damn dog don't get away from me."

"Are you threatening me?"

"Damn right I am."

The three priests upstairs heard the screen door open and the dog's running gait as he skittered across the kitchen linoleum on the way to his supper dish in the dining room.

Sparky Larkin rushed up the stairs. He went to the bar, red-faced, and poured himself another scotch, spilling most of it on the bar's Formica top. "I gotta get rid of that guy," he announced. "He's not fit to be a priest. I'll go to the bishop, that's what I'll do," he said, gulping down his drink.

Jerry Donnelly said, "You already lost one assistant last year, Sparky. Another one so soon and the chancery will be asking questions. You may not get any help for a while and this is a big parish. Why don't you go careful on this one?"

"I can handle this parish on my own. Besides, I hear I'm due for a new assistant," he said, nodding his head at Joe Denzer, who cringed, and hoped that he had done so unobtrusively.

"Krebs isn't a bad guy, Sparky. You're just not hitting it off," Carl Kalina said.

"What do you know?" Sparky Larkin said.

"You told me the same thing about what's-his-name, uh, Capry, and look what a jerk he was. Should never a been ordained."

"That was your doing, Sparky, not Tony's. He lost his priesthood here," Carl Kalina said.

"He lost his priesthood, he lost his priesthood," Sparky Larkin mimicked. "You don't lose your priesthood. You either have what it takes or you don't and that guy didn't."

"That's not true, Sparky," Carl Kalina said. "He was okay until he came here."

"Yeah? How do you know that? I was his pastor and I think he was a first-rate screw-up."

"He did his deacon year at my parish, Sparky. He was good, the people liked him, and … What's the use?"

"And what?"

"I was his mentor, too," Carl Kalina said.

"His mentor?" Sparky Larkin said. "What the hell is that?"

"He came to me for advice. I told him that he should be patient with you, that you would come around. What a jerk I was."

"What did you say to him when he told you that he was in the sack with a married woman?"

"That didn't happen until after you drove him out of the rectory."

"I don't know any such thing, except he was a skirt-chasing dago."

"Shut up, Sparky. The guy was my friend," Carl Kalina said.

"My, how the dagos stick together."

"How many times do I have to tell you before it gets through that thick Irish skull of yours. My family was Polish, not Italian."

Carl Kalina looked at the man. They had known each other for decades, a friendship born of sharing many common enemies: their professors in the seminary, the hard-set pastors they had served as young priests, the various bishops of Rocksburg

234

that had come and gone in the last thirty years. They had started St.Gregory's Seminary together in 1927, two kids fresh out of grade school, and their names, Larkin and Kalina, meant that they would have classroom seats near each other, room assignments next to each other, work assignments with each other, forever afterward. It had never occurred to the rigid men who ran St. Gregory's in those days to do anything out of alphabetical order. So the two of them became friends, almost of necessity.

Carl Kalina could still recall Visitors' Sundays, when Sparky Larkin's parents would show up, his mom in a series of loud, floral print dresses, carrying a suitcase-sized box of chocolate chip cookies that she had baked for her boy and his friends. And the man with her, shy and quiet, in an ill-fitting suit and four-inch wide tie.

When visitors' day was over, it was always the same. The Larkins stayed to the last possible moment, to the visible embarrassment of their son, and Mrs. Larkin would say as she left, to the priests on the staff and the other students, "Take care of my boy, take care of my boy."

And Carl Kalina had taken care of Sparky for years. But he had finally lost his patience.

"You are incredible. I should have gotten rid of you when I had the chance," Carl Kalina said.

"You? You get ridda me? Whaddaya talkin' about?"

"I should have blown the whistle on you when I had the chance. At least then Tony Capresi and who knows how many other poor souls might still be around."

"Whaddaya talkin' about? Sounds like you got somethin' on me. You got nothin' on me."

"Don't push me, Sparky. We've known each other for a long time. Let's just forget this whole thing."

"No. It was you brought it up. Say what you wanna say."

"Forget it, Sparky. It was nothing."

"Goddam right it was nothin'. You got nothin' on me. You're just another big-talkin' dago."

"Okay, Sparky. That's enough."

"No, it's not enough. You said you had somethin' on me, and the truth is you got nothin'. I just want present company," he threw out his hands to encompass Joe Denzer and Jerry Donnelly, "to realize that you were blowin' smoke, that for over thirty years I been a good priest."

"You know, Sparky, I always wondered, when your mom and dad came on Visitor's Sunday at St. Greg's, they never held hands, never even sat next to each other, and when they left, your mom always gave you a big hug, and the man just waved good-bye. I wondered, were you estranged from your dad or what. First, I thought, well, they're Irish. The Irish aren't good at showing their emotions, unless they're drunk, of course, when there is no holding them back. But it was strange. You never made a friendly gesture towards the man, and he barely looked at you.

"Every summer, back then, I got a political job because my mom was a Democratic committee woman in Rocksburg, 4th Ward, 10th District. One summer I was working in the County Courthouse, in the records office, and there was not a whole lot to do there after about two in the afternoon, so I got the idea to start looking up the records of folks I knew, the marriage licenses of all my relatives, my mom and dad, my aunts and uncles. Their birth certificates, too. Then, when I was done doing that, I started on friends, like you. I found your birth certificate. ..."

"Oh," Sparky Larkin said.

"Odd, you know. In the space for father, it was blank. Maureen Larkin, mother and father blank. I figured it was a mistake, so I went looking for your parents' marriage certificate. But there was none.

"The reason was pretty obvious. You are a bastard in the real sense of the word, Sparky. I won-

dered who the Thomas Larkin was who showed
up every Visitor's Sunday, so I kept looking. Your
mom had a brother named Thomas, born a year
before she was. So it wasn't your parents visiting. It
was your mom and your uncle.

"The problem is, Sparky, when we were ordained in 1940, bastards weren't allowed to be
priests. The Code of Canon Law prohibited it.
When you drove Tony Capresi out of the priesthood, I was so mad I called Hank DaSilva, and
asked him if there was any legitimation in your file.
He said there wasn't."

"Hank DaSilva knows? You son of a bitch,"
Sparky Larkin said.

All of a sudden, Sparky Larkin rushed at Carl
Kalina, as if he wanted to tackle him. Carl stepped
aside and Sparky crashed, head first, into the front
of his bar.

At first, they thought he was unconscious. But
then he sat up on the floor, his eyes weaving circles,
his face flushed.

"Nah, nah," Sparky Larkin said, shaking his
head.

Jerry Donnelly asked, "What are you saying,
Carl? None of this makes any sense to me."

"It makes sense to Sparky. The man who pretended to be his father was really his uncle. Sparky
doesn't have a father, at least not a legal one."

"Nah, nah," Sparky Larkin mumbled, still sitting on the carpet.

"Oh come on, how'd he get ordained then?"
Jerry Donnelly said.

"He hid it. And someone must have jiggered
his baptismal certificate to show a father. Probably the parish secretary did it for a few bucks, or
because she was Sparky's cousin. Who the hell
knows? But that's all the diocese looked at in
those days, was Church records. The chancery never asked to see birth certificates. That's what the
farce on Visitor's Sunday was all about. When his

uncle came out and pretended to be his father."

"C'mon Carl, give him a break. You don't know that."

"No, Jerry. I'm tired of giving him a break. He's been picking on meek souls for years, since the seminary, and we've been laughing at it and letting him get away with it. I watched him torture Tony Capresi, and never said a word, figuring it was just Sparky, you know, just the way he was, and things would get better. You heard him today with Krebs. What did the guy do to deserve that tirade?"

"I should never have opened that damn window," Jerry Donnelly responded.

"You should have kept quiet about what you saw," Carl Kalina said. "You know how easy it is to set this lunatic off."

"Nah, nah," Sparky Larkin said, still sitting on library carpet.

"Something's wrong with him," Joe Denzer said.

"No, Joe, nothing's wrong," Carl Kalina answered. "It's just that after thirty years, this guy's finally heard the truth about himself.

"Carl, look at him," Joe Denzer said. "His eyes are glazed over and he's not making any sense."

"Nah, nah," Sparky Larkin mumbled again.

"I think we should call a doctor," Joe Denzer insisted.

"No, he'll be all right. Sparky always comes out of everything all right," Carl Kalina said. "Hank DaSilva told me that even though he wouldn't have been ordained if they had known he was a bastard, it still wasn't null and void. Some canonical mumble jumble about *ecclesia supplet*. The Church makes up for its own mistakes," Carl Kalina said. "Lucky bastard. I'm going. You need a ride, Joe?"

"No, thanks, Carl," Joe Denzer said. "Jerry's taking me home."

After Carl Kalina left, Jerry Donelly and Joe Denzer put an addled Sparky Larkin to bed and asked a perturbed Mike Krebs to keep an eye on him. Afterwards, in the car, Joe Denzer asked Jerry Donnelly if he truly believed that Sparky Larkin would be all right.

"He's a tough guy, Joe. He'll be okay."

"I never heard anybody treat anyone like what I saw today, I mean him and Mike Krebs, and then him and Carl."

"You'll get over it, Joe. Priests can be pretty rough when they're alone with each other, without any people around. The worst things I ever heard anybody say about a priest were said by another priest. It sort of goes with the territory."

"Then I think I'd like to move."

"Too late, Joe. It's *usque in aeternitatem*, 'even unto eternity,' remember?"

XIII

Shoelaces

The tall, thin, ascetic looking young priest thought
that he heard the two Italian monsignors titter as he
walked past them, down the marble-lined corridor
of the Congregation for Clergy. He knew why they
were laughing. Another American *pazzo*, a crazy
person, had shown up at the Congregation's doors,
seeking help from this important Vatican department, and the junior American priest had been del-
egated to take care of his bothersome co-national.

It happened frequently now that the Vatican
Council was over. The doors of the Church had
been flung wide, and when people had problems
with their pastor or their bishop, they thought
nothing of getting on a plane to Rome and rushing
through those open doors, going directly to the Vatican for help, especially the Americans.

He was sure that the Italian monsignors saw
some sort of poetic justice in it. An annoying
American shows up on our doorstep, let the fledg-
ling American priest on staff handle him. Since
the Congregation for Clergy was the only Vatican
department headed by an American, John Cardinal Rooney, former bishop of Rocksburg, it was a
veritable lightning rod for distraught Americans, in

trouble, one way or another, with their Church.

Often, all the young priest had to do was hear them out and refer them to the proper Vatican department for help. But this morning's problem sounded more serious. The drop-in *pazzo* was a priest himself, and he was complaining about some problem with his bishop, or so the Italian monsignor who had summoned Father Tuigg had said.

The short, spare, elderly priest was waiting in the reception room of the Congregation. The walls of the room were hung with the photographs of past and present Cardinal Prefects, all of them dour looking Italians, except for the picture of the incumbent, a smiling, double-chinned John Cardinal Rooney.

Sitting in one of the small gilt and red satin brocade chairs that lined the walls of the waiting room, the visiting priest was bent over like a pretzel. His legs were crossed and he was holding his arms clasped against his chest. He jumped up when Father Bill Tuigg entered the room and rushed at him with his hand outstretched. He looked like a tightly-compressed spring that had just been let loose from a very confined space and was now flying towards freedom.

"Good morning, Monsignor," the little priest said as he vigorously shook Bill Tuigg's hand. "Father Augustus Diamond's my name."

"Pleased to meet you, Father Diamond, but it's not monsignor. I'm Father Bill Tuigg."

"Oh," the old priest said, "I thought all of you fellows over here were monsignors."

"No, not all of us. Some of the new arrivals are still simple priests. I'll probably be a monsignor next week and a bishop soon after that," Father Bill Tuigg said with a smile.

"It happens that fast, does it?" the diminutive priest said.

"I'm sorry, Father. I'm not being serious. It takes quite a long time, if ever. Right now, let's just call each other 'Father,' all right?"

"Are you sure that you can help?" the old priest drew back, disappointed at Father Bill Tuigg's lack of ecclesiastical standing.

"Why don't you tell me why you're here and I'll let you know?"

The aged priest looked at him quizzically. "Have you read my file, Father?" he asked.

"No, no, I haven't," Bill Tuigg replied. The Italian monsignor who had summoned Father Tuigg had neglected to tell him that there was a file.

"I guess I could explain it all over again," the old priest said in a dispirited tone.

"You won't have to do that, Father. Just wait a few minutes. I'll find your file and we can talk in my office while I look it over. Do you know your protocol number? It will make the file easier to find."

"I think I have it on this letter I got two years ago." The man fished a crinkled letter from his suit coat pocket and handed it to the young priest who checked the protocol number and went away to fetch the old priest's dossier.

Minutes later in his office, Father Bill Tuigg was flipping through the documents in the folder while the elderly priest chattered nervously away.

"It's about my pension, Father," the old man said. "Bishop Manley is refusing to give it to me. And it's not fair. It's only a matter of months, and the pension rule wasn't even made until I was already there."

Father Bill Tuigg put up his hand in a gesture to stop. He was trying to focus on the file, but it was impossible with the man prattling on.

"I'm sorry, Father Diamond, maybe it would be best if you just tell me the story in your own words." He put the folder down.

"It's in the file, I'm sure," the old priest answered. "You see, I was a priest for the diocese of Duluth, but then I developed this lung problem.

I was only forty years old and my doctor said I needed a change of climate. I had to go somewhere warm and dry if I wanted to get well. So with the permission of my bishop, I moved to Nogaces, New Mexico and I became a priest of that diocese.

"I've worked there for almost thirty years, Father, longer than I was a priest in Duluth. I have one of the largest parishes, and my people, my people," the man paused, choking on his emotions, "my people, a lot of them are Aztecs, can you imagine that, Father, Aztecs? But they love me. I've been with them for years. Then two years ago, all the priests in Nogaces got letters from the chancery, telling them what their pension benefits would be. My letter said zero. I was getting nothing. So I called the chancery. It had to be a mistake, right?"

"But they told me, no, it wasn't. I was forty years and three months old when I moved to Nogaces. When they put the pension plan in, they had a restriction, any priest who joined the diocese after his fortieth birthday was not eligible. So I went to see Bishop Manley. He was very apologetic, but he said he had been getting a lot of requests from priests up north if they could come to his diocese. They wanted to spend their last years someplace warm. He says there's no way his diocese could support all those snowbirds, he called them. There had to be a line drawn somewhere.

"I said to him, 'But, Bishop, all this happened after I got here, this restriction in the pension plan. It's not just. It shouldn't affect me.' He said, 'Before you got here, there was no pension plan. So if you insist on when you got here, you're still entitled to nothing.'

"That's when I wrote to Cardinal Fischetti, the fellow who was here before Cardinal Rooney, but I never got an answer from him, just some clerk. Here it is, two years later, I'm ready to retire, and my only pension is social security. So I decided to come to Rome. I thought I could see Cardinal

Rooney, him being an American, I thought he
would understand. I know if I could only explain
my situation to him, he would help me. He's a fair
man, I'm sure. Will that be possible, do you think,
Father, to talk to him?"

"Perhaps," Father Bill Tuigg said, "but why
don't you let me see if I can help you first?"

"Certainly, Father. No disrespect meant for
you."

"How long will you be in Rome, Father? Perhaps you could allow me some time and I could
work on this for you."

"I guess. I've been waiting so long another few
days won't hurt. But you know, it's so expensive
to stay here. I never dreamed Rome would be so
expensive."

"Where are you staying, Father?"

The old priest named a *pensione* near the train
station. "Father," Bill Tuigg said, "that's not a very
good area."

"There was this young fellow, when I got off
the bus from the airport, he offered to carry my
suitcase, and I was so tired. He took me right to this
place, said it was one of the best in Rome. He was
very kind. He wouldn't take a penny for helping
me with my bag."

"Father, those men are paid by the *pensione*
owners to do that. He got a commission on you."

"Oh," the elderly priest said, "I didn't know
that."

"How much are you paying?"

"Twenty dollars a day, twelve thousand lira."

"Father, for half that you could stay with the
German nuns, across the square here, near the Vatican. You would be safer. There are a lot of gypsies
and muggers near the train station."

"Father, thank you for your concern. I would
like to save the money, but, at my age, moving
around like that is a lot of trouble. By the time I
pack my bag and find somebody to help me with it,

and get a taxi …"

Bill Tuigg persisted. "Father, I am very serious. It can be dangerous near the train station, especially at night. I would feel responsible if anything happened to you. Look, it's practically lunch time. Why don't we have a bite nearby and then I'll get my car and help you move. All right?"

"Lunch would be nice, Father. I've been having trouble finding any good food here. They don't make too many American dishes, do they? It's just all this macaroni."

On their walk to the restaurant, Father Bill Tuigg noticed that the aged priest was wearing black orthopedic shoes with thick, tattered laces and gummy crepe soles. The soles squeaked on the hard Roman cobblestones, but Father Diamond appeared not to be aware of the noise he was making as they walked along. The big, clodhopper shoes with their frayed laces made Bill Tuigg feel even sorrier for the man.

They went to Roberto's, a small, pleasant restaurant on the Borgo Pio, much frequented by minor curial officials. Father Diamond allowed Bill Tuigg to do all of the ordering and the excellent rigatoni alla carbonara convinced him that there were some kinds of macaroni he could live with.

The old priest ate in quiet ritual, taking small bites and chewing everything very thoroughly, but he assured Father Bill Tuigg that it was all very delicious.

In Father Bill Tuigg's Fiat 600, they left the Vatican area and went to Father Diamond's pensione on the Via Principe Amedeo where they collected the old priest's belongings and transported them to the German nuns' guest house at the top of Borgo Santo Spirito, a few hundred feet away from the grandeur of St. Peter's Square, and right across the piazza from the Congregation for Clergy.

"This is much better, Father," the old priest said when they got to his room at the German nuns.

Father Bill Tuigg had been heart-sick when he

saw the pensione on the Via Principe Amedeo. It was dirty and foul-smelling. The lobby area had been full of slovenly characters, who looked as if they would knife you as easily as say hello. He had thought that Father Diamond was oblivious to it all until the elderly priest remarked how much nicer the German nuns' guest house was. Perhaps the old guy is not as detached as he seems, Bill Tuigg thought.

They parted on the promise that they would meet in a few days, after Bill Tuigg had had a chance to review the records and talk to Cardinal Rooney.

Father Bill Tuigg returned to his office at the Congregation and examined the file. It was not an extensive one. There was Father Diamond's initial letter to the Congregation, two years ago, complaining about being deprived of a pension. There was a letter from a *minutante*, a minor official in the Congregation, acknowledging his letter. There was a subsequent letter from the secretary of the congregation, an archbishop, to Bishop Manley, enclosing a copy of Father Diamond's letter and asking him to reply to the charges of unfairness that Father Diamond had made. Finally, there was Bishop Manley's letter, enclosing a copy of the diocesan priests' pension plan, and explaining that under its terms, Father Diamond did not qualify.

After that, there was nothing in the file, no analysis, no notes, no memorandum, no indication that anyone at the Congregation had ever looked into Father Diamond's complaint. Father Bill Tuigg had learned that this was a typical Vatican method of action. Gather the facts and then wait, one year, two years, three years, a decade, a century. After all, time was on the Church's side, and it was amazing how many problems, when ignored, went away.

But this one had not gone away. Father Diamond was in Rome, demanding an answer to the complaint he had lodged against his bishop.

Examining the file documents, Father Bill Tuigg

could see that there was no pension plan in Nogaces in 1941 when Father Diamond, an infirm priest from Duluth, just over forty years of age, had transferred into the diocese. When the pension plan was established in the early sixties, it had an exclusion for late incardinations, men who had joined the Nogaces diocese after turning forty. By its technical terms, Bishop Manley was right. Father Diamond did not qualify for a pension from the Nogaces diocese.

But there was another issue here, the young priest thought. What about simple justice? Was it fair that a priest who had worked almost thirty years for a diocese would get nothing from it in his old age?

The young priest spent the rest of that day and the next drafting a decree for Cardinal Rooney's signature, instructing the Nogaces diocese to include Father Diamond in its pension plan on grounds of basic fairness.

He chose his words carefully, not wanting in any way to imply any fault on the part of the diocese. He knew that the decree would get nowhere if it made the diocese look bad. He quoted all of the relevant portions of the documents of the recent Vatican Council, especially *Presbyterorum Ordinis* on the rights of priests. He took frequent walks down the hall to confer with the Redemptorist friar who served as the canonical consultant to the Congregation, so that all his citations to canon law were correct.

When he was done, he had a document that he was proud of, one whose rotund phrases even the Italians in the Congregation would have to agree were as polished and as self-effacing as their own.

He showed it to Cardinal Rooney the following day, briefly reviewing the facts of the file with him. The Cardinal nodded approvingly as he read his young secretary's draft decree.

"Bill, this is fine work," the Cardinal said when

he had finished.

"Thank you, your Eminence," the young priest replied.

"But," Cardinal Rooney continued, "you and I are both still new here. I think before I sign this, I should check with the coetus when we meet the week after next."

"Oh," the young priest said, his shoulders slumped. The coetus was a group of senior officials in the Congregation, mostly Italians, all left over from the administration of the previous Cardinal Prefect. They met with the Cardinal once a month to discuss the workings of the Congregation, and the young priest often felt that their job was more to impede than to inform the Cardinal, making sure that this American in the papal curia did not become a bull in St. Peter's china shop.

"If you think you have to, your Eminence," the young priest said. "I did tell Father Diamond to stop back today."

"Today?" Cardinal Rooney asked, his eyebrows knit together in disbelief. "This is Rome, Bill, not Rocksburg. Nothing happens overnight in Rome. Why, I'm continually surprised that the Roman sun makes it up on a daily basis."

"I know, your Eminence, but I just thought that since Father Diamond had already waited over two years for an answer."

"Bill, we can't help that. Tell Father that we'll have an answer for him as soon as possible, and we shall not be as dilatory as the previous Cardinal Prefect. That will have to do," the Cardinal said as he put both hands flat on his desk, indicating that the topic was closed for now.

Father Diamond arrived very late that morning. He apologized to Bill Tuigg. "I was walking around in St. Peter's church and I forgot the time, Father. Gosh, that place is so big. I never saw a church so big. You know, they have a statue of St. Peter in that church, people have kissed the foot so much, his toes and even the laces on his shoes are all worn away."

Bill Tuigg could hardly believe the man's ingenuousness. He was disappointed to have to tell him that he could not keep his promise.

"Oh, well, I guess it was too much to hope for, Father. I'm sure that you tried," the old priest said. "Should I stop back later this week?"

"Father Diamond, the Cardinal wants to take this to his consultors, and they don't meet until the week after next. It won't be before then, and even then, there's no guarantee that they will reach a decision on your file immediately."

"But, Father, I will have to go home by then."

"I'm sorry, Father. I tried. I truly did."

"You know, Father, sometimes I think people just hope I will die so they won't have to answer my petition," the old priest said as he turned to leave.

"Father, that's not so. Cardinal Rooney asked me to tell you that he won't delay on this."

"All right, Father, if you say so," the aged priest said as he continued to walk away.

"I'll see that we write you as soon as there's a decision, Father," the young priest called after the old man as he walked out the large doors of the Congregation's offices.

In two weeks, when the Cardinal came back from the meeting of the coetus, he summoned his secretary into his office.

"Bad news, Bill, I'm afraid," he said as he placed Father Diamond's file carefully on his desk. "They wouldn't buy it, said it sets too dangerous a precedent, interfering in the financial affairs of a diocese."

"Are you happy with that, your Eminence?"

"Bill, hard as it may be for us to admit, they do have much more experience in these matters than we do. Maybe they know better," the Cardinal replied.

"And what about Father Diamond?" the young

priest asked. "He doesn't get his pension?"

"I know Bishop Manley, Bill. He was a contemporary of mine at the College in the thirties. He doesn't bend the rules, but he won't let a retired priest of his diocese starve, either."

"But, your Eminence, why should it be a matter of the bishop's charity when Father Diamond has worked for his pension?"

"Bill, I am put in mind of Jesus' words on how we ought to pray. Hound the Father until he gives in, is that it?"

"I'm sorry, your Eminence. I didn't mean to sound like that."

"Let me see what I can do, Bill," Cardinal Rooney said as he reached for the grey telephone that sat on his large desk. He picked up the receiver, dialed a number and spoke to one of the efficient Italian nuns who worked the Vatican switchboard. *"Per piacere, vorrei parlare col monsignore Manley, il vescovo di Nogaces, Nuevo Messico, negli Stati Uniti d'America, appen'e` possibile."* He told the sister to connect him with Bishop Manley in the States.

The call took ten minutes to go through, but the nun finally established a connection between Nogaces and Rome.

"Bob, this is Jack Rooney in Rome."

His secretary, sitting there in the Cardinal's office, could hear the squawk of Bishop Manley's voice coming from the receiver.

"Yes, Bob, I know it's very early in the morning over there, but you sound in fine fettle. How are you doing?" the Cardinal said.

"That's good. I'm doing well, too, Bob. The place agrees with me. Tell you why I'm calling, Bob. A priest of yours was in to see us the other week about his pension, Father Diamond."

More squawks from the line to Nogaces.

"Yes, Bob, I could see why you think he's a stubborn person, but then I've heard people say the same thing about you."

The Cardinal paused while Bishop Manley spoke.

"I understand, Bob, but thirty years is a long time to work in a diocese and not get anything for it when you retire, don't you think? Why don't you talk to your finance people and see if you can't squeeze something out of them? I would count it as a personal favor."

The young priest heard more screeches from Nogaces.

"Great, Bob. I genuinely appreciate that." There was a long pause while Bishop Manley continued talking.

"No, I didn't know that. That much? Are you sure?" the Cardinal said and then he broke into a loud roll of laughter.

"Fine, Bob, fine," the Cardinal said, "I won't forget what you're doing," and then he ended the call.

Cardinal Rooney looked up at his secretary who had observed the entire telephone exchange in complete incomprehension.

"Well, Bill, Bishop Manley has agreed to give Father Diamond a small pension based on his years of service."

"Thank you, your Eminence. I'm sure that Father Diamond will appreciate that."

The cardinal looked at him. "Do you really think so, Bill?"

"Your Eminence, it's all that he has, that and his social security."

"Bill, did Father Diamond ever tell you that exactly?"

"No, but he implied."

"Bill, what would you say if I told you that Father Diamond doesn't need his pension, that he is, in fact, quite wealthy?"

"Your Eminence, that can't be. You should have seen the place he was staying before I moved him to the German nuns. And his clothes ..."

"A lot of rich men are parsimonious, Bill. Father Diamond wouldn't be the first. Do your shoes have shoelaces, Bill?"

"Yes, your Eminence," the young priest said, looking down at his elegant black Italian leather shoes with their stylish pointed toes and fine, thin laces.

"See the ends, those little pieces of plastic that keep the laces from fraying, so you can tie your shoes in the morning? Father Diamond's father invented the machine that makes those little plastic tabs. Every time a pair of shoelaces is sold, at least in the United States, Father Diamond gets half a cent royalty. Think about that, Bill. It's a lot of money."

"Then why was he so worried about his pension?"

"It was undoubtedly a matter of principle, Bill. He felt that he had worked for it, and he had. But now at least I understand why Nogaces was being so difficult."

The young secretary sat there in disbelief, red-faced in front of his superior.

"I'm embarrassed, your Eminence."

"Don't be, Bill. How could you know?"

"I should have asked, but the way he acted, the way he dressed, I never doubted that he was as poor as a church mouse."

"Some mouse, Bill. Some Church," the Cardinal said, as he handed Father Diamond's papers back to his secretary. "I think we can mark this file happily closed. I wish they were all this easy."

XIV

Forgiven

He was hunched over the kitchen table, writing one of his lists. His mother came in from hanging clothes in the back yard and asked, good-naturedly, "What are you writing, Ernie?"

"Oh, nothing, Mom," he said as he slipped the note paper and stubby pencil into his pants pocket. And then he realized that he had done it again. He had lied to his mother. Was that a violation of the Fourth or the Eighth Commandments, he wondered. Probably both, he thought, and he went up to his bedroom, sat down at his study desk, and wrote it down both ways.

It had only been two days since his last confession and his list was already a long one. Last night he was watching *The Beverly Hillbillies* on television when he had the idea to go to his room and say some prayers, but he decided to keep watching TV instead. That was putting false gods before him, and so he had put a violation of the First Commandment on his list.

Sister Marie Francine, his sixth grade teacher, had said that. She had said that today, in the 1960's, we didn't worship golden cows, but instead we made idols of other things, like money or sex or

TV. He had made television his idol because he had preferred it to Jesus, and that was a sin, probably a mortal sin.

He had not taken the Lord's name in vain or said any bad words. He had never done that. He had thought some bad words, but he had never said them. He was not sure if thinking bad words without saying them was a sin. Probably it was, because you could sin by your thoughts as well as by your deeds. He left that a question mark on the Second Commandment.

He was always stepping on cracks in the sidewalks that looked like the cross of Jesus. That was blasphemy, dishonoring the cross of Christ, if anything was, and blasphemy was a definite sin against the Second Commandment. On his list, under the Second Commandment, he wrote down "sidewalk cracks," and beside it he had a lot of hash marks.

It was the middle of the week and he could only violate the Third Commandment, not honoring the Lord's Day, on Sundays so he was missing that sin on his list.

He had violated the Fourth Commandment a lot. He was always lying to his parents and disobeying them. They knew about his lists and told him to stop. But he had to keep his lists, otherwise he would be forgetting his sins and making a bad confession.

One Monday, on his way to school, when he was walking along the driveway to St. Teresa's Church to go to confession before early mass, he had met Father Donahue. Ernie liked Father Donahue because he would visit the parish school and talk with the children. The pastor, Father Larkin, never did that. Anyhow, on weekday mornings, before the early mass, only the young priests were in church to hear confessions.

Father Donahue asked Ernie if he was serving the early mass. Ernie said no, he was just there to go to confession. Father Donahue said, "Didn't the whole school just go to confession last Thursday for the First Friday Mass?" and asked Ernie why he was back so soon. Ernie knew that he could not lie to a priest, that was surely a mortal sin, so he explained about his list. As they walked towards the church, the priest asked to see Ernie's list and, after reading it, said that nothing there was a sin. He said that Ernie should skip confession and just go on to school.

Father Donahue had even called Ernie's parents and told them what Ernie was doing. He said that Ernie needed help, maybe a psychiatrist. But his parents couldn't afford a psychiatrist. Ernie had been lying to his folks about his lists ever since.

He thought that Father Donahue was wrong not to have heard his confession. A priest should never turn away a repentant sinner, Ernie thought. What if he had been killed by a car crossing the street to school that morning?

Then he would have died in a state of mortal sin and his damnation would have been all the fault of Father Donahue. The loss of a soul, what a terrible thing to have on your conscience, especially if you were a priest.

After that, he had decided that Father Donahue was probably not a very good priest. Father Donahue shouldn't have called his parents. That was very close to breaking the seal of confession.

Then he wondered what kind of sin it was to have evil thoughts about a priest. Ever since Father Donahue had refused him confession, Ernie was always having evil thoughts about him, imagining all the gruesome ways a priest could die.

He couldn't think of any commandment that exactly fit under. He knew that unjust anger was a sin against the Fifth Commandment, Thou shalt not kill, because it led to murder, so he listed his murderous thoughts about Father Donahue under the Fifth Commandment, but he underlined it, because, involving a priest, it had to be a serious sin.

His list was full of sins under the Fifth Commandment. He had a lot of vengeful thoughts about Father Donahue and other people that he wanted to die, mostly his classmates who had started calling him "Ernie Burnie," after he told some of them how afraid he was of the fires of hell that Sister Marie Francine talked about so often in class.

He was happy when the bishop had moved Father Donahue to another parish. The priest who replaced him, Father Capresi, had been kind. He had tried to explain to Ernie that mortal sins were very hard to commit, but then he ran away with a married lady from the parish, and that showed that he really didn't understand what sins were.

Father Denzer who had just come to St. Teresa's was another brand new priest, like Father Capresi. Every time that Ernie went to confession to him, Father Denzer told him this was a phase he was going through and he would grow out of it. Remember, he told him, the Lord is kind and merciful. Don't think about your sins so much. Just remember how much Jesus loves you.

But how could he do that? How could anybody who sinned as much as he did forget about his sins? What if he went to confession and left out a sin? Then that would be a bad confession and none of his sins would be forgiven. No, that did not seem like good advice.

And how could Jesus love anybody who sinned as much as he did? Ernie wondered what they were teaching these priests nowadays. It wasn't the same religion that Sister Marie Francine was teaching her sixth graders at St. Teresa's grade school. And Father Denzer had been trained at Rome, too. Maybe that was what Sister Marie Francine had meant when she said that the fish rots from the head down.

He had mentioned to Sister what Father Denzer had said in confession and Sister did not think very much of his advice either. He felt bad, telling on Father, and he thought that maybe it was a sin, but Sister Marie Francine said it was okay, because he was serving a higher good.

She even asked Ernie to tell her more things Father Denzer said that sounded like heresy. She was compiling a report for the bishop, she said. Ernie had to ask what "heresy" was and Sister explained that it was a denial of the sacred truths of the Faith, the truths she taught the children every day in their religion, English, history, geography and math classes.

Sister Marie Francine said that the whole Jesuit faculty at the Gregorian University in Rome where Father Denzer had studied was full of heretics who were trying to undermine the Church. The whole Vatican Council was the idea of the Jesuits and it had been the ruination of the Church, Sister said. She told Ernie that most of those Jesuits were probably communist sleeper agents.

The communists hated the Church for sure. Ernie knew that. Look what the communists did to the Church in Vietnam. Whole parishes had fled south on foot, led by their priests, when they had heard that North Vietnam was going communist. And the communists had tortured and persecuted the Catholics who had stayed behind.

Sister Marie Francine had read that part of Dr. Tom Dooley's book, *Deliver Us From Evil*, out loud to her class, how the Vietnamese communists had pounded nails, in imitation of Jesus' crown of thorns, into the head of a priest they caught teaching religion to children and then they slit his tongue so he couldn't preach anymore. Then they had pounded bamboo sticks into the children's ears, breaking their eardrums so they could never hear about Jesus again.

It had made the whole sixth grade class queasy, but Sister Marie Francine had said that no one had to listen if they didn't want to. Of course, no one was allowed to leave the room, either, so it was hard not to listen.

Ernie had walked home for lunch that day from St. Teresa's grade School, but he had had no appetite. His mom and his granddad, who lived with them, had asked what was wrong. But how could he tell them what was wrong? How could he tell them that he was so scared if the communists ever came to Rocksburg?

Sister Marie Francine had discussed that possibility with the children, but she had said that they shouldn't worry about it. When the communists came, Catholic grade school children would only have a short period of suffering. The communists wouldn't waste any time trying to brainwash them because of their Catholic education. They would be killed straight off, together with their priests and nuns. The communists would simply get the Catholic school enrollment lists and go house to house. The communists would have a better chance working with the faithless Protestants and Jews, she said.

Ernie hated the communists and he wanted to kill them. He put a lot more marks next to the Fifth Commandment on his list.

The Sixth Commandment was "Thou shalt not commit adultery." He was too young to commit adultery, but Ernie knew that it meant more than just that. The Sixth Commandment was impure thoughts and words and deeds, and he had a lot of those. It seemed like he always had those. He was a raving sex maniac.

He was in love with Ellie Greenock, who sat in front of him in school. She had just started wearing a training bra, and he could sometimes see the strap through the back of her blouse, at least when she wasn't wearing a sweater. He found himself hoping, "Ellie, please don't wear a sweater today," and that was a sin of desire, a ton of sins, because he stared at her back a lot.

This afternoon while he was working on his airplane models in the basement, he had sat back on his haunches and touched his rear end with the backs of his heels. He had touched his ass, he thought as soon as he did it. That was certainly an impure touching. And he had thought another bad word too.

Yesterday at school when Charlie Morrison farted, he felt his nose pucker. Oh my God, he thought, he had tried to smell it. He had tried to smell Charlie Morrison's fart. Farts were certainly impure. He had debated for a while if that could be a sin. He had never heard of sins of smell, but then he decided that there must be such a thing. After all, when you were dying, the priest anointed all five senses. Why would he anoint your nose if you couldn't sin with it? No, a priest wouldn't waste time like that, especially with a dying person. Smelling farts had to be an impure act forbidden by the Sixth Commandment, so it went on his list, too.

Had he stolen anything, he wondered, violating the Seventh Commandment? Well, he had looked at Ellie Greenock's math homework yesterday, and then when he did his own, some of the answers were the same. He had stolen Ellie's work. That was another sin, pure and simple. He better put it down.

He was always lying to his parents about his lists, so he put a lot of hash marks beside the Eighth Commandment, "Thou shalt not bear false witness."

Had he broken the Ninth Commandment and coveted anybody's wife? There were some actresses on TV that he really liked. He was sure that they were somebody's wives, probably second or third wives in Hollywood. Sister Marie Francine said Hollywood was the sin capital of the world. Still they were married women and he had desired them. He put more marks down besides "coveting wives" on his list under the Ninth Commandment.

What about coveting anybody's property, the Tenth Commandment? Well, he wanted Billy Zimmerman's bike and Walt Cushner's baseball glove. That was two right there. He added these to his list.

Then he went on to the Six Precepts of the Church and the Seven Deadly Sins. When he was done, his list was two pages long. It was time to go to confession again. But it was afternoon. He could not get to confession until next morning on his way to school.

What if he should die before then? Some of these sins on his list were definitely mortal sins. He would go to hell. He thought about what sister Marie Francine had said about the fires of hell and he put his head down on his desk and he started to cry.

His granddad, who had the bedroom next to him, heard him crying and knocked on the door.

"What's the matter, Ernie?" he asked.

"Nothing, Pappy. Nothing's wrong."

His granddad came in and sat on the bed. "You've been crying a lot lately, Ernie," he said. "Why? You're only twelve years old. What could be worrying you so much?"

"I can't talk about it, Pappy. It's a secret."

"Why is it a secret, Ernie? What kind of secret?"

"It's about my sins, Pappy. That's why it's secret."

"Your sins? Ernie, you're a good boy. What sins do you have?"

"I can't say, Pappy. I'm only supposed to tell my sins to a priest."

"I wish you could talk to me about it. It worries me to see you so unhappy like this."

"I can't, Pappy."

"Only a priest, then?"

Ernie nodded his head.

"Why don't you come with me. I know a good priest you can talk to."

Ernie followed his granddad downstairs and they both put their coats on.

In the kitchen, Ernie's mother asked them where

they were going. She could see the tears fresh on her son's face and she had an idea what was wrong.

"I'm taking the boy to the monastery. He needs to talk to a good priest and Father Larkin's the man."

Ernie's mother pulled her father aside. "Dad, are you sure that's a good idea? They took Father Larkin babbling like a baby away from the rectory. They say he's at the monastery for a rest cure. The stroke, it did something to his brain."

"For fifteen years, when this family needed a priest, Father Sparky Larkin was there. He's a good man. He'll help Ernie, you'll see."

She heard the tone of reproach in the old man's voice, and she knew that her father did not think she and her husband were doing enough to help her son out of his depression. She was at her wit's end and she agreed that they could go.

The monastery sat high on a hill overlooking the Conemaugh River and the steel mills that lined it. Downtown Rocksburg was on the other side.

The old man rang the monastery's bell and was led into the front waiting room with his grandson.

"We've come to see Father Larkin," he announced.

The mousy young man who answered the door asked if they had an appointment.

"No, we don't. But just tell Father Larkin that Jim O'Hara is here with his grandson. He'll see us."

The young man nodded and left through a set of heavy wooden doors. He came back in a few minutes and asked them to follow him.

He led them through the doors, around a corner and up a very steep set of stairs to a long, wide, dimly-lit corridor. He knocked at the third door on the right and told Father Larkin that his visitors were here.

Sparky Larkin opened the door, smiling. He was wearing sports pants, a polo shirt and a golfing sweater. He looked the picture of health.

"Father Larkin," Jim O'Hara began, "it's very

good to see you. Thanks for taking the time to see us."

"Jim, anytime. Not many of the old parishioners from St. Teresa's make it over here. Maybe they don't know that I'm taking visitors. But you let them know it, Jim. You'll let them know it, won't you?"

"Sure, Father. Be glad to."

"Is this your grandson you have with you? You're an altar boy at St. Teresa's, aren't you? Let's see, Eugene, isn't it?"

"No, Father, Ernie."

"Ernie, that's right. But I was close, wasn't I?"

The priest turned and winked at Jim O'Hara. "I tried to learn all of the boy's names. I did."

"I'm sure you did, Father. It's Ernie that wants to talk to you."

"Certainly. Come on in," the priest said as he threw open the door to his room.

As they were about to enter the priest's room, Ernie looked up at his grandfather. "This is secret, Pappy."

"Oh, of course. I forgot. Is there some place I could wait, Father? The boy wants to talk to you alone."

"Sure, Jim. At the end of the hall. A big sitting room, newspapers, magazines, TV, bowls of hard candy and all. You just make yourself at home there. Tell them you're my guest."

Sparky Larkin asked Ernie to sit on the bed. He took the easy chair next to it. "Now what is it you want to talk about, son?"

"It's my sins, Father."

"Your sins?"

"Yes. I have a lot of them. Can this be a confession, Father?" Ernie asked.

"If you want it to be," Sparky Larkin replied.

"I do, Father. I want to get everything off my conscience."

"Well fine, then," said the priest. He opened

his nightstand, removed a long purple sacramental stole and put it around his neck. "Why don't you start?"

Ernie knelt down in front of Sparky Larkin's chair and said, "Bless me, Father, for I have sinned."

"Hold on there young man. There's no need to be so formal. You just keep sitting on the bed there."

Ernie looked up and said, "Are you sure?"

"Sure," Sparky Larkin nodded and pointed to the bed.

Ernie wasn't certain you could make a good confession without kneeling down, but he figured the priest must know. So he sat back on the bed and continued, "It has been two days since my last confession." He consulted his list and said, "Since that time, I have placed other gods before me, once. I have blasphemed six times."

"Wait a second, there, young man, would you? How is it you've taken other gods and blasphemed? You're not cussing at your age, I hope."

Ernie told him about watching TV instead of praying and stepping on sidewalk cracks that looked like the cross of Christ.

"Jesus, Mary and Joseph, those aren't sins," Sparky Larkin said.

"They're not?" Ernie looked up hopefully, but then he had a thought and he was upset again. "But I thought they were sins when I did them, Father. If I thought they were sins when I did them, that's enough, isn't it? Sister Marie Francine is always telling us about the girl who thought it was a mortal sin to wear striped socks. She said that even though the girl was mistaken, every time she wore striped socks, she committed a mortal sin, because she thought that it was a mortal sin and she did it willfully."

"That's a whole lot of theology that Sister's trying to give you in a small, little example, young man.

There may be a wee bit of truth there, I suppose, but not very much. Sister shouldn't be so strict with you. And what's that paper you're reading from?"

"That's my list, Father. I keep a list so I won't forget any sins. I wouldn't want to make a bad confession if I forgot any sins."

"Eugene, at your age you can't have that many sins to remember."

"Ernie, Father. But I do. I have so many."

Ernie told him about disobeying his parents and his hateful thoughts about others. Sparky Larkin nodded his head. Then Ernie told him about his impure thoughts and deeds.

"What are you doing? Are you touching yourself down there?" Sparky Larkin asked.

"No, Father. I wouldn't do that."

"Well, what then?"

Ernie told him about leaning back on his heels and about Ellie Greenock's bra strap and about smelling Charlie Morrison's farts.

"None of those are sins," Sparky Larkin said.

"But, Father, when I did them ..."

"I know, you thought they were sins, and Sister Mary Whatsername says if you think it's a sin, then it is. Well, Sister doesn't know. Listen to me. None of these things you're telling me are sins. Sins means you've done something to hurt someone. Have you ever done that, Ernie?"

"No, Father. I would never hurt anyone."

"Listen to me, then. That's what sins are. We can't see Jesus in this world. He's gone away to heaven. We can only see our brothers and sisters that He's left behind. The way we hurt Jesus isn't by sidewalk cracks or watching television or by our thoughts. The way we hurt Jesus is when we do something bad to another person. Do you understand?"

"I think so, Father."

"And about those impurities."

"Yes, Father?"

"It's the same way. Impurities means using other people for our own pleasure, without caring about them. Have you ever done that with your little friend who sits in front of you, what's her name?"

"She's Ellie, Ellie Greenock. But I haven't, Father."

"No, I didn't think so. Now what else have you got to tell me?"

Ernie tore up his list and put the paper scraps back in his pants pocket. "Nothing, Father."

"Fine, that's fine," Sparky Larkin said. "Every time, before you're thinking about going to confession, I want you to use this rule. It took me a long time to learn this rule, Ernie, but after my stroke, in the hospital, flat on my back, I spent a lot of time alone with my thoughts and my God, and I learned a few things, lying there helpless. So here's what I want you to do. Before you go to confession, I want you to think what people you've hurt, on purpose, not by your thoughts, cause thinking's not sins, but only by something you actually did. And if you haven't hurt anyone, there's no need for confession because you haven't done any sins. Do you understand?"

"Yes, Father."

"And do you promise me that's what you'll do?"

"Yes, Father."

"No going back? No going back to those little things Sister Mary Whomever was saying? I'm sure she was trying to be helpful, but none of those things she was telling you are sins."

"Yes, Father."

"Now I'm going to give you absolution, even though you don't really need it, but it will make you happy and it brings you grace regardless. We could all use a little grace."

Sparky Larkin reached out and touched the boy's head with his left hand while he quickly said the Latin words and made the sign of the cross over him with his right hand. When he was done, he said, "Now, for your penance, Ernie, please recite for me Father Larkin's rule."

"Father, the only way we sin is when we hurt other people on purpose."

"Good, Ernie. Are you happy now?"

"Yes, Father. I feel lots better."

"Ernie, you are truly without sin. So, can I ask you a favor, Ernie without sin?"

"Sure, Father. What's that?"

"Will you forgive my sins?

"What sins do you have, Father?"

"I was a hard man, Ernie. I hurt people without hesitating. I neglected to see Jesus in them. I took advantage of them, I was mean to them, I lied to them, I lied about them. Do you forgive me my sins, Ernie?"

"Sure, Father, if you're truly sorry."

"I am, son. Thank you. I am truly, truly sorry."

XV

The Life of the World to Come

The jangling of the telephone beside his bed startled Joe Denzer from his sleep. He had played a game of pick-up basketball in the high school gym after the Catholic Youth Organization meeting that night and he was very tired.

In his dream, he was in Rome again, strolling down the Via Giulia, on his way to class at the Gregorian University. It was a walk he had taken many times, past the Renaissance palazzos, with their intriguing courtyards of trickling fountains, tall thin cypress trees and broken Roman statues. He remembered walking down the street, thinking what am I doing here, I should be in Rocksburg, and then the telephone woke him.

It was the night nurse from the Rocksburg Veterans' Hospital. A dying soldier needed the last rites, she said.

The massive hospital structure stood on top of a hill overlooking St. Teresa's parish, and, on the regular chaplain's day off, the priests from St. Teresa's covered for him.

He dressed hurriedly in his black slacks and clerical shirt, threw on his heavy coat and walked through the drifting snow to the parish church.

From the tabernacle, he took a consecrated wafer and put it into a golden pyx that he carried on a chain inside his shirt. He had brought the sacramental oils with him from the rectory.

His hands trembled as he handled the host. This was the first time that he has been asked to anoint a dying man.

The snow plows were out, with their looping yellow lights, sweeping the snow from the city streets. He crept behind one in his car all the way to the top of the hill where the hospital was.

The Veterans' Hospital was decorated for Christmas. A large tree, hung with plastic ornaments, stood in the lobby. Tinsel garlands drooped down each hallway.

"He's in here, Father," the night nurse said as she pushed against the wide wooden door to the hospital room on the eighth floor.

The light from the corridor slanted across the bed and half a man in it, inside the darkened room.

The hospital corridor was quiet. The nurses and orderlies went silently about their rounds.

Inside the room, illumined only by a small night light, was the person Joe Denzer had been called to see.

He was a young man. Joe Denzer was surprised at that. He had expected someone older.

In the bed, under the sheets, Joe Denzer could see the stumps of the man's legs. The nurse had told him that they had been amputated above the knee to stop the gangrene but it hadn't worked.

"This is a brave one, Father," she had said when the priest arrived on the floor. "He's been putting off his pain-killers because he wanted to talk to you."

The priest bent over the bed. "I'm Father Joe Denzer. What's your name?" he asked the man.

"I'm Ben, Father.

"How are you doing, Ben?"

"Not too good, Father."

"I'm sorry to hear that. They said you wanted to see a priest. Do you want to go to confession and be anointed, Ben?"

"I don't think. I mean the other priest, the regular chaplain, he did that yesterday."

"Oh," Joe Denzer said. He thought he had been called for an anointing, and now he wondered why he was there. He was tired.

"I want to, I want to just talk. Is that okay, Father?"

"Sure," he said. "Whatever you want."

"Father, I'm afraid bad. I don't want to die."

"Ben, that's just human. I'm afraid to die, too. But who says you're dying?"

The night nurse had told him over the telephone, when she called him, that it was only a matter of hours, and he did not mean to lie to the man, but the person in the bed was alive and talking, and it was only natural to question. Perhaps it wasn't so. Who knows? Doctors weren't always right.

"I know it, Father. Yesterday, they moved me to a room by myself. That's the sign, otherwise you're in the ward. They don't want nobody else to see, so they put you in by yourself. 'Sides, the other guy, the regular chaplain, he gave me the last rites. That's a sure sign, innit?"

"No, that's all changed. We don't even call it the last rites anymore. It's the sacrament of the sick now." Joe Denzer rambled on, as if the change in nomenclature made after the Second Vatican Council could somehow convince the man.

"Okay, Father, I guess you know."

The simple confidence overwhelmed him. In the first months of his priesthood, Joe Denzer was just learning to accept the unquestioning trust that people placed in their priests.

"That's right, I know. Just relax now. It'll be okay. I brought you," his voice faltered, "I brought you communion."

"I already did this morning, Father."

"That's okay. You can go again. It's the next day already."

"Maybe. I don't know."

"What?"

"I don't know."

"Ben, are you all right?"

The man seemed to be turning a ghoulish yellow.

"Could you hand me the ice chips, Father? It's there on the night stand."

Joe Denzer took the paper cup and held it to the man's lips.

"Thanks, Father."

"If you went to confession yesterday, I'm sure it's all right to receive now," Joe Denzer said.

"There's something I been feeling, Father. I don't know. I didn't tell the guy yesterday."

Joe wondered what secret sin the man might have withheld. Whatever it was, it could not be as serious as the man thought.

"You can tell me. I'm here to help you. That's why I came."

"I'm scared, Father. I don't want to die."

"Sure. It's okay to be scared. It's normal. There's nothing wrong with that. But they tell me you're a very brave man. This medal here means something, doesn't it?"

Joe Denzer touched the Purple Heart medallion that was propped up in a box on the man's bed stand.

"That's for being wounded, Father. You don't have to be brave to be wounded, just unlucky."

"I'm sure you are brave."

"Nah, Father, it was an accident ..."

"How'd it happen?"

"We was out on patrol. I wasn't even point. I don't know how it happened. There must a been a wire or something I didn't see. I don't know. It was a booby trap. The gooks use lots of them. I heard the explosion and then I tried to run but I didn't have no feet. Then a firefight started, and the choppers, they couldn't get in. I was medevacked the next day, but I was too late. They operated stateside, and cut me …" His voice trailed off as he started to cry.

Joe Denzer did not know what to do. He watched the tears stream down the man's face and wished that he could do something to stem them.

"Listen, it's going to be all right. You are a brave man," he finally said. "You should be proud, Ben. People like me, we owe a lot to you."

"How old are you, Father? You look my age."

"I'm twenty-five. You?"

"Twenty-two. Were you there, Father?"

"No. I was out of the country."

"You didn't go to Sweden or Canada, did you, Father? You weren't one of them?"

"No, I wasn't one of them. I went to the seminary right after high school, so I missed the draft in college. After that, the diocese sent me to Rome to study theology. I was away for most of the war. I've only been home a few months."

It was during his seminary years in Rome that the war had really exploded. He could remember walking by the Piazza Dodici Apostoli on his way to classes at the Gregorian University when the piazza was full of Italians protesting the war. Their red banners and anti-American slogans had angered him. What did a rag-tag band of Italian communists know about the burdens of being the world's greatest power? We should never have saved them from fascism, he thought more than once as he hurried by the protesters crowding the Roman streets.

But even his classmates at the Greg, seminarians from England and West Germany, rode him about the war. What, they asked, do you think you are doing there? Why have you made yourselves the world's policeman? Don't you realize this is a civil war, a war that wouldn't even be happening if the Americans weren't there?

But that's all it was, theoretical conversations

with other seminarians in a Roman coffee bar. All the while he was defending his country with the fervor of an expatriate, he never thought that what he was really talking about was people dying, people like this very young soldier in the bed beside him.

He suddenly felt so guilty, as if he had something to confess, and perhaps he did, he thought.

"You were lucky. It was terrible over there."

"I'm sure. I'm sure I can't imagine."

"It was like hell. I don't think hell can be worse than that. I figure, Father, I'm not going to go to hell, I already been there."

"No, of course not. Don't even think that way."

"But I'm afraid, Father."

"It's okay to be afraid, Ben. That's not a sin. There's nothing wrong with that."

"No, Father. I don't think it's okay to think what I'm thinking. The other guy, the regular chaplain, says that if I die, I'll see God. I'll be with him. But you know, Father, you know?"

"What?"

"I don't want to see God."

"Sure you do. We all do"

"No, Father, not me. I hate him. I hate God."

"Why?"

"Why? Why? Look what he done to me. I never had a life. Right out of high school I went to the service. Six months of training and then overseas. The only girls I ever had were the whores in Saigon. I don't know nothing. I never had a life."

"Your life's not over yet. You don't know what's in store."

"Nah, Father, don't lie. I know."

"No, I wouldn't lie."

"You know, Father, you're a bit like me, I mean, besides our age and all."

"What's that?"

"We both swore off women. We'll never have another one."

"No, I guess not. I mean, I won't."

"Father, look at me. Who'd wanna?"

"You never know. Lots of women."

"I told the other guy, I tried to jerk off. I tried, but all I could see was my legs weren't there, and I couldn't."

"You're not well. You're taking medicine. Who knows after?"

"Father, there ain't gonna be no after. Did you ever, Father?"

"What?"

"Jerk off. Don't lie to me, Father."

"Maybe. Sometimes. When I was younger. Not now."

"I used to, a lot. I told the other guy, but no more. I can't no more. I look at my legs, where they was, and I can't."

"That's not the most important thing, Ben. There are other things."

"No, Father. I need that. Do you think it's a sin, Father?"

"What?"

"To hate God."

"I can't say. A lot depends. It's not an easy answer." Joe Denzer paused, struggling for the words. "I think," he finally said, "I think that God loves us so much that we're allowed to hate Him."

"We are?"

"I think so. I mean, he gave us everything. Our lives, this world, and when we tried to throw it all away, He gave us His Son."

"So if I hate God, I'm not going to hell?"

"No, you won't go to hell. It's like I said. It's okay if we hate Him. He understands. Listen, did your folks ever yell at you or punish you when you were a kid?"

"Sure, lots of times. I was a hellraiser, Father."

"And when they punished you, did you ever get mad at them and say you hated them?"

"Yeah. Kids do that a lot."

"Do you think they ever believed you, that you hated them?"

"No."

"That's how it is with God. He doesn't believe you when you say you hate Him."

"My folks were just here till yesterday. My dad had to go back for his job. I miss them, Father. I wish they were here."

"Where are you from, Ben?"

"Near Youngstown. You, Father?"

"Right here in Rocksburg. Is that what was bothering you?"

"What?"

"That if you hated God you would go to hell?"

"Yeah."

"Okay. So don't worry about that. God understands."

"I wish I could be sure."

"You can be sure. I wouldn't lie to you."

"What's the other guy mean, that if I, you know, I'll be with God?"

Joe Denzer had not expected this conversation. He thought that he would just come to the hospital, say the words that accompanied the sacramental gestures and be done. But the soldier in the bed deserved, needed, an answer. Joe tried to recall what he had learned in the seminary about heaven and the Eternal Presence, but it all seemed so irrelevant now. And then, he was aware of a voice. Was he simply hearing his own thoughts, or did it come from somewhere else? "In my Father's house there are many mansions, and I will be there, preparing a place for you."

"You know, Ben," he started to say, thinking slowly as he spoke, "I think heaven, I think heaven is like coming home after you've been away for a long time. Did that ever happen to you, when you were in training, and you were away from home for a while, and then you went back to your parents' house? Remember how good it felt to be home, with all the people who loved you, waiting for you, caring for you?"

"Yeah."

"I think that's what it's like to be in heaven. It's like going home, after being away a long time, to be with Someone who loves you."

"I like that. That's good. Going home. Father, if you don't mind I'm gonna call the nurse now."

"Okay."

The man pushed the buzzer on the chord tied to his bed rail, and soon the night nurse looked in and then came back with a hypodermic needle. The man was crying in pain and then he had the injection and he was mostly quiet again. Joe Denzer sat in the chair next to the man's bed during the procedure. At the end of it, the man turned to the priest. "Father, could you do me a favor?"

"Sure. What's that?"

"Hold my hand."

Joe Denzer reached out and grabbed the soldier's hand. He sat there, in silence by his bedside, holding onto the man's hand and watching in the shadows, waiting for the man to say something more. But the man only whimpered and then he was asleep.

Joe Denzer relaxed into the chair, keeping the sleeping man's hand in his, listening to him breathe in fitful starts. The next thing the priest knew, the night nurse was shaking him. "Wake up, Father. Wake up."

"I fell asleep."

"Yes."

There were orderlies in the room now, putting the body, wrapped in a sheet, onto a gurney. Joe Denzer stopped them and slowly made the Sign of the Cross over the dead man, whispering the words of absolution that would see him home. Then he let them take Ben from the room.

"I can't believe I fell asleep," he said to the nurse. "He needed me and I fell asleep."

The night nurse turned to him. Her eyes were brimming with tears. "You were here," she said. "He wanted you and you were here. Isn't that what priests are for?"

Driving back to the rectory, Joe Denzer felt the chill of the metal pyx against his skin. He remembered then that the consecrated wafer, the Body of Christ, was with him still, in its golden container. He had never given the man communion. It had been his first anointing and he had not done anything right.

XVI

Return to Rome, 1995

Bill Tuigg, the bishop of Rocksburg, did not like to be kept waiting. A highly organized man himself, with a seemingly immense capacity for work, he never kept others waiting. After all, he thought, their time is as important as mine.

But he had to admit, if he had to wait, this was an impressive place to do so, with its patterned marble floor, its coffered ceiling and the Italian renaissance paintings on the walls. He had spent a good part of his life here in Rome, fours years as a theology student at the North American College and then ten more as a young priest, secretary to John Cardinal Rooney, in the Vatican's Congregation for Clergy.

He wondered who was sitting there now, in his old office at the Congregation, in his old chair. And had they ever air-conditioned the place? In the years he was at the Congregation, the answer to Rome's summer heat was simply to close up shop from the end of July through mid-September. The world and its affairs could wait. It was just too hot to do any work in Rome, and if the rest of the world did not understand that, well, Rome would always be Rome, and they should.

Such spare time as he had as the Cardinal's

secretary—which was not much, since Rooney was
a famous workaholic himself—he spent studying
for a doctorate in Sacred Theology at the Gregorian
University. He was one of the very few American
bishops who actually had a real, not an honorary,
Doctorate in Sacred Theology. That distinction had
earned him a post on the American bishops' doc-
trinal committee and, last year, an appointment by
the pope as a consultor to the Congregation for the
Doctrine of the Faith.

Tuigg was in Rome now for a meeting of the
consultors. At the end of yesterday's session, Cardinal Hildebrand, the Prefect of the Congregation,
had whispered in his ear, in his slightly accented
English, "The Holy Father would like to see you
tomorrow. Call Monsignor Dziwisz and arrange a
time."

He asked Cardinal Hildebrand if he knew why
the pope wanted to see him, and in reply all the
Cardinal did was to put his forefinger to his lips
and smile.

And now he was in the apostolic palace, waiting on the Holy Father, wondering why. Lately
his normally tightly-regulated life had been full
of surprises. On the day before he was to leave for
Rome for the consultors' meeting, his secretary in
the Rocksburg chancery rang him and said there
was a Mr. Capresi there to see him. Once the best of
friends, he had not seen or heard from Tony Capresi
since he had left the priesthood, almost twenty-five
years ago.

Although the visit was unexpected and un-
scheduled, he knew that he had to make time for
his old friend. As Tony entered his office and sat
down, Bill Tuigg wondered at Tony's grey hair.
Then he realized that he might be looking in the
mirror. Somehow, without his noticing it, his own
hair had thinned and silvered. Despite their age,
seeing Tony again made him feel as if they were
twenty-three year olds again, sitting in a car at the

Park and Eat, pondering life's improbabilities. Bill could tell that Tony needed or wanted something. He wondered what it could be.

"Tony, you should have called. What brings you here?"

"Our oldest daughter, Olivia, is going to be a freshman at the University of Rocksburg, and I drove her up from South Carolina for the start of the school year. Being in town, I thought maybe I could stop by and thank you, since I never did, for your help with my laicization."

"Thank me? That was decades ago, Tony," Bill Tuigg said, thinking there must be something else.

"The Rocksburg Tribunal wouldn't give Connie her annulment from her husband, you know."

"No, I didn't." Was that it? Did Tony want him to nudge the Tribunal some way? He should know better.

"Years of going to mass and not being able to go to communion. It kind of makes you feel guilty."

"The tribunal has its rules, Tony. You know that."

"That's not why I'm here, Bill. Joe, Connie's husband, never did get his life back together. He started drinking and lost his job at the university, then a few years ago he ran his car into a pylon on Route 22. It was a lousy way to die."

"I am sorry to hear that," Bill Tuigg said, wondering where this was going.

"But it meant that Connie and I could finally get our marriage validated in the Church. Our pastor down in Myrtle Beach did the ceremony in the rectory."

"So you've been in South Carolina since you left?"

"It's where we ended up. We couldn't come back here. Both of our families were madder than hell with us. They were for years, till the grandkids started coming, and then everything changed. Funny thing, neither of us had any real job skills, so Connie started walking dogs for all the tourists down on the beach. I always thought it was strange that people would take their pets on vacation, but Connie is really good with animals."

"And you?"

"We opened a full-time kennel. I know, me at a kennel. Go figure. But Connie helped me get past my fear of animals. We do pretty well there. The vacationers have lots of pets, and more and more, the high class beach condos don't allow animals, but their owners still want them nearby."

"Tell me about your children."

"Two daughters. They both look like Connie, thank goodness. Olivia's the oldest. She's the freshman at Rocksburg. Connie's folks and mine are in good health, so she has her grandparents nearby for any first year college crisis, plus a little bit of home cooking. Olimpia is still in high school, deciding whether to be a veterinarian or an actress." Okay, Bill thought, the ask is coming soon.

"Bill, I was wondering if you could help me?"

"What would that be?"

"The parish over from us is looking for a director of religious education. I have a masters in theology, from the seminary, and I was wondering if you could give me a reference? A letter from a bishop would mean a lot. And I could finally get back to doing what I was trained to do."

So that was it. Poor Tony. He was still conflicted. He could never really leave the Church. It was a harsh mistress. And he obviously wasn't as happy at that kennel as he said.

The pope's time was important, Bill Tuigg knew, a bit more important than the time of a bishop from a small American diocese. He paced back and forth and occasionally parted the window curtains to look down into the courtyard below. He could not sit still in the uncomfortable baroque chairs placed around the ante-room for visitors. There were some

Swiss guards on watch down in the courtyard, and there were two guards on either side of the heavy wooden doors to the pope's study. He heard the door open and Cardinal Hildebrand walked out. The Cardinal came over to him and, even though they had spent most of yesterday in meetings together, asked how he was.

"Well, your Eminence. And you?"

"Tired, your Excellency, tired. This position is no longer what I accepted. The world has changed. The Church has changed. It's time for an old priest to rest. Please, listen to the Holy Father," he said in parting.

"Listen to the Holy Father," Bill Tuigg thought to himself. What else would a bishop do? And then he heard himself being summoned by Monsignor Dziwisz into the papal study.

He remembered the last time he had been there. It was just after John Rooney had died. He had accompanied the cardinal's body back to Boston, where he was buried beside his mother and father. Then he had returned to Rome to clean out their apartment. On his last day in Rome, as a courtesy, he had asked to see the pope, to say good-bye.

"So, you are leaving me," the pope had said.

"It is time to go home, Holy Father. I have spent more than a third of my life in Rome. I need to go back to Rocksburg. I need to do what I was ordained for, something priestly."

"And what I am doing here is not priestly?" the pope had asked.

Bill Tuigg's face turned a bright red. "No, I did not mean that, Holy Father. But I would like to be in a parish, among the people," he said, realizing that he was digging himself a deeper hole as the pope smiled awkwardly.

"Fine, you are a priest of Rocksburg. You should be with the people of Rocksburg," the pope had said.

But fate had played a trick on Bill Tuigg almost as

soon as he was home. During a game of handball on the seminary courts, Don Himmelreich, the rector of St. Gregory's, the Rocksburg diocesan seminary, had collapsed from a mild heart attack. He asked to take a lighter load, to step down from the rectorship of St. Gregory's. Bill Tuigg, newly returned from Rome, with his doctorate in theology, was the logical replacement and Marty Phelan, Rocksburg's aging bishop, had appointed him seminary rector.

Although he had wanted parish life, St. Gregory's was a pleasant assignment. Being around the seminary students made him feel younger than he was, and the time flew by. One day, seven years later, sitting in his rector's study, reading a volume of Rahner's *Sacramentum Mundi* and preparing for the Christology class he was about to teach, the telephone rang. It was the papal nuncio. Bishop Phelan, old and ill, had asked for a co-adjutor bishop to help him with the see. The nuncio told him that the pope's choice had fallen on him. Bill Tuigg never did get to that parish.

The pope was sitting at his desk, but he got up when Bill Tuigg entered and offered his hand in greeting. "Thank you for coming on such short notice, Bill," the pope said in his very good English.

"Certainly, Holy Father. It is not often that the bishop of a small diocese gets summoned to see Your Holiness outside the quinquennial visit."

Bill Tuigg had known the pope for a long time. As the archbishop of Krakow, the pope had visited Rocksburg, which had a large Polish population. The archbishop was staying with Father Carl Kalina at Visitation of the Blessed Virgin Mary Parish in the Little Poland section of Rocksburg, but had stopped by the chancery to pay his respects to the bishop of Rocksburg, John Rooney. As usual, Rooney was running late, and Bill Tuigg, Rooney's young secretary, had spent a pleasant half hour talking with the archbishop until Bishop Rooney was available. To the surprise of the world, the archbishop of Krakow had been elected pope in the last year of John Rooney's time in Rome. Those years had not been easy since Rooney spent them in a wheel chair after serial hip surgery operations in the United States.

"So, you have returned to Rome?" the Holy Father said.

"Only for a meeting, your Holiness. I go back to Rocksburg tomorrow."

"Yes, I remember Rocksburg, and Father Kalina. How is he?"

"He is on pension, living in the retired priests' home, your Holiness. The last time I saw him he was doing quite well. He has outlived all of his classmates, but he's happy and in decent health."

"I would like you to stay."

"In Rocksburg, Holiness?" Bill Tuigg deflected the pope's obvious meaning. "That would make me very happy."

"No, I mean here, in Rome."

"In what capacity, Holiness?"

"Cardinal Hildebrand has not talked to you? He would like to return to Austria. You would be his successor."

"No, he has not talked to me, Holiness."

"But it is logical, no? You have a doctorate in Sacred Theology. You have the experience of working in the Curia. You are already a consultor to the Congregation for Doctrine of the Faith," he paused. "And then there is the American problem," the pope said. He rifled a stack of manila folders on his desk. "Do you know what these are?"

"No, Holiness."

"These are files from the Doctrine of the Faith. Files of priests, almost all Americans, who have molested young people. They require only my signature to be dismissed from the priesthood."

"I am aware of the problem, Holiness. Even in my own diocese ..."

Bill Tuigg still had tremors from that terrible day a month before he had left for the consultors meeting in Rome, when his chancellor, Monsignor Joe Denzer, had walked into his office with Sister DeeDee Moriarity, head of diocesan social services. There was a crisis, they told him. Sister DeeDee had just met with a family from St. Edmund Campion parish. Paul Lorenz, their pastor, had befriended the family, had showered them with attention, and then had taken advantage of their trust to sexually abuse their ten-year-old son. It was a nightmare.

"Joe, have you talked with Lorenz?"

"I just got off the phone, Bishop."

"And?"

"He says he was drunk and can't recall anything."

"But we're talking about more than one time here, right? Was he drunk all the time?"

Joe Denzer shrugged. There was no answer.

"How often was he alone with the child?"

"Often," Sister DeeDee said. "The parents really trusted him. He took the boy out to the movies, for ice cream, and obviously more ..."

"Do you believe them, Sister?"

"They seem very credible, Bishop. There's no reason to make this up. And from what Monsignor Denzer says, the pastor's not really denying anything."

"What do you want us to do, Bishop?" Joe Denzer asked.

"Call the cops."

Sister DeeDee interjected. "The family doesn't want that. That's why they came to us. They are afraid of any publicity for their son. They just want Lorenz removed from the parish and kept away from other children."

"Then let me talk to them," Bill Tuigg said. "We can't keep something like this under wraps. Joe,

have you talked with Art Darner? This is a canonical crime, too."

"No, I haven't."

"Well, talk to him. I want Lorenz out of the
parish today, suspended, and talk to Darner in the
tribunal and get a canonical process started."

Bill Tuigg had met with the family, against the
advice of his lawyers who told him that all contact
with the family should be avoided lest he make a
damaging admission of liability that could be used
against the diocese in a civil lawsuit.

"But these are my people," Bill Tuigg had said.

"Better to think of them as future plaintiffs,
Bishop," one of his lawyers had said.

"I can't do that. The Church has harmed these
people. They need our care, not our disregard."

"We can only tell you the risks, Bishop. You decide
whether to take them or not," the other lawyer added.

Bill Tuigg had decided to take the risk. He had
gone to the family's home for dinner. His heart
broke when he walked in the front door and saw
the little boy, sitting on the living room couch between his parents.

The first thing he said was, "I am so sorry."
And then they embraced and cried together.

With the family's consent, the diocese had
reported Lorenz to the authorities. He had been
arrested and, unable to make bail, was in prison
now awaiting his trial. In a few years, his file would
probably be on the pope's desk.

It had been the worst experience of his life. The
press had been all over him. What did he know
about Father Lorenz and when? And what was the
Church asking of him now? To deal with child sex
abuse cases from all over the world?

That one case had been so hard. How could he
do dozens, hundreds? A part of his heart would
fragment with every one.

"What you ask is a terrible responsibility, Holy

Father. Can I please have some time to think, and to pray?

"How could I ask you not to pray or to think?"

"I will delay my return to Rocksburg, your Holiness. Will tomorrow be all right?"

"The Church works in eternities, Bill. Tomorrow will be all right."

He took the elevator down to the San Damaso courtyard, was saluted by the Swiss guard and walked down the street and out through the Porta Sant'Anna. A quick right and he was in the middle of St. Peter's Square, headed for the basilica. He entered the elegant renaissance structure and walked down the nave, past the columns with the statues of all the saints, past the statue of St. Peter with the laces of his sandals worn away from the kisses of the faithful, towards the stairs, near the main altar that led down to the grottoes where the popes were buried.

But when he got to the stairs, they were chained off with a sign that said *"Chiuso per Restauro,"* Closed for Restorations. He knew that in Italy that could mean anything. It was the sign that restaurants put up when they were going out of business and did not want anyone to know. It was the sign the authorities put up at the antiquities sites when too many guards called off sick for a sunny day at the seashore.

Deprived of the papal tombs, Bill Tuigg changed directions and headed down the side aisle to the chapel of the Blessed Sacrament. He parted the heavy grey curtains that shielded the chapel from the touristy hub-bub of the basilica, and knelt down in front of the baroque tabernacle and the presence of Christ.

"Lord, what are you asking of me?" he prayed silently. "I did not expect this? What do You want? What should I do? I do not want this. But if it's Your will …" hoping for a voice from the tabernacle that never came.

After a half hour of silent prayer, he left the

chapel, and was about to leave the basilica when he had an inspiration and headed across the nave to the elevator that carried tourists up to the roof of St. Peter's. When the usher saw the gold chain and pectoral cross on Bill's black vest, he held the elevator door open for him to get on at the last minute.

The roof of St. Peter's was an uneven mix of terra cotta tiles and small cupolas that let light flow down into the basilica below. There was a gift shop on the roof, staffed by very efficient nuns, who sold Vatican souvenirs. Bill Tuigg stopped in to buy some rosaries and prayer cards for his staff back at the Rocksburg chancery. He would ask the Holy Father to bless them tomorrow.

Then he walked to the front of the basilica's roof where the best views were, between the huge travertine statues of Christ and his apostles looking down from the facade of St. Peter's onto the grandiose square. Up close, Bill Tuigg could see that the metal cross that Christ held over his shoulder was rusting. Not a surprise after a few centuries of exposure to the elements.

Walking back to the center of the roof, Bill Tuigg entered the inside of the dome. From this vantage point, the Latin words ringing the dome that looked so small from down below, were huge. *"Tu es Petrus et super hanc petram aedificabo ecclesiam meam et tibi dabo claves regni caelorum—*You are Peter and upon this rock I will build my Church, and I will give you the keys to the kingdom of heaven." It was amazing he thought, how your perspective changed from where you stood. Peter was calling him. What should he do? What could he do?

He took the pair of curving stairs inside the dome up to the lantern at the very top of the cupola. The internal stairs started out wide enough but as they got higher within the dome, they narrowed and he had to bend his body inward to negotiate the turns. It wasn't the easiest thing for a fifty-three year old man, and he felt a bit dizzy as he climbed.

Bill Tuigg thanked all those mornings that he had spent on his treadmill back in the basement of his small suburban home in Rocksburg that had kept him in shape.

Exiting from the stairs, into the fresh air, Bill Tuigg saw that there were only a few tourists at the top, and he was able to walk around the entire circumference of the lantern unhindered, each pass giving him a different view of Rome and of a different time in his life. There, on top of the Janiculum Hill, was the North American College where he had studied theology as a callow young man before ordination.

Bordering St. Peter's Square was the Palazzo of the Congregations, where he had worked with Cardinal Rooney. Those years had started out happy, but as the turf wars with the other Vatican bureaucrats intensified, and as John Rooney's health worsened, they turned sad. Then there was a blow-up with the Spanish bishops that made Paul VI very unhappy, and Rooney had not been able to speak to the pope for over a year. And once Rooney got sick his life was a constant refrain of hospital trips to the United States. Rooney was happy at the election of John Paul II, but was too old and ill to stay and serve him.

Behind the Palazzo, on a small square filled with green city busses, was the apartment house where he had lived with Rooney. He remembered his late night discussions with the cardinal, after dinner, trying to decide the right way to handle the challenges that confronted the Congregation, and then trying to predict the Roman way. He had matured as a person and as a priest during those years. Rooney had been a good mentor, but he was not so sure that he could make the same sacrifices that Rooney had made. Cardinal Hildebrand lived in that apartment now, he thought, and, if he said yes to the pope, Hildebrand would soon be moving out.

The winds picked up around the lantern. It was

the highest spot in Rome. Unprotected on all sides, it was famous for its gusts, the salty western squalls that blew in from the Tyrrhenian Sea, the sand-filled southern currents from the Sahara, and the chilly northern blasts rushing down from the Alps. He felt caught in a whirlwind. From this great height, he could see the world that he was being offered. Buffeted by the breezes, he grabbed onto the railing on the parapet of the lantern, steadied himself and looked down, but he no longer saw Rome.

He saw Rocksburg, its valleys and its rivers, its hills and its bridges, its people and its priests, his small suburban home, and his loyal staff in the chancery. It was home. It always would be.

About the Author

Nicholas P. Cafardi is a well-known Catholic author whose works have appeared in *America* magazine, *U.S. Catholic*, *Commonweal* and the *National Catholic Reporter*. His book, *Before Dallas*, has been called the definitive history of the child sex abuse crisis in the Catholic Church. This is his first work of fiction.

www.ingramcontent.com/pod-product-compliance
Lightning Source LLC
Chambersburg PA
CBHW051245260626
47162CB00002B/619